Death of a
Dishonorable
Gentleman

To the Kingston Library

Best wishes *(signature)* 1/22/2015

TESSA ARLEN

Death of a
Dishonorable
Gentleman

MINOTAUR BOOKS
A THOMAS DUNNE BOOK
NEW YORK

A THOMAS DUNNE BOOK FOR MINOTAUR BOOKS.
An imprint of St. Martin's Publishing Group.

DEATH OF A DISHONORABLE GENTLEMAN. Copyright © 2014 by Tessa Arlen. All rights reserved. Printed in the United States of America. For information, address St. Martin's Press, 175 Fifth Avenue, New York, N.Y. 10010.

www.thomasdunnebooks.com
www.minotaurbooks.com

Library of Congress Cataloging-in-Publication Data

Arlen, Tessa.
    Death of a dishonorable genteman: a mystery / Tessa Arlen—First edition
        pages   cm
    ISBN 978-1-250-05249-0 (hardcover)
    ISBN 978-1-4668-5427-7 (e-book)
    1. Countesses—Fiction.   2. Great Britain—History—Edward VII,
1901–1910—Fiction.   I. Title.
    PS3601.R5445D43 2015
    813'.6—dc23

                                                          2014032395

Minotaur books may be purchased for educational, business, or promotional use. For information on bulk purchases, please contact the Macmillan Corporate and Premium Sales Department at 1-800-221-7945, extension 5442, or write to specialmarkets@macmillan.com.

First Edition: January 2015

10 9 8 7 6 5 4 3 2 1

To Chris—the love of my life

Acknowledgments

I first described my idea for this story to my husband in 2009, and he told me to stop talking and start writing. Without his unwavering belief that I am a writer there would be no book.

It is with deepest gratitude that I thank Chris Arlen; my daughters, Chloe Nichol, Toby Horvitch, and Georgia Arlen; my sister, Deborah Bell, and my dear friend Sandy Kirsopp—their willingness to read many iterations of my original manuscript and offer me nothing but encouragement to continue was kindness unto itself.

Kevan Lyon, the most diligent and generous of agents, took me to the next step and deserves my greatest thanks. Without her help and professional guidance I would still be pestering my family to listen to yet another chapter.

At St. Martin's Press, grateful thanks to: my talented and insightful editor, Toni Kirkpatrick; her hardworking editorial assistant, Jennifer Letwack; David Rotstein, who gave me the book jacket I hoped for; and to my publicist, Shailyn Tavella.

Thanks also go to Lindsy Spence, Deanna Raybourn, Anna Lee Huber, and Christine Trent for the generosity of their time and the kindness of their words; and to Lisa Samuelson of

Samuelson Communications, who initiated me into the mystifying world of social media, and to Jen Pennington of Rhizome Designs and James McGrath of McGrath Media for my beautiful Web site.

And last of all to my parents. Thank you for my outstandingly eccentric childhood and for teaching me, quite unintentionally, to be independent and open to new experiences no matter what they were, and for the valuable quality of emotional resilience. May I remain forever an optimist!

Death of a Dishonorable Gentleman

Chapter One

On the morning of Lord and Lady Montfort's annual summer ball, their housekeeper, Edith Jackson, was up, washed, and almost dressed by six o'clock. She unraveled her long bedtime plait, brushed out her hair, and, with a mouth full of hairpins, swept the thick auburn swath into a twist at the nape of her neck, deftly securing it in place. The glance she cast into the looking glass was brief, made only to reassure that she was presentable. Then she rang for the third housemaid to bring breakfast up to her parlor.

As Mrs. Jackson sat down to eat her bacon and eggs, she mentally prepared herself for a day that would be packed with complicated, overlapping timetables and countless calls on her patience and tact. She was quite certain the house was ready for the greatest event of its year, but she did not allow herself to be complacent about her ladyship. The countess often awoke to her best ideas on the morning of the ball. In past years, dancing by the lake or midnight supper in the ruin of the old moated castle were inspirations that had struck Lady Montfort only at the last moment. Mrs. Jackson knew from long experience that it did not pay to be overconfident about readiness where her ladyship was concerned. *Don't tempt fate,* the housekeeper told herself, *not until after your meeting with her at nine o'clock.*

She finished her second cup of tea and washed her hands before leaving the sanctuary of her rooms to descend three flights of stairs to the servants' hall. Walking past the kitchen, she increased her pace as she heard the strident voice of the cook harrying her kitchen maids to greater efforts. She was careful not to turn her head in case she caught Mrs. Thwaite's eye; an early encounter with Cook, who was of a garrulous nature, would certainly slow her down. Fortunately, Cook was wholly absorbed in straining a large copper pan of veal stock, and Mrs. Jackson made her escape out of the scullery door, unnoticed.

Once outside, she rounded the tall laurel hedge at the edge of the kitchen yard. The house and its gardens lay before her, glorious in the morning light. These hours in the garden, when the day was fresh and new, were a favorite time for Mrs. Jackson. The only movement was the swoop and flutter of birds as they caught insects and drank fountain-water, the only sound the jubilant trill of their early morning song. She stopped, turned her face up to the sun, closed her eyes, and took a slow breath. The air was fresh with the earthy fragrance of rainwater and the sweet, rich scent of freshly mown lawns and scythed meadow grass. She allowed herself a few moments to enjoy the peace and solitude of the garden, a brief respite from the clamor belowstairs in the house. Glancing at her wristwatch, she saw that it was nearly seven o'clock and set off at a fast clip along the drive. *Whatever you do now,* she told herself, *don't fritter away your time, or you'll lose the day.*

When she stepped through the green, arched wood door in

the brick wall of Iyntwood's kitchen garden she was transported from the empty, smooth lawns, groomed parterres, and shrubberies of the house into a different world altogether, but one she found just as pleasing in its own way. Abundant ranks of vegetable, fruit, and flower beds stretched before her, bristling with frames, trellises and bamboo stakes supporting the lush crops of early summer. An orderly vegetable garden never failed to gladden her practical heart; there was comfort in the sight of such well-tended profusion.

In the middle distance she saw Ernest Stafford chest-deep in rows of vivid blue delphiniums. He was obviously ready to wait on her in the cutting garden rather than the elderly head gardener, Mr. Thrower. Momentarily confused, she came to a halt and became engrossed in the list of instructions in her hand, to give herself time to adjust to this change in plans. When she moved forward she was conscious to keep the tenor of her meeting with Mr. Stafford formal; their past few exchanges had left her with the distinct impression that he was one of those men who didn't pay quite enough attention to the importance of social convention. He was often direct with her, which she had no objection to, but on occasion his demeanor bordered on unwelcome familiarity.

In Mrs. Jackson's limited experience, men who worked in the open air were often withdrawn and not given to conversation. But Ernest Stafford was a cut above the average gardener: he was a landscape architect, which presented a puzzle to her rather hierarchical cast of mind and stern regard for social distinctions. That he was an educated man who held a job where his hands were often dirty no doubt contributed to Mr. Stafford's disconcerting social manners, she thought. And most certainly his success with the new sunken garden, and Lady Montfort's entranced enthusiasm for everything he had accomplished there, had rather gone to his head.

Mrs. Jackson allocated exactly twenty minutes to spend in the kitchen garden before she moved on to the more important tasks of her day, and as a result she was a little brusquer than she intended to be as she said good morning.

"I know what's on your mind," he said in his easy way, oblivious to her stiffening back. "The delphinium—no need to worry, they are perfect despite the rain and should open up completely by this afternoon, once you have them inside. But I think we need something for contrast; lime-green amaranths would set off those stunning blues beautifully, don't you agree?" She nodded, and couldn't help but admire Mr. Stafford's unerring sense of balance when it came to color; Mr. Thrower would undoubtedly have suggested a commonplace and insipid pink. Mr. Stafford's creative eye for composition awoke all sorts of possibilities and she eagerly asked which roses were at their best.

An unhurried litany on flowers took place between them, of which colors, scents, and contrasting foliage choices were the only topic. On safe and familiar ground, Mrs. Jackson regained her composure. With decisions made for all the rooms in the house, she finally lifted her chin and, without turning her head in his direction, risked a tentative glance. It was difficult to judge the expression on his face, as his eyes were hidden by the shadow of his hat brim, but she noticed that the set of his mouth was good-humored and relaxed.

Mrs. Jackson was tall for a woman, almost as tall as Stafford. She carried herself well with an upright, quiet dignity that was accentuated by the simple cut of her clothes. Now in her middle thirties, she believed that once, when she was young, she might have been quite a good-looking woman. She certainly didn't think she was now.

Emerging from her moment of introspection, she was embarrassed to see Mr. Stafford watching her, as if he knew what she had been thinking. She swallowed slightly and felt a complete fool.

"The lads will carry them all up to the house for you immediately, Mrs. Jackson. I'd better go and help Mr. Thrower."

She heard Mr. Thrower's cracked old voice, clearly audible even at this distance, lifted in cries of alarm and impatience from the direction of the vegetable beds in protest against the clumsy handling of tender lettuce and purslane.

Set at ease by everyday ritual and past the worst of her anxiety, she realized their time had come to an end. She thanked Mr. Stafford for his help and watched him turn and walk back down the path toward the men in the vegetable garden. She noticed that he held himself upright: back straight, broad shoulders squared, when most gardeners were often round-shouldered and stooped. She ran her hands down the front of her skirt to smooth its folds, fixed her attention firmly forward to the business of the day ahead, and set off back the way she had come.

When she entered the kitchen courtyard, she saw the first of the wagons from the dairy parked outside the kitchen door. She called out a greeting to the driver, and walked through the doors and down the steps to the orderly and familiar world over which she held dominion: the storerooms, pantries, larders, laundries, and the servants' hall, which stretched in a subterranean maze beneath the ground floor of Iyntwood, Lord Montfort's country house.

* * *

The private rooms of Clementine Elizabeth Talbot, Countess of Montfort, were situated in the west wing of the house and looked out over the rose garden. Her bedroom was spacious and airy with tall windows on two sides; the walls a deep Wedgwood-blue silk damask, the furnishings in soft grays and silvers. It was in these elegant and supremely comfortable surroundings that Lady Montfort awoke to her day, and on this particular day, long before her breakfast tray was brought up by her maid Pettigrew.

Her first groping thought as she emerged from a deep sleep was whether it was raining, and with this concern she was immediately awake. It had been drizzling off and on throughout the preceding afternoon and evening, and she had gone to bed praying it would clear in the night. She sat up, swung her legs out of bed, walked to the nearest window, pulled back the heavy velvet curtains, and gazed out onto a sun-drenched lawn. Perfect! She turned her gaze upward—not a cloud in sight. Even better! Elated that somehow she had cheated the weather, which was so often unpredictable in June, Clementine clapped her hands together and turned to face the day with even greater energy and resolve.

Through the open window the sweet morning air poured into the room and she felt a momentary thrill of eager expectancy, like waking up on Christmas morning when she was a child with the prospect of a huge treat in store. She would forgo her morning ride, she decided, as there was far too much to do in preparation for the ball tonight.

She rang for her maid, but when Pettigrew arrived with her tray, Clementine was too charged to linger over breakfast. She distractedly nibbled toast and marmalade, her attention focused on last-minute plans. Having had a moment to think over all that must be done as she sipped her tea, her mood of anticipation and pleasure at the prospect of tonight's magnificent ball was intermittently eroded by underlying anxieties that would be hers until she met with her housekeeper and was reassured that no problems had emerged since their meeting the evening before.

Clementine planned the festivities for her annual summer costume ball with scrupulous care. It was a significant social occasion and stood for something a little more momentous than the opportunity to get together to enjoy good food and dancing in the company of their friends and family. It was important to remind their friends and neighbors that despite whatever new economic upheavals might be imminent in their twentieth-century lives, the Talbots' wealth was copious, their holdings and estates were plentiful and productive, and their place in society was therefore secure. Unlike the many brash *arrivistes* who had bought their way into upper society, Clementine was careful to ensure that her ball did not smack of vulgar ostentation but displayed the elegant, understated style that stood for the effortless security of coming from an ancient family entrenched in the county for centuries.

She walked to the west windows and looked down on the rose garden, which had been carefully tidied to remove all traces of yesterday's rain. She watched several men from the estate stringing pretty, painted, paper Japanese candle-lanterns across the garden and into the surrounding trees. Immediately below on the terrace, she was pleased to see that every potted palm, scented shrub, and small flowering tree had already been carted up from the glasshouses and the dowager's conservatory and were now being arranged to create intimate bowers on the terrace for her guests to sit out and enjoy supper. She hoped this would transform the terrace from an austere blank of gray flagstone into a fairyland found only in the balmy, soft nights of the Mediterranean, or perhaps, she thought with a little stab of apprehension, the set of Gilbert and Sullivan's production of *The Mikado*. They must be careful not to overdo the paper lanterns.

As Pettigrew withdrew after helping her mistress dress, Clementine was already running her eye and pencil down one of several lists that her maid had brought up on her breakfast tray. She stopped work for a moment and threw down her pencil. She rather wished that Althea, their middle daughter, who was on a walking tour in Switzerland with friends, and their eldest daughter, Verity, married and living in Paris with her young family, were able to join Iyntwood's festivities this year. This would be the first time since the girls had come out that they would miss the fun. It just wouldn't be the same, she thought, without the shared silliness of getting ready for the ball together with her grown-up daughters.

Harry would be with them, of course, as he was coming home today from Oxford for the long vacation, and Harry was tremendous company. But sons, she had reluctantly come to realize as their children had grown, who were so much more independent than daughters, somehow had the knack of staying in a house without actually being present.

A new thought crossed her mind, and, discarding her lists, Clementine wandered into her dressing room to take a good long look at her costume for the ball. She had taken the idea from the little Sèvres porcelain figure, in the library, of an eighteenth-century French milkmaid. Holding her dress up against herself, she gazed critically at her reflection in the looking glass. It was certainly very elegant, she thought, as she twisted from side to side to take in all angles. The jade-and-ivory silk of the skirt à la polonaise was finely embroidered, and the flat, rolled-straw hat would look quite the thing and rather chic with curled and powdered hair falling about her shoulders.

She transferred her attention away from the dress and leaned in to gaze thoughtfully at her reflection in the glass. Large gray eyes with delicate, dark brows stared back; her rich brown hair was still glossy but it was beginning to show gray at her temples. She peered closely at fine lines gathering in the corners of her eyes. She knew she wasn't considered pretty by the rather lush standards of the day; her elegant, slender frame was far from that of a pouter pigeon, and she liked to think hers was a lean and intelligent face that would bear up over the coming years. Bone structure was a valuable asset, she reminded herself, as she turned herself sideways and spread the skirt of her dress around her slender hips.

Her reverie was interrupted by the welcome arrival of her housekeeper, Mrs. Jackson, who was holding several lists of her own and appeared fully in charge of her day. Jackson, always self-possessed, looked positively rigid with intention this morning, which caused Clementine to shed most of her anxieties about Iyntwood's preparedness. She was always reassured by her housekeeper's composure and equanimity; Jackson was such a soothing individual and so extraordinarily capable. George Hollyoak, Iyntwood's butler and majordomo, was a faultless person, but she saw her housekeeper as Iyntwood's internal-combustion engine, propelling a household, with upward of sixty rooms and a staff of fourteen resident servants, resolutely forward to meet each day with unfailing and dedicated service.

TESSA ARLEN

"Morning, Jackson, how are things?" Mrs. Jackson was standing at a respectful distance by the door. "Yes, do come in. Have you seen Mr. Thrower this morning? Please, before anything else, tell me the rain hasn't ruined the flowers."

"Not at all, m'lady, everything is at its best."

"Well, that's a relief. Anything horrid I should know about, any last-minute surprises?"

Clementine seated herself in a comfortable chair by the window and Mrs. Jackson took two steps toward her so that she wouldn't have to raise her voice. There *was* a surprise, Clementine thought. She could tell by her housekeeper's hesitation, but she knew Mrs. Jackson would have a solution to go with it, as no problem was ever mentioned without one.

"Mr. Evans of the Market Wingley orchestra sent a message over last night: his first violinist has sprained his wrist and is unable to play."

"There's *always* something at the last moment, isn't there? How many violinists do they need, for heaven's sake?" Clementine did not allow herself to overreact, but patiently waited for Mrs. Jackson's way out.

"The Market Wingley usually plays with three, m'lady. I sent Dick over to Mr. Simkins, as the schoolmaster is a very accomplished player, and he sent word this morning he would be happy to join the orchestra tonight." Mrs. Jackson produced her perfect resolution to the problem with pacific calm, and Clementine made sure it was properly acknowledged.

"Oh, well done, Jackson, five steps ahead as always. I thought we had a real problem on our hands for a moment. Mr. Simkins? Why, that's Violet's father. If she's up-to-the-moment on her duties, will you make sure she spends some time with him?"

Clementine relaxed and then tightened up again. "What about oysters—did we manage to get some?"

"A bit difficult at this time of year, m'lady, but we were fortunate. They arrived from Billingsgate on the early train with the other fresh fish this morning. We are completely prepared in the kitchen."

"Well, it appears we are on top of things. I'll join you and Hollyoak after luncheon for a quick walk-through, if you are sure you will have the flowers done by then."

Mrs. Jackson assured her that she would.

"Now here are my lists, no real changes." Regardless of how unnecessary she knew it was, she went about the task of updating her long-suffering housekeeper with her annotated lists of last-minute needs and wants. Her annual summer ball must always surpass the spectacle of luxury and the cachet of previous years and nothing must be overlooked. But what Clementine did not foresee was that it would become one of the most talked-about events of the season.

Chapter Two

Ralph Cuthbert Talbot, the 6th Earl of Montfort, did not share his wife's unrestrained enthusiasm for their ball. Lord Montfort was tucked away from the commotion of preparations in the house and was enjoying the solace of the morning room. Sunlight poured in through the leaded panes of the large stone-mullioned windows, creating a comforting pool of warm light where he sat at the table. One of the casements was open a little, and he briefly became aware of the pleasant sound of bees working sturdily among the wisteria blossoms in the quiet of the room. He was enthusiastically applying himself to a large and substantial breakfast of the sort that was referred to in Europe, and especially by the French with a slight shudder, as the "Englishman's breakfast."

The thought that half of London society would turn up at his house this evening dressed in costumes so ridiculous that it would take days for him to eradicate them from his memory caused him to snort with irritation. He firmly believed that costume balls had the tendency to make fools out of most of his friends. *All the more reason,* he said to himself as he stretched his legs out under the table, *to enjoy this quiet hour and the luxury of uninterrupted thought.* Lying open on the table to his right was a copy of *The Times.* He read ominous reports of the ferocious opposition by Ulster Unionists against the latest Home Rule Bill, as he champed stoically through a plate of the fried, the grilled, and the scrambled. On his left, a neat pile of the morning's first post awaited his attention.

As James poured a second cup of coffee, Lord Montfort turned with irritation from a particularly depressing editorial on trade unions and opened the letter on the top of the pile. It was from the proctor of Oxford University, Dr. Everard Bascombe-Harcourt.

As he cast his eye over Bascombe-Harcourt's opening lines, the day quite lost its beauty. The initial flash of alarm and anger as he took in the sentence that began, "I regret to inform you . . ." was replaced with the dull and miserable acceptance he often experienced when he was informed of the more distasteful exploits of his ward and nephew, Teddy Mallory. He read on to the foot of the page, conscious of a twinge in his stomach where his grilled lamb chop and sautéed mushrooms had landed with such contentment a few moments ago.

The warm, sunny room pleasant five minutes earlier now felt confined and airless. With the beginnings of severe indigestion and memories of Teddy's past indiscretions, Lord Montfort felt trapped and suffocated. He got up from the table, stuffed the letter into his coat pocket, and left the house, walking briskly toward the stable block. He always did his best thinking on the back of one of his horses.

Less than an hour later, he crested the ridge of Marston Downs astride his favorite hunter, Bruno. A stiff southwest breeze picked up and he jammed his hat down tightly on his head. His horse's ears pricked back, asking if he was ready. Lord Montfort leaned forward and gave him the go-ahead and felt the animal's stride lengthen in a powerful thrust of muscle and intention. All thoughts were mercifully blanked from his mind in a rush of cold air as his horse stretched out in a long, measured gallop. Horse and rider raced along the top of the ridge as one in the pure physical enjoyment of the moment, without a thought between them. Ahead was a wide ditch brimming with rainwater, followed by the fallen trunk of a beech tree, and, farther on, to the right a hedge with a barred gate. Lord Montfort usually slowed his horse for these obstacles, but today he felt reckless, and his horse, familiar with them all, covered the ditch, took three strides, cleared the log, and went on to lift effortlessly over the five-bar gate. "Now that," Lord Montfort said to the horse as he clapped him on the shoulder, "is more like it."

Half a mile on, his mind returned to Dr. Bascombe-Harcourt's regretful letter. He knew there was nothing he could do about his nephew's present dilemma; Teddy had apparently run the full course of his self-destruction. And really when it came down to it, what was there to do, except maintain as much dignity as he could in the face of his nephew's coming ostracism and disgrace? The proctor's letter had been formal and to the point, but his son, Harry, when he arrived for luncheon would be able to fill him in on Teddy's latest fiasco. And more than likely Teddy was also on his way to Iyntwood, so he had that interview to look forward to as well. There was no point in ruining his wife's enjoyment of her ball, so he decided to wait until Monday before he told her, if he could. He turned his horse and they cantered back along the gallop.

Returning to his house, he chose to enter the park by the southeast gate. He trotted his horse alongside the drive, passing under the spread of immense chestnut trees with their white candles still in bloom, the filtered shade of beech, and the deeper shade of elms. At the edge of the park they broke clear of the woodland, and his horse briskly increased the pace, snorting rhythmically down his nose in anticipation of oats.

When they came to the south edge of the lake, which curved in a crescent up and around the base of the gardens and the northeast side of the house, he slowed Bruno to a walk and crossed the bridge where the lake narrowed into a shallow bed of water lilies fringed with flag iris. And here the principal facade of his house came into view: sunlight glinted on the handsome Elizabethan stone mullioned windows which formed such a feature of the house. At the sight of the familiar mellow stone walls glowing against a backdrop of dark Lebanon cedars, Lord Montfort halted his horse to enjoy the contentment this scene always instilled within him. The sun was warm on their backs as horse and rider cantered forward, followed by a flock of swallows skimming along the surface of the turf behind them to catch the insects that flew up from the grass disturbed by Bruno's hooves.

Just before luncheon, Clementine was on alert to the arrival of their son, Harry. She heard the rough purr of the two-seater Bugatti long before the butler came to announce that Lord Haversham had just arrived and to ask if they would need to hold luncheon.

She said no, she felt sure that Lord Haversham and Mr. Ellis would be quite ready to eat at one o'clock, and walked out to greet her son as he pulled up at the east portico of the house with a spray of gravel and a shout of greeting.

Used to her son's habitual energetic exit from his motorcar, she was surprised to see him open the door and climb out with what appeared to be the burdened weariness of a middle-aged man. Intrigued, she immediately glanced at Ellis Booth, whom she regarded as a steadying influence on her son's often exuberant and unchecked disposition, but Ellis's round and rather placid face was studiedly noncommittal. There was a brief, muttered exchange between the two young men as they divested themselves of caps, goggles, and the huge gauntlet gloves they insisted on wearing whenever they traveled in Harry's open motorcar, and she caught a rather admonitory glance pass from Ellis to Harry before her son walked up the steps toward her.

She noticed that as he grew older Harry resembled his father more closely. They were both tall men, athletic in build, and had the same high-crowned shape to the head and the dark, almost-black hair of the Talbot family. But most of all she realized that they shared the same air of authority that riches, rank, broad acres, and ancient lineage bestow on men with the providence to be born first in line to the right family. Harry certainly resembled his father, she thought, but there the similarities ended. Her son differed from his father's entrenched traditional views, and like many young men of his generation he had a fascination for the modern world and a love of mechanized speed and motorcars; whereas her husband viewed all change with concern and, if given time, with some sort of reluctant acceptance.

"Well, here you are, and so admirably early." They were already half an hour late. "You look like you were certainly spanking along in that motor of yours, what's it called again?" She could never manage to remember the stupid thing's name.

"A Bugatti T-22, Mother. It goes like the devil, did close to sixty the other day up the Great North Road." It didn't take much to restore Harry's good humor, she thought. But goodness, why were they both so disheveled and dusty with their hair all over the place? She laughed as if she approved of Harry's rather dangerous love of speed, which she didn't, as she was determined not to appear too critical when he had only just arrived.

"We are taking luncheon outside by the lake, so we can keep out of the way of the final flurries to get us ready for the ball tonight. Join us when you've had a moment; your father is outside already." She knew he would understand her polite code for *Don't keep him waiting; cut up to your room for a wash and brush-up, and be quick about it.*

When Harry and Ellis came down to join them they were almost on time for luncheon. Clementine was sitting under the loggia, enjoying the business of doing nothing as she watched her husband encourage his Labrador to retrieve a small tree limb, twice the dog's length, from the center of the lake. At her feet lay Harry's old dog, Percy, asleep with the sun on his belly, his feet twitching as he dreamed of past quests for game birds.

Lord Montfort turned to greet his son with a welcoming, "Harry, well here you are." He placed an affectionate arm across his son's shoulders and walked with him to the loggia to say hello to Ellis.

"Good drive down?" he asked them both. "You're on time for once, must have been cracking along! What's that new motor of yours again?" Harry and Ellis rushed to interrupt each other as they related the glories of the motor and what it was capable of, until Hollyoak bent to inform Clementine that their luncheon was ready.

When they had finished their meal, she was pleased to see

that all three men were relaxed and enjoying the afternoon. There seemed no trace of the ill humor Harry had displayed upon his arrival, or of her husband's grim preoccupation when he had returned to the house after his morning ride. If their son seemed a little inattentive, his father seemed not to mind. He had glanced in Harry's direction several times during their meal, obviously as happy as she was to have him home for the summer.

"Always feel I might be in Valtravaglia when we eat out here; we should perhaps go back there." Her husband turned to look at her as he sat back in his chair and reached for a delicate peach from the estate's glasshouses.

"I'd love to. Let's make a plan for next spring. It will be beautiful then," she said as the butler bent to speak in her ear. "The first of our guests have arrived, sadly too late to join us. Teddy and Oscar Barclay are being given something to eat in the house; I'll pop in on them later."

At the mention of his cousin's arrival, Harry came out of the preoccupied state he had fallen into since they had finished their meal. "Father, perhaps I could have a word before tea?"

"Yes of course, why don't you walk over with me to the estate office. I have an appointment with our new agent, Archie Pommeroy, and it would be a good time for you to meet him. Ellis, what about you, want to walk along?"

"Thanks, but I think I'll run up to the house and say hullo to Mallory and Barclay." Ellis was already on his feet.

Their luncheon over, her husband and son left in the direction of the estate office in the stable block and Ellis wandered off in search of Teddy Mallory and his friend Oscar Barclay, leaving Clementine to join the butler and housekeeper for one last walk-through of the house.

* * *

With her inspection complete to her utmost satisfaction, Clementine decided to take a stroll before her guests arrived at five o'clock. She put on her hat and set off in the direction of the lime walk to spend a happy hour with Mr. Stafford, discussing under-plantings for shade and to see what was happening with the new garden before she had to change for tea.

On her way back to the house she chose the path that came from the lake through a dense shrubbery of tall rhododendrons and azaleas. Their somber, heavy foliage concealed her approach as she came up to the back of the boathouse building. But as she drew closer she heard, quite distinctly, voices lifted in anger. She stopped, uncertain for a moment what to do. She listened as the shouting started again and was surprised when she recognized one of the voices as Harry's. Walking forward, she could clearly see into the boathouse garden while remaining well hidden among the tall shrubs.

Standing on the back steps of the building were Harry and Teddy. Teddy had his back to her, but she saw Harry's face and he was furious. She had never seen her son so angry before.

She watched Harry haul Teddy toward him by his shoulder and shirt collar with both hands. Harry's face was red and distorted with anger and at that moment he appeared immense, almost unrecognizable. He shook Teddy so hard that his cousin would have fallen if he had not been held in such a strong grip. Seeing them close together, she realized how much taller and heavier Harry was than his cousin; his anger seemed to have increased his size. His hostility was so palpable that she felt a thump of adrenaline surge in her stomach. *He's going to hit him!* she thought. *This simply can't be happening.* But it was happen-

ing. In one lunging, stiff-armed push, Harry shoved Teddy down
the boathouse steps and onto the lawn. Teddy sprawled on the
grass, drew up his legs, and raised his arms over his head. He
cringed as Harry bore down on him from the top of the steps.
Harry pulled him to his feet and started to shake him again.
He was even angrier now and gave Teddy a shove back toward
the path leading into the orchard.

In considerable alarm, Clementine withdrew into the shrubbery and retreated down the pathway. What on earth was happening? This was quite awful. Harry's voice was so magnified
by rage that even at this distance she clearly heard some of the
words he was shouting.

". . . Get out of here . . . you bloody little swine . . . I'll break
your damn neck . . ."

Despite her horror and disgust, Clementine couldn't help but
walk forward to see what was happening. Harry was at least
making a supreme effort to pull himself together: he had turned
from his cousin but was still beside himself with rage. She
watched Teddy brush grass and dirt from his trousers, saw him
shrug his shoulders back into his coat and reach into his pocket
for his cigarette case, bending his head to light a cigarette. He
threw a nervous look at Harry and, reassured that his fury had
passed, sauntered off through the boathouse garden-gate into
the orchard and disappeared in the direction of the adjoining
stable block as if nothing in the world had happened. Clementine was aware that her heart was beating rapidly and her throat
felt tight and dry.

She was not so naïve that she didn't understand that young
men sometimes fought, but she imagined that by their early
twenties they would surely have outgrown adolescent pos-
turing and moments of mad violence. She was frightened to

see her considerate and civilized son behave so brutally, and couldn't begin to imagine how Teddy could have had such a profound and ugly effect on him. Something had gone quite terribly wrong between them. She stood still for a moment, trying to make sense of what she had seen. She fervently hoped this was the end of their quarrel and not the beginning of something more disturbing.

Chapter Three

When Clementine came downstairs to join their guests before dinner, the red drawing room was thronged with glossy, glittering, and impressively attired men and women, all of them the product of the minute attentions of their valets and maids. She briefly tuned in to her husband's conversation with Colonel Jack Ambrose and Sir Hugo Waterford—on Purdy's or Holland's for guns—and quickly walked farther into the room.

There was an exclamation and a shout of laughter from her son, Harry, and she turned to see him with Oscar Barclay, Ellis Booth, and Lucinda Lambert-Lambert in a tight group at the far end of the room, having the time of their lives. How loud they were! What on earth could they be drinking? She signaled to Hollyoak not to serve them any more. At the rate they were going, they would be pickled by midnight.

Turning away, she crossed the room to where Lady Agatha Booth sat in a low chair, her large square head supporting a heavy Victorian tiara of dingy diamonds. On her lap she clutched a little dog of the sort of breed that had a squashed and crumpled face, and on either side of her stood her eighteen-year-old twin daughters. Pansy and Blanche were casting yearning looks in the direction of Harry and Oscar but not daring to leave their mother's side.

"Clemmy darling, how lovely . . ." Constance Ambrose, pretty, diminutive, and all shining gold curls, looked up gratefully at Clementine's arrival and patted the sofa next to her. Lady Harriet Lambert-Lambert, large, stately, and handsome, turned her dark head and shot her a look of exaggerated resignation. Clementine assumed that she had interrupted one of Lady Booth's pronouncements.

". . . I simply won't go to that dreadful play, it's ridiculous and unbelievable; a cockney barrow-girl can't be coached to act and speak like a lady. These things cannot be taught, they are bred-in." With a large gloved hand Lady Booth indicated her daughters and the generations of marriage to cousins they represented. Clementine could see out of the tail of her eye that Harriet's shoulders were shaking.

"I nearly wore my new Fortuny this evening, deep yellow, such a gorgeous shade." This from Constance, who was no doubt anxious to divert from a lecture on well-bred young girls, thought Clementine.

"I avoid yellow, such a strident color and only looks well with a swarthy complexion. Oh my dear, what has Gertrude Waterford got on, she looks quite half dressed!" Lady Waterford was a favorite of Clementine and she quickly glanced over to see what her friend could have done to cause such an exclamation from Lady Booth.

Gertrude Waterford, who always looked to Clementine as if she were made of alabaster, ivory, and silver-gilt, was wearing a magnificent narrow dress of filmy, indigo silk that elegantly but clearly whispered *Paul Poiret*. It was cut so low at the bosom and back that it was evident she could not possibly be wearing a corset of any kind whatsoever. She reclined against the cushions on her sofa, eyes half closed, as Lord Albert Booth broke away from his conversation and bent over her to light her cigarette in its amber quellazaire. If Gertrude was surprised by such close proximity in public she made no sign, and Clementine could have sworn that Lord Booth's hand brushed lightly against Gertrude's upper arm. Lord Booth, usually ebullient with charm and charisma, was uncharacteristically subdued this evening, Clementine thought, as she watched him seat himself at a respectable distance from Gertrude on her sofa and start a conversation about a mutual friend who was interested in buying his mare.

Clementine smiled to herself and looked across the room in time to see Teddy Mallory's late arrival. Sleek and well groomed as always, she thought, as she watched him saunter across the room to talk to Lady Shackleton. *How do some people do that?* she asked herself. *Behave as if nothing has happened at all, when they have been given a thorough trouncing just a few hours ago.* Teddy was standing with his fair head bowed as he listened to Lady Shackleton's account of her recent dinner party; Clementine was close enough to hear Olive quite clearly.

"He was just about the dullest man you could possibly imagine, so dreadfully reserved, it was an awful disappointment."

"What? Who was?" It seemed that Teddy was unimpressed. He made no effort to conceal his boredom. In fact he almost yawned. *How impertinent he could be sometimes,* thought Clementine. She rose to her feet as Olive answered.

"Kenneth Grahame, you know, *The Wind in the Willows*. He ate a tremendous amount at dinner and seemed quite disinterested in all of us." Olive Shackleton laughed good-naturedly at her failure to recognize a dud in lion's clothing.

"Probably speechless because he was shot at three times in his bank." Teddy was obviously enjoying his own inner joke, and Clementine decided to make sure it remained that way. She steered Harriet across the room toward Olive.

"Teddy dear, how on earth do you know a thing like that?" Olive Shackleton exclaimed as they joined her. "Was he shot at because of the book?"

"Well, I hardly think so. No, this was a socialist demonstration of some sort at the Bank of England. I think he just happened to get in the way." Teddy looked around for someone else to talk to and had already turned away as Clementine and Lady Harriet joined them.

"I simply loved *The Wind in the Willows*." Clementine narrowed her eyes at Teddy, touching him on his elbow, insisting he turn back into the conversation. "An utterly enchanting poem to pastoral England; Althea and I had such fun deciding who among our friends were Ratty, Moley, Badger, and Toad. The Wild Wooders of course are all up in London shooting at people in the Bank of England." Clementine laughed, inviting them to play the game with her.

"Oh . . . I see . . . well, that's easy," said Teddy, and he lifted his voice to include everyone within earshot. "Lord Booth is the Badger with his silver-and-black hair, and those terrifically broad shoulders; but, there again, perhaps not. Badger was an uncouth, old country bachelor and Lord Booth is evidently not interested in . . . bachelor ways."

Clementine glanced over at Lady Waterford on her sofa, exhaling a thin stream of smoke over the top of Lord Booth's head as Teddy, far too pleased with himself, continued.

"Sir Wilfred Shackleton is Mole—dreaming of adventure on

his dig in Egypt." Olive nodded her head in agreement. "So who is Ratty? The poet, the true countryman, immersed in his love of the bucolic paradise that is England?"

Teddy lifted his voice to be heard and Clementine discerned a slight sharp edge: "Well of course, my uncle, Lord Montfort, is undoubtedly Ratty," Teddy laughed, "which leaves us with Lord Booth as Badger—at heart a dedicated bachelor."

There followed one of those natural pauses that sometimes occurs among large gatherings, and Clementine was horrified that Teddy's voice had carried clearly across the room.

"And you, Teddy, undoubtedly you are the Toad." This came from Lady Waterford, reclining on her sofa. "A conceited, puffed-up, and naughty little Toady." Uncertain laughter greeted this, and Teddy made an acquiescing bow, but the expression in his eyes was not kind, and neither was there a smile on his face.

Clementine was utterly grateful when Ellis Booth lifted his voice to distract attention from his father and fill an awkward gap.

"Did any of you hear about the Derby today? Apparently, some deranged woman, wearing the suffragette flag wrapped around her middle, threw herself under the king's horse at Epsom this afternoon." This news had inevitable reactions.

"Which horse . . . oh, surely not Anmer?"

"Mind you, that horse didn't have a hope of winning!"

"What's wrong with these ruddy women?" Lord Booth's fruity tones were dropped in favor of an outraged male bellow, but he was careful to stand up and rejoin Lord Montfort and Jack Ambrose.

Clementine glanced over at Hollyoak. There passed between them the silent understanding that perhaps there had been enough parlor games on empty stomachs for one evening, and Hollyoak announced, "Dinner is served, m'lady!"

Lord Montfort offered his arm to Lady Booth, and Clementine took a quick look around to make sure their procession into dinner observed precedence, and saw Lucinda Lambert-Lambert standing at the far end of the room, her back to everyone.

She walked across to her and put her arm lightly around the girl's waist. "Lucinda, dear, are you unwell?" She looked searchingly into Lucinda's face. Had the girl had too much to drink? Lucinda straightened herself in the traditional schoolroom response to authority.

"So sorry, Lady Montfort, quite all right, thank you." The expression on her face conveyed distress and hurt. Clementine was reminded of the stunned expression of a child who has been too harshly chastised.

"My dear, you need some fresh air straightaway, so stuffy in this room when the weather is this close."

Even as she said this, Clementine hesitated over the wisdom of handing Lucinda over to Teddy, who was waiting to take her in to dinner; the girl was clearly upset and Teddy had rather a cruel streak. *Oh dear, she thought, this is unfortunate but there's no one else and I must go in.*

"Teddy, take Lucinda outside for a moment for some air, she'll be fine then, won't you, my dear?" The girl nodded her reassurance, and Teddy tucked her arm into his as he escorted her from the room.

Walking behind them with Lord Booth, Clementine heard Teddy say as they walked across the hall, "Poor old Lucy, such a dreadful shock, come and tell me all about it," and watched

Lucinda jerk her arm free of Teddy's and cross the hall ahead of him, ignoring him completely when he caught up with her to open the door to the terrace.

Well now, Clementine said to herself. *This is certainly rather interesting. Is everyone upset with Teddy today?*

Chapter Four

After dinner the Iyntwood house party reassembled in full costume and crowds of guests arrived to join them for the ball, filling flower-laden rooms with a shifting carnival of colors. Standing in the hall with her husband, Clementine's sense of occasion was completely gratified as they welcomed their friends, dressed in a vivid array of flamboyant outfits representing half the world's monarchy, at one time or another, as well as their more infamous subjects. Music cascaded from the ballroom, and she reminded herself to tell the orchestra to include more modern dances. Pretty paper lanterns were lit to illuminate gardens, pavilions, and hidden walks to the lake. Hollyoak and his brigade of footmen offered champagne throughout the house and on the terrace. Amid flickering golden candlelight, the creamy scent of roses and the chatter of voices lifted in greeting and delighted laughter, the Talbots' summer ball was fully under way.

After the ball, Clementine turned over in bed just as dawn was breaking, barely an hour since she had come up to her room.

The new day was obscured behind heavy clouds and she heard the rattle of rain outside her open windows. As the ball had drawn to an end, heavy black clouds had started to roll in from the southwest, sealing in the thick, humid night air. Clementine usually enjoyed untroubled sleep and she wondered what had awakened her as she lay listening to the rain.

There was a blue-white flare of lightning, and out of childhood habit she counted, one-one thousand, two-two thousand, followed by a heavy crackle and thump of thunder as the storm moved rapidly toward them. She hopped up and stood in the window closest to her bed. As if the thunder had been a signal, the rain tripled its efforts and smashed straight down, hitting the terrace with the force of a monsoon.

"Poor roses, they'll be a mess tomorrow," Clementine said as she closed the casement window, scrambled back into bed, and snuggled up to her sleeping husband.

Another flicker of lightning lit the room and this time the crash of thunder was immediate as the storm moved in overhead. She was vaguely aware of a sense of foreboding, as if she had forgotten to take care of something. The greatest social event of her year had exceeded all her expectations and she should have slept soundly, delighted with the outcome. But Clementine didn't feel particularly elated, or even complacently relieved at its success, instead there was a restless unease and she found herself anxious and wakeful. To distract herself as she waited for sleep to come, she settled back among the pillows with her arms crossed behind her head and sought to replay the highlights of her ball. It had been a resounding success. An event fit for London's society columns to gush over the details; an invitation to her summer ball had become one of the most sought-after occasions of the season. Smiling to herself in the dark, she remembered Constance Ambrose in a ravishing costume, representing strumpets through the ages, surrounded by admirers. Lord Booth as Bluff King Hal, whirling partner after partner, except for Gertrude Waterford, who, with her inevitable élan, had chosen to dress as la Dame aux Camélias, obviously inspired by Sarah Bernhardt; Lady Staunton got up in her favorite costume, which was supposed to be an accurate reproduction of Madame de Pompadour from Boucher's portrait, and miraculously for once not wearing her famous diamonds; and with an inward giggle she remembered Lady Booth as Britannia, a gleaming bronze Corinthian helmet clamped firmly down over her eyes, champing slowly and deliberately through a generous plate of lobster salad.

Clementine relaxed her jaw, let her shoulders sag, and consciously slowed her breathing as she drifted back into a deep, dreamless sleep.

Chapter Five

The following day after luncheon, Lord Montfort, grateful that his social duty was done, and done thoroughly well at that, retired to his study to enjoy the company of his closest friends, Sir Hugo Waterford, Lord Booth, and Colonel Jack Ambrose. Happy to accommodate his friends in a comfortable chin-wag on one of their favorite topics—the end of England's rural life as they knew it—Lord Montfort settled back in his favorite chair and made himself comfortable. He completely accepted that their afternoon discussion would be a heated one as his friends aired their fears for the future of a world in which they had been bred, born, and educated to serve, and which they now felt was doomed to an unspeakable end, nominally at the hands of free trade and the middle classes. He surrendered to the inevitable, knowing this conversation could go on all afternoon. He closed his eyes and allowed himself to drift off.

The door opened and, across the room thick with cigar smoke and heated rhetoric, he saw his butler standing on the threshold with such an overtly serious expression that he was already halfway out of his chair as Hollyoak reached his side. As his butler bent to speak in his ear, mild concern was replaced with confusion and then alarm. Excusing himself to his friends, he followed Hollyoak out of the room. Once Lord Montfort was penned up in a dark corner of the hall, his butler dismissed a footman in waiting, before he spoke.

"Theo Cartwright has come to the house, my lord, and wishes to speak to you rather urgently. He is most agitated."

"Oh really? Did he say what it might be about?" Lord Montfort could not imagine what his head gamekeeper could possibly want at this time of day.

"It appears that he has found the body of a dead man in Crow Wood, and is convinced it must be one of our guests."

"Good God!" His words were loud in the silent hall and he stared at his butler for so long that the man was about to repeat himself when Lord Montfort came to his senses and asked in a low tone, "Did Cartwright say who?"

"He wouldn't say, my lord."

"Well then you'd better tell him to wait for me at the terrace door. I'll meet him there. In the meantime, better keep this to yourself."

"Yes, my lord," said the worthy Hollyoak. "I thought perhaps you might need someone other than Mr. Cartwright with you, he's so badly shaken. I took the opportunity of asking Mr. Stafford to come over to the house."

"Thank you. Did you tell me where Lady Montfort was?"

"She's in the long drawing room. Shall I alert her, my lord?"

"Not yet, but I would like you to send someone over to the dower house to find out if Colonel Valentine is still a guest of my mother. If he is, ask him to come over immediately to Crow Wood in the pony and trap. We will need his help, and we should have a vehicle at hand. Please make sure someone directs him to that part of the wood."

Lord Montfort joined his gamekeeper and Mr. Stafford on the south terrace and they walked the entire distance from the edge of the gardens to the stable block and from there down the lane past the home farm and through the pasture to Crow Wood, in silence.

As the three men drew near to the edge of the wood, the oppressive sky darkened and a light shower of rain came down on them. Grateful for the protection of the trees, they proceeded in single file deeper into the wood. The fresh, light green of trembling beech leaves formed a filigree canopy high overhead, providing a translucent roof between woodland floor and gray cloud above and offering a little protection from the rain.

When they approached the area where Iyntwood's gamekeepers reared the young pheasants for the yearly shoot, Lord Montfort noticed that Cartwright's hand stole upward to his mustache and beard, carefully and protectively grooming them as if seeking comfort before confronting the sight he had discovered earlier. When Lord Montfort had met him on the terrace, he had been disconcerted by Cartwright's agitated manner. And then as he listened to Theo describe how he had come across a young man's body hanged by his neck from his gamekeeper's gibbet he saw, with concern, beads of sweat break out on the man's forehead.

"Who is it, d'you know?" Lord Montfort asked him.

"I can't be sure, my lord, the body is in bad shape and some of the crows have been at him." Cartwright looked like he was going to be sick.

Now Lord Montfort walked forward with a feeling of dread and unease building in his stomach. He cast a glance at Cartwright, who became paler as they went deeper into the wood.

He had always found gamekeepers' gibbets gruesome and

depressing. Wooden posts with crossbeams pinned above the main supports, on which were nailed the rotting carcasses of birds and animals that were thought to prey on young pheasants. Lord Montfort, a true countryman, was committed heart and soul to the preservation of his lands, woodlands, and wild game but had long ago come to the secret conclusion that predators were not deterred one jot by the sight and smell of the dead and rotting carcasses of their kind. He found the pitiful, shriveled bodies of animals and birds exhibited this way repellent, but forbore to comment to his gamekeeper on what he felt was after all Cartwright's business.

He was familiar with this particular gibbet, which was of unusually impressive size. Two tree trunks set ten feet apart supported several heavy horizontal boughs bolted four feet distant of one another; the top rail was of a substantially greater thickness than those below it, and one end jutted out beyond the tree that supported it. The carcasses of foxes, weasels, stoats, and even a badger were nailed at intervals along the length of the beams, with a line of birds, mostly crows, on the lowest rail forming a depressing underscore to the larger animals hanging above them. It was an ugly and dispiriting sight and one, he believed, that truly proclaimed the ignorance of the country dweller at that time. But it did nothing to prepare him for the appalling spectacle at the far end of the gibbet's heavy top rail.

The shock of what he saw made it hard for him to focus for a moment, and then the image before him sharpened into dreadful clarity and he felt his stomach convulse and his gorge rise as his mind finally caught on to what his eyes were telling him. He was looking at the body of a young man dangling like a shabby, broken doll in front of him, his feet barely six inches off the ground. He was hanging by his neck; he must have choked slowly to death. Lord Montfort struggled for reason and found none. The dead man's head drooped downward and to the left in the stiff, unnatural pose of a body that has been made to die. The tight noose had dug deeply into his neck, his face was distorted, and his tongue protruded black and swollen between lips drawn back in a fearful grimace. The crows had been at work where his eyes had once been.

Lord Montfort turned his head away and gave himself a moment before he made himself look back again and then he had to force himself to take in the terrible details. The murdered man's arms in the torn coat of his evening suit were bound tightly behind his back, and his legs had been bound twice, just above the knees and again at the ankles. Inconsequentially, he noticed that the body was missing a shoe; the other one, a black patent leather evening shoe, was still on his foot.

In Lord Montfort's entire life he had never seen anything as fearsome and atrocious as this pitiful scrap of humanity proclaiming the anguish of his death as clearly as if he still had words to speak. He heard Stafford's cry of horror as he rapidly gained the privacy of a large tree and was violently sick.

Lord Montfort managed his horror, and his stomach, though he still felt bitter bile rising in his throat. He suddenly became desperately cold and felt a startling snatch of fear in his chest. It was only absolute discipline that stopped him from crying out. The yellow hair, even though it was plastered with mud and rainwater, was an unmistakable clue to the victim's identity, as was its slight, youthful build. He knew, with absolute certainty, he was staring at the body of his nephew, Teddy Mallory.

"I know who this is," he said quietly, his heart hammering in his chest and adrenaline coursing through his body, causing the muscles in his legs to cramp and the hair on his nape and his forearms to rise in stiff, harsh prickles. It was difficult to breathe in the clearing. The trees shut out the air. The sight of the eyeless sockets of foxes and birds hanging alongside Teddy made him feel panicky and terribly nauseated. He fought down a natural urge to turn and make for home. His senses were so heightened that he could hear the rain pattering on the canopy of leaves high overhead, the rustle of small animals and birds foraging in the undergrowth around them, and his pulse sounding inside his head, loud and slightly accelerated. Above this, coming insistently toward him, was the homely sound of a pony trotting up the dirt track toward the wood.

He turned to Cartwright, who had avoided looking at the body of the murdered man ever since they had arrived. Lord Montfort realized that Cartwright had probably recognized Teddy Mallory when he had first found the body. His orderly countryman's mind would have had difficulty in understanding that a member of the aristocracy, born and bred in the county, could possibly be found so thoroughly abused, dead and covered in mud, swinging from his gibbet. He was evidently struggling with what he had found, and Lord Montfort noticed that his hands were trembling.

He walked over to Cartwright and rested what he hoped was a reassuring hand on the older man's shoulder. Offering comfort to his gamekeeper helped Lord Montfort to recover his wits. Stafford emerged from behind his tree wiping his forehead and mouth with a large blue handkerchief, and the three men waited for Colonel Valentine, who, driving up in the pony and trap, was more than equipped for what he found waiting for him.

Lord Montfort knew Colonel Valentine reasonably well; he appreciated Valentine's reserved, courteous manner and believed him to be fair-minded and steady. He had certainly contributed well in his capacity as chief constable for the county town of Market Wingley and its surrounding villages and smaller towns. He knew the colonel was a retired professional solider, a veteran of the Boer Wars. Valentine had probably had enough excitement in Africa to last a lifetime and had retired to this pleasant backwater where nothing ever happened, except the odd drunken brawl on a Friday night, petty theft, and of course poaching. It suddenly flashed into his mind that in the old days the executed bodies of criminals—highwaymen, footpads, and murderers—were hung in cages at well-traveled intersections of the country's highways, a dreadful warning of the consequences of a lawless life.

Leaving the pony and trap at the edge of the wood, Valentine walked toward Lord Montfort carefully inspecting the ground and the surrounding area as he made his approach. He stopped and took a long, thorough look at the area under the gibbet before joining Lord Montfort, who was now standing apart from Cartwright and Stafford. "Terribly shocking thing to find. I had hoped you would wait and let me be the first to arrive. Looks to me like it's young Teddy Mallory. Would you agree?"

"Yes, I am afraid it is." As he heard himself acknowledge that the dead man was his nephew Lord Montfort felt grief and anguish for a young man who had been a part of his household since he was a boy. His throat constricted and he put his hand up to his eyes and felt tears seep through his fingers. He pushed back hard into the corners of his eyes to stem the flow of misery and sadness.

"It looks as if some motor vehicle has been drawn up under this arm of the gibbet. Unfortunately, the rain has been going on long enough to disguise any real activity." Valentine paused in thought for a moment or two before continuing.

"When we get back to the house, I would like to go straight to your study to begin my inquiry. Can we rely on your men here not to talk about what has happened?"

"Undoubtedly." Lord Montfort's voice sounded hoarse, as if it were about to break, and he made the supreme attempt to pull himself together. "Where do you want them to take Teddy's body?"

"Somewhere under cover, your carriage house would do. If you would wait awhile, I need to make sure everything is carried out properly."

Lord Montfort stood under the shelter of a large tree and watched as Colonel Valentine gave instructions to Cartwright and Stafford. Stafford was sent off in the pony chaise to bring Constable Standish from the village and Cartwright was sent with him to bring up the dray from the home farm.

Lord Montfort's feet felt like ice; he was cold through and through. He almost envied Valentine: busy and purposeful as he investigated the ground under the gibbet and jotted down notes in a small book pulled from his coat pocket. As Valentine finished up and started to walk toward him, Lord Montfort heard the dray's engine coming up the track from the home farm toward the wood.

Chapter Six

When Lord Montfort returned to the house with the chief constable, he felt like an altogether older and quieter man than the one who had left his house, more than two hours earlier, so decisively in the company of his gardener and gamekeeper. As he approached the terrace door he saw that Hollyoak must have been waiting for them. His butler walked ahead to open the door into his study.

"Hollyoak, show Colonel Valentine to the telephone room and then wait for me in the hall, please." He watched Hollyoak usher Colonel Valentine into the pokey room that had been built into an out-of-the-way, dimly lit corner of the hall, which offered minimal privacy in its cramped and stuffy interior, before gaining the sanctuary of his study.

Lord Montfort did not dare allow himself a speck of respite from the locked-down self-control he had summoned up in Crow Wood. There were many miles to go, he realized, before he could allow himself the indulgence of introspection. In the few moments he gave himself, before Valentine returned, his face showed a fleeting glimpse of the cold horror he felt. He had never particularly liked Teddy and his brutal end now added considerably to his confused emotions.

He believed his sister's only child had been quite terribly spoiled throughout his life. When Teddy was eight years old, and his father had been killed in a shooting accident, he had become the sole focus of his mother's life, when she had time for him at all. On her brief visits to England, Christina Mallory spent days with the boy at Montfort House in London, lavishing attention on him and including him in her busy social life. But her visits were few and far between and inevitably bored with playing mother, she increasingly returned to the sophisticated pleasures of the Marlborough set in Biarritz or Baden Baden, abandoning her son to the comparatively dull and prosaic existence of family life at uncle's house in the country, This on-again, off-again arrangement had proved disastrous for Teddy. As the years had gone by Teddy, now at Eton, had become more isolated from his mother and had turned away from the simplicity of Talbot family life at Iyntwood. Lord Montfort thought of himself as a well-intentioned man, and as Teddy's legal guardian he had tried hard to show patience and forbearance toward his nephew, while he daily thanked God that Teddy was not his son. As he tried to come to terms with Teddy's death, he believed he had let his nephew down. He believed he had let his sister down, too.

He sat down at his desk and began to make up the list of his guests, as Valentine had requested. As he wrote down their names he was aware that each of them would be severely impacted by Teddy's death simply by staying in his house. He was finishing this task when Valentine came back from making his telephone call to the coroner's office.

"Will you tell me a little about your nephew, Lord Montfort?

I know he is your sister's only child and that he was up at Oxford . . . Christ Church wasn't it? What sort of young man was he?"

Before he answered, Lord Montfort paused in thought. What kind of young man had his nephew been? At any other time, it would have been so easy to answer this question. Now it was impossible with the image of Teddy hanging from the gibbet. It was as if his mind refused to obey direction, hopping from one inconsequential thought to another in the strangest way. With a great summoning of effort he forced himself to answer the question.

"He was on the whole rather a difficult young man; I had trouble getting through to him, which seemed to get worse as he grew older. Yesterday morning I received a letter from the proctor at Oxford in which he told me that Teddy had been expelled for cheating at cards. I heard the rest of it from Harry later on."

"Oh I see. Did Teddy keep company with Lord Haversham?" Valentine asked, and Lord Montfort was grateful for Valentine's matter-of-fact question that included his son, as it helped him focus on the reality of the situation.

"They shared few interests. Harry moved in different circles."

"What do you know about this cheating business?"

"The proctor's letter was to the point with very few details. But Harry told me that Teddy had set up some sort of informal gambling club at Oxford: high stakes games and so on. It appears that there were quite a few young men involved. Teddy was caught by one of them, cheating." He stopped for a moment; he had been appalled when his son confided this news to him yesterday.

"Must have been quite a showdown." Valentine's voice and expression were noncommittal.

"Yes, I expect it was. Harry said it got quite rough, not that he was there," he hastily added. "Of course Teddy denied it because . . . well he would, wouldn't he?" Lord Montfort paused and then added, "The stakes were quite large apparently . . ."

"Any idea how large?" Valentine asked.

"I don't know exactly. Harry named a sum that was almost preposterous, it's probably hugely exaggerated." As he related his conversation with Harry, he was aware that no one in his family knew yet what had happened to Teddy. They would have to tell everyone in the house.

"I would like to talk with Lord Haversham as soon as possible since he was up at Christ Church with his cousin and the other young men here in the house who knew Teddy at Oxford. Let's see now, that would be Oscar Barclay also up at Christ Church and Ellis Booth at Balliol, am I right?"

"Yes, that's right."

Lord Montfort turned his head as Hollyoak returned and announced that a Detective Sergeant Hawkins and Constable Dixon had arrived at the house for Colonel Valentine and, with an expression of disapproval on his face, that Theo Cartwright had come at Colonel Valentine's request and Hollyoak thought it best to keep Cartwright in the gun room until he was needed. The gamekeeper's boots were very muddy.

"Thank you, Hollyoak," Lord Montfort said, grateful to hear that his voice sounded quite normal. "You should know in complete confidence that it was Mr. Teddy who we found in Crow Wood." He walked out into the hall with Hollyoak and politely accepted his butler's condolences.

"Hollyoak, please make yourself available to Colonel Valentine. Now I want you to round up all our guests and gather them together in the long drawing room. Important you don't say why. Colonel Valentine will address them." He turned to go back into the study but, realizing that Valentine's investigation was now under way, decided it was time to leave him to it. The only thing he could think of was that he wanted to be with his wife.

Chapter Seven

Clementine was in the long drawing room with her friends, where they were idly indulging in the inevitable gossip that is always on offer after a large event in the company of close friends. It was nearly time for tea to be brought in and Clementine was surprised when Hollyoak appeared before them, standing in the doorway with his head bowed.

"What is it, Hollyoak?" She turned as he walked toward her and asked her to join Lord Montfort in the morning room. It was unusual for her husband to stir out of his study when they had a lot of people in the house and she was a little perplexed by Hollyoak's rather portentous manner. Always correct and self-contained, no matter what occurred, she could tell that something was troubling him: there was a greater intensity in his demeanor than was usual. He seemed almost furtive as he gave her Lord Montfort's message. She was grateful to excuse herself. Agatha had been boring on endlessly about her father's glory days in the House of Lords as a young man, where he single-handedly held the line against the Commons and their determination to prevent factory owners from using child labor.

She was completely unprepared for the sight of her husband sitting on the window seat of the morning room, his dogs in a sad heap on the floor, gazing abjectly up at him, at a loss to understand his mood. He was staring out of the window, his face haggard and drawn, with such a palpable air of despair about him that Clementine immediately thought of their daughter Althea, who had started her walking tour of the lower slopes of the Jungfrau yesterday morning.

"What is it, Ralph? What's happened? . . . Are you all right? Is Althea . . . ?" She stood in the doorway, determined to remain calm. He rose at once and crossed the room, gathered her to him, and held her very close until she gently pushed him away so she could look up into his face.

"My darling, it's Teddy. He's been found dead in Crow Wood, murdered. Theo Cartwright found him early this afternoon." She knew she looked horrified, because he stopped and guided her to the sofa, where they sat down together. He held her hands in his and continued.

"Morris Valentine was still staying at the dower house with Mother and he came over to the wood immediately. He's going to conduct an inquiry into Teddy's death."

She nodded, but couldn't quite take in what he was saying. After a moment she asked if Teddy had been shot and was completely unprepared for his response that he had been hanged. She gasped, and her hands came up halfway to her face, as if to protect herself from seeing the hideous image that had jumped into her mind. Her husband put his arms protectively around her, pulled her to him, and held her until she was able to understand what had happened.

"Ralph, did you see Teddy?" she finally asked.

"Yes, my dear, a terrible death. I can't imagine who would

want . . . He was heedless and selfish, but nothing he could have done . . ." His voice trailed off. She saw how wretched and uncertain he was as he turned away from her to stare out of the window again. She reached out and took his hands in hers, shaking them gently to regain his attention.

"Ralph, you did everything you could to help him grow up to be a decent man. Christina was always so distracted. Teddy either had too much attention from her or none at all. Now what are we to do?" Clementine knew immediately that things had to be done and was ready to move into the next phase, the one she was always most comfortable with, the business of doing. "Does Valentine have any idea how long his inquiry will take?"

"Probably a couple of days; after all, no one here killed him and we know our local poachers are not murderers." He almost smiled. "Valentine will break the news to our guests. Harry's in there now with him." He waved a hand toward the study.

"Harry's with him!" Clementine straightened up. Her eyes were fixed on his face and she was holding her hands tightly together, alarm flashing through her body. "Why is Harry with him?"

"Steady on, darling, no need for alarm. Of course he has to talk to Harry; they were all up at Christ Church together. He'll be talking to all the boys—they know more about Teddy's life than we do."

Clementine said nothing. But she felt cold and her mouth went dry as she remembered the awful incident she had witnessed at the boathouse yesterday afternoon, when she had heard her son threaten Teddy with his life: *I'll break your damn neck . . .*

She came out of this awful reverie to find that Hollyoak had arrived and was asking Lord Montfort to join Colonel Valentine in the study.

"Ask Lord Haversham to come in here while I am gone, Hollyoak. Lady Montfort should not be alone." Her husband stood up and left the room and within minutes the door opened again and Harry joined her.

Lost in her thoughts and struggling to regain equanimity, Clementine could barely trust her voice to speak when her son came into the room. But she was sufficiently recovered to watch his face closely. Did he look tense? He was wary perhaps, she thought—yes, definitely wary. But it was so hard to tell with Harry.

"Mother, come and sit down. What can I get you?" He was as solicitous as if she had been caught in a rainstorm and still had wet feet.

"Harry, I . . . Teddy . . . I'm quite shattered."

"Well, Mother, it's a shattering thing. Poor old Teddy, I can't quite take it in." Harry led her back to the window seat and sat down in a chair facing her. She stared into his eyes and all she found looking back at her was kindness and concern. How could she suspect him of something so dreadful? Her son could never have done this terrible thing, it just wasn't possible. But she asked, "What did Valentine say?" and kept her eyes on his face, watchful of every flicker.

"He asked me to tell him about Teddy, which I did. You see, Teddy was caught cheating at cards . . ." Harry then filled her in on Teddy's gambling club at Oxford. Clementine was not particularly shocked about the reason for Teddy's expulsion. It was not surprising news. She remembered the incident at Eton when Teddy's fag had been thrown down the stairs for not cleaning Teddy's shoes properly; the incident had started with an irritated shove on Teddy's part and ended up with the boy in a wheelchair. And then there was that business with other boys' postal orders, and forged signatures. It was not surprising that Teddy could have systematically set about cheating his friends at cards.

As she listened, her mind went back to the boathouse and she saw Harry raging at his cousin as he threatened to break his neck. She knew her son well; he was not a complicated individual. She believed he was fair-minded, a decided champion of the underdog, with all the hallmarks of a gentleman and none of the bully. She made an evaluation of Harry's level of anger based on her new knowledge of Teddy's disgrace at Oxford. However angry Harry had been, she did not believe it was Teddy's misbehavior that had infuriated him. There was something else, something that cut deeper than Teddy's dishonesty.

"How was Teddy when he came to the house yesterday afternoon, did you have the chance to spend any time with him?" she asked, doing her utmost not to assume the tone of interrogator. She knew she'd succeeded because he answered her quite easily, and there was no change in the expression on his face or in his voice.

"I hardly saw him, there were so many of my friends here. I told all this to Valentine, by the way." If her questions annoyed him after his session with the chief constable he didn't show it. But then Harry's manner often bordered on the matter-of-fact; it was how young men often behaved, thought Clementine, especially when confronted with emotional women. She scanned his face. So this was how Harry looked when he lied, she thought. He might have "hardly" seen his cousin, but the few moments he had shared with him had been violent ones.

"Harry, darling . . ." She was tentative, unsure how to proceed. Mothers did not as a rule interrogate grown sons on their conduct and certainly did not question the code of behavior that governed their bewildering masculine world; these things were best left to their fathers.

"Yes, Mother?"

"Harry, I saw you and Teddy by the boathouse." She paused to let this bit sink in. "After luncheon, just as I was coming back to the house before tea." She cursed herself for sounding accusatory; he knew when he had fought with his cousin and where.

"Ah, I see." He colored slightly, looked away for a moment and then back to her. "And after seeing that . . . that exchange between us, you think perhaps I might have killed Teddy?"

His tone was quite level, polite even. He didn't sound upset but he frowned. Was it annoyance? Perhaps he was embarrassed. Whichever it was, he respectfully waited for her answer.

"Of course not. But you were very angry and you . . . well, it was all *very* loud. It looked so bad, so violent."

"Yes, I suppose it did. Would you like me to tell you why I gave Teddy such a going-over?" The frown disappeared. They might have been talking about anything other than his shoving his cousin backward down the boathouse steps and threatening to break his neck.

She nodded. "Yes, Harry, under the circumstances, I think perhaps I would."

He cleared his throat and getting up from his chair he joined her her on the window seat. "Very well then. I was walking back to the house from my meeting with Pommeroy and Father. I took a shortcut around the back of the boathouse. As I came round the corner, I heard a good deal of splashing out on the lake and I wandered around to the front of the boathouse to see what was up. And there was Teddy." Her son paused, lips compressed, hands pushed down hard on either side of him into the chintz cushions of the window seat. He shook his head and shot her look of hurt and disgust at the memory of what he had seen.

"Teddy had thrown a heavy stick out into the middle of the lake and encouraged Percy to retrieve it."

"Percy?" She couldn't help but interrupt. "He threw a stick for Percy?"

At fifteen, Harry's dog was far too old and arthritic to do much more than gently amble from his bed to his food dish. It was unthinkable that he had actually gone into the water, as the lake was still bitterly cold at this time of year. But Percy's stubborn Labrador heart would never accept that his glory days as a retriever were over. It would only have taken some enthusiastic egging on to get him to go in after the stick.

"The stick was waterlogged and terribly heavy and the foolish old man was floundering, but he wouldn't let go and it was beginning to pull him down. I peeled off, swam out to him, and somehow managed to get him in. The poor old chap was nearly done for. All this time, Teddy was standing there smoking a cigarette and watching me. I carried Percy into the boathouse, dried him off, and wrapped him up in a rug to keep him warm. Then I went out to Teddy and he said, 'Sometimes it's kinder to let them go out the way they lived. If he was my dog I would have had him shot a year ago. Put him out of his misery.' I saw red, it was the last straw and I thumped him."

Why wasn't she surprised by any of this? This was Harry through and through. He could turn stoically away from Teddy's bad behavior at Oxford, put on a brave face as Teddy dragged the family into yet another scandal, but it was beyond him to ignore the cruelty of bullying. Especially to an animal as helpless as his much loved old dog.

Clementine felt a momentary lessening of the load. For the first time since she had been told of Teddy's death she could actually move her shoulders.

"There was something not quite right about Teddy in that area," was all she could think of to say, her relief was so immense. "He could never be trusted with small children or animals. I think it was the way he was made; something was lacking."

Her son reached over and patted her hand. "It's all right, Mama," he said. "Please try not to worry. Teddy's life was more awful than you could possibly imagine. We will never know what he was mixed up in. His death has nothing to do with anyone at the house, I'm sure of that. And if I gave him a trouncing it was bad of me, but I certainly didn't kill him."

They both turned to gaze out of the window, and with deep regret and considerable confusion Clementine thought of the very young man who had been an uncomfortable and difficult member of her family. What a troubled and unhappy boy he had been. What caused some children to turn out so badly and lose their way? Anxiety started to chip away her earlier reassurance. Harry was wrong. His cousin had died a violent death and now a police inquiry would reveal exactly what Teddy had been "mixed up in." Every question asked, every statement made would bring another of part of Teddy's unsavory life swimming up to the surface, and God only knew what else would come with it.

These disturbing thoughts were interrupted by her husband as he opened the door of the morning room.

"Valentine is going to talk to Oscar and Ellis now." Lord Montfort seemed to have regained some of his equilibrium, but she thought his face still appeared haggard and wretchedly tired.

"As soon as he has finished with them, he will meet with all of us. In the meantime we should just sit here and wait." He came farther into the room and sat down with them.

Clementine was grateful that they could all sit still with their thoughts and not feel the need to talk. Her mind was trundling around so many what-ifs that she felt sure it could be heard in the quiet room. She would never understand how men managed to conceal their feelings so thoroughly. She was sure her face was an open book. She was scared. Ever since her husband had told her of Teddy's death she had been scared—scared for so many reasons that she could barely count them.

It was only twenty minutes before Colonel Valentine opened the door to the morning room, but to Clementine it felt like an ancient and dusty age had crept coldly by as they sat silently together. She looked up at Valentine standing in the doorway. Oscar, behind him, looked distinctly green about the gills, she thought. Ellis, standing next to Oscar, appeared calm, but as he glanced at Harry, Harry looked away.

Anxiety had focused Clementine's vigilance to a razor's edge. She noticed Ellis's glance, took it as significant, and felt her body react with panic. It occurred to her as they all walked across the hall toward the long drawing room that their lives in that moment had completely changed. A brutal murder of someone in their family had been committed here, where they lived, and probably by someone they all knew. She wondered how long it would be before they knew who had murdered Teddy and understood with a feeling akin to hopelessness that much would have to happen before that time and at the end of it would be shame and more awfulness. Teddy's very short life had ended as regrettably as it had been lived.

* * *

Their guests were waiting for them in the long drawing room, and the group turned expectant eyes on them as they came into the room. Clementine avoided catching anyone's glance. *Is this what happens?* she asked herself. *Do we feel culpable when a member of our family is brutally killed, as if we had done the awful, unimaginable thing ourselves?* But someone *had* done the unimaginable, maybe someone standing close to her in this beautiful room. She must pay attention. Valentine was telling them that Teddy Mallory had been found dead on the estate.

There was a moment of stunned silence. Clementine made herself look around the room at the sea of bewildered faces before her.

Lady Agatha Booth, sitting in a chair in the middle of the room and attended by her daughters, was the first to speak with exclamations and exhortations for something to be done immediately for the "poor dear boy." Paying no attention to her loud, distracting cries, Clementine noticed that Lady Waterford's head jerked up and that she gripped the arms of her chair, but she was quick to recover her self-possession, and asked if it had been an accident. Lord Booth, in the act of lighting a cigar, seemed almost prepared for the announcement of Teddy's death, as he continued to draw on his cigar, hands steady, eyes speculative as he glanced around the room. Olive Shackleton and Constance Ambrose were clutching each other rather melodramatically. Clementine looked over at Sir Wilfred Shackleton, stiff as a board; he remained absolutely still and let his eyes swivel around the group as he carefully licked his lips, like a cat when it smells something unpleasant.

Jack Ambrose looked altogether far too eager as he cleared his throat. "Are you going to conduct an inquiry into the death, Valentine?" he asked—almost enviously, she thought.

"For the time being," Valentine answered, and Clementine noticed that he kept his eyes on their faces, as if watching for reactions.

She saw Jack nod and then he asked if it had been some sort of accident, and when he received no answer he said, "Oh, I see, that's bad. I expect you'll want to talk it over with all of us one at a time . . . right? So we should be prepared to spend a few more days with Ralph?"

"Yes, you will all need to extend your stay here for a couple of days, perhaps more, I am not sure. If you will all wait together here for the rest of afternoon, I will call you when I need to speak with you. I need hardly say, of course, that the less you discuss this among yourselves, the easier my job will be."

Colonel Valentine's voice is so calm and detached, thought Clementine who had only met the chief constable at local charities and dinners. *I've never seen him doing his job.*

Finally the question that she was waiting for was asked, and it was Lord Booth who asked it: "How did he die?"

"It is hard to be precise about cause of death but it looks like strangulation. More than that I am not prepared to say at the moment."

Clementine was surprised to hear a loud gasp from Gertrude Waterford, echoed immediately by Constance; Lord Booth looked blandly ahead, puffing out gales of cigar smoke. Olive Shackleton—never blessed with the best of nerves, Clementine afterward remembered—exclaimed, almost shouted, "Good God," so loudly that Lady Booth burst into tears. Harry and

Ellis stood off to the side of the room, looking serious. Oscar seemed as if he might pass out.

Clementine's eyes turned back to Valentine as he stood looking at the group for a few more minutes. He had Lord Montfort's guest list in his hand, which he had been studying, glancing up occasionally before returning his gaze to the list. He finally lifted his head and said, "Lucinda Lambert-Lambert? Where is she? I asked everyone to be called . . ."

They all looked at one another and around the room, and Lucinda's mother said plaintively, "Lucinda, not here?"

Clementine's eyes went to Pansy and Blanche, who stood behind Lady Booth, their pale-lashed eyes blinking nervously, as everyone turned interrogatory eyes toward them.

"Pansy, Blanche, have you seen Lucinda today?" Lady Booth demanded. They shook their heads, incapable of speech, it seemed. Their mother twisted around as much as she could in her chair.

"Answer! *When* did you last see Lucinda?"

"Last n-night—" Blanche stammered out, "at the ball. Not today, not at all," and Pansy nodded in agreement. "No, not today . . ." she murmured.

"I will send Hollyoak to find her. She has to be here somewhere," said Lord Montfort. "Was she with us for luncheon?"

"Lucinda doesn't often take luncheon if she is studying," her mother said, but she didn't appear to be reassured by her words. Harriet turned to her husband, and Clementine thought there was something rather accusing in the look she gave him.

"Perhaps in her room?" suggested Clementine.

They waited for an agonizing twenty minutes as Hollyoak was sent to look through the house. He came back and spoke quietly to Lord Montfort.

"Lucinda does not appear to be in the house," Lord Montfort said, relaying Hollyoak's information. "Perhaps she has gone for a walk."

"If you would send word to the stables and the gardeners' room to have the grounds checked?" Colonel Valentine had to raise his voice over the excited babble of conjecture and further exclamations that now broke from people who rarely raised their tone above a well-modulated murmur. Hollyoak looked inquiringly at Lord Montfort, who nodded his directions.

Clementine said, "Hollyoak, I am sure tea is ready . . . please ask James." She crossed the room to Lady Harriet and Gilbert Lambert-Lambert, who were standing side by side. *How miserable and embarrassed they look. Of course they feel thoroughly in the wrong,* she thought. *Who wouldn't if you didn't know where your daughter was when a dead body has just been discovered in the woods.*

"I expect Lucinda has taken herself off for one of her long walks," she said to Lady Harriet as she reached out a hand toward her friend.

"In this?" Olive, standing next to Lady Harriet, gestured to the window and everyone obediently turned their heads and gazed politely at the summer rain as it poured resolutely down, the lawn soaked and puddles forming on the drive.

"Well quite . . ." said Constance Ambrose, and speculative eyes turned to Lady Harriet before everyone remembered themselves. The large room became silent as they waited.

Clementine looked around at her friends, such a voluble, chattery group. People she had known for years now sat apart from one another, worried that they might say the wrong thing, and so said nothing. She noticed that all eyes turned continually to

Colonel Valentine, who was sitting in the corner, in quiet contemplation of his notebook. After a while he looked up.

"Lady Harriet and Mr. Lambert-Lambert, I take it the three of you all came here together?" He got up and walked to the door.

"Lucinda drove down from Cambridge in her motorcar and met us here," said Gilbert Lambert-Lambert.

"Then we must send to the wash-down to see if it is still there. Perhaps we should go up to your daughter's room." Valentine stood aside in the doorway for the Lambert-Lamberts to precede him, giving another glance at the throng before the three of them left the room.

"Did he say *Lucinda's* motorcar?" Lady Booth was already looking for allies in her disbelief and outrage. "Whatever will it be next? Young gells driving themselves about alone in their *own motorcars*."

"We assume she wasn't naked. What are you implying, Agatha? Many of us drive motors." Gertrude glanced coldly at Lady Booth before turning to Olive Shackleton with a look of helpless indignation on her face. *Oh dear,* thought Clementine, *I hope these two can manage to be polite; there is so much more to come before we are done.*

Hollyoak reappeared at her elbow. His was a busy afternoon, she thought.

"I have sent Dick over to the stable block to find a couple of lads to help him look over the grounds for Miss Lucinda, m'lady, and James and John are bringing tea." Clementine nodded. Her butler seemed to have endless reserves of people to send on errands hither and thither about the estate. He also appeared to have attained greater height as the afternoon had worn on, and was it her imagination or was he still full of portent?

Clementine, grateful for an occupation, automatically sat down to prepare tea for her guests as Hollyoak bent to speak a private word in her ear. As she listened, she was so startled that she barely managed to avoid pouring hot water into Gertrude's lap. With commendable self-possession she carefully set down the cup and saucer she was holding.

"You are certain?" she said under her breath as she looked up at the butler, convinced that she had misunderstood.

"Yes, m'lady, absolutely certain."

She had always found Hollyoak to be a master of understatement, but she thought she detected a little tension lapping around the edges of his impassive demeanor.

"Very well then, please meet me in the morning room with Mrs. Jackson, after tea."

And she turned back to the task of giving her guests a sustaining cup of tea to allay the shock of their afternoon.

Chapter Eight

Earlier that day, Mrs. Jackson had taken up a command position in the wide corridor belowstairs that was the arterial route between servants' hall, kitchens, and workrooms. Her head ached and her feet hurt. She had been directing efforts to put the house in order after the ball long before her breakfast, keeping her fellow servants bent to the task of staying on schedule. After the endless hours of preparation for yesterday, culminating in the excitement of arriving guests, dinner, and the ball, she was running on less than three hours of sleep.

The sound of Cook's harsh voice, a continual backdrop to the morning, wore on her nerves as Mrs. Thwaite and the kitchen maids flogged through the last of the preparations for luncheon upstairs. Painfully aware of Cook's grating and shrill glottal stop and her dropped aitches, Mrs. Jackson often found herself wondering how someone as coarse in voice and sensitivity as Mrs. Thwaite could produce food of such delicate subtlety and complex flavor.

Determined to find a quiet spot until it was time for the servants' midday dinner, Mrs. Jackson shut herself away in the china and crystal pantry to inventory all the plates, glasses, and serving dishes that had been used for the ball. As she ticked off the last item of Sevres in the ledger she was thankful to hear that Mrs. Thwaite's voice had become less caustic and her tone a little kinder. She emerged from her pantry and realized with a sinking heart that it was merely because Mrs. Thwaite was indulging herself in her favorite pastime: gossip.

"What's going on with this new maid do you reckon?" she heard Mable Thwaite ask her kitchen maid, Iris White.

"She's all right really, not a bit stuck up for all her father's a schoolmaster."

Mrs. Jackson cocked a protective ear and walked into the kitchen as they were obviously talking about her new third housemaid, Violet Simkins.

"I didn't say what was wrong with her, I meant what was *up* with her. She looks really miserable all the time. There's something broody about that girl."

"I dunno, I think she has mood problems or something."

Mrs. Jackson filled a kettle with cold water and set it to boil on the hob.

"Well I never—mood problems, is it?" Mrs. Thwaite's voice was triumphant. "That's the sort of behavior we expect from upstairs with young girls, not down here. Down here we work through our mood problems and no time to think, neither."

Mrs. Jackson took a cup and saucer from the pine kitchen dresser and decided she would stay out of it, unless things got too unkind, but Mrs. Thwaite's next remark hit home.

"And where was Miss Violet all afternoon yesterday, off in the rose garden reading a book?" Mrs. Jackson heard a snigger from the listening kitchen maids and decided that things had gone too far.

"Her dad was pulled in to help out with the orchestra last night and Vi was given a half hour off to have a cuppa with him in Mrs. Jackson's parlor, ladyship's instructions," Iris blundered on.

"Well, I never. A cuppa tea with her dad, whatever will it be next? Mrs. Jackson getting too easy in her ways, is she?"

Mrs. Jackson measured tea leaves into the pot and poured hot water from the kettle, and a woody, astringent aroma lifted up in a pungent cloud of steam. She firmly put the lid on the teapot. It was high time Mable Thwaite's gossip came to an end; the woman was the limit. She came farther into the kitchen so that Mrs. Thwaite could see her.

"In this house we do not speculate on Lady Montfort's orders, or mine, Mrs. Thwaite." She kept her tone level. "Violet is doing a good job in the house, despite her homesickness."

"Homesickness?" Mrs. Thwaite tempered a bowl of butter. "Well, we all get homesick, Mrs. Jackson, no doubt about that, but we don't get to sit about with a nice cuppa tea in the middle of the afternoon, taking our ease."

Using her most repressive voice, she answered, "I would have thought you were too busy right now to waste your time on how the new maid is settling in."

She watched Mrs. Thwaite set the butter down and start to break eggs, deftly separating whites from yolks.

"That's as may be, but a little talk about the facts of life wouldn't go amiss. Violet's got James and John making complete fools of themselves," Cook said, referring to the footmen who, Mrs. Jackson had to silently agree, had been showing off for Violet's benefit ever since she had started at the house eight weeks ago.

Mrs. Jackson closed in on the kitchen table and said, "Servants' dinner is in two minutes. I hope you have things in hand, Mrs. Thwaite, we must not be late," and she left to walk down the corridor to take her place at the top of the table on

Mr. Hollyoak's right, as the servants filed in to take their places for their midday meal.

Mr. Hollyoak was clearly irritated as he took his place at the head of the table, and waited for the visiting servants to seat themselves in the order of their masters' precedence. She followed his glare to its far end and Violet's empty chair next to the scullery maid, Mary. Mrs. Jackson did not tolerate unpunctuality for meals, nor did the butler; latecomers forfeited their dinner. She caught his eye as he cast a glance of silent criticism in her direction. She lifted her eyebrows, tilting her head a little, mutely asking for tolerance after the arduous weeks they had all been through. Catching his minimal acquiescing nod, she sent Mary up to the room she shared with Violet.

When Mary returned, Mrs. Jackson listened to the tiny whisper that everyone strained to hear: Violet was not in their room. She turned her head to catch Mr. Hollyoak's frown. He made no comment but proceeded to say grace, and Mrs. Jackson said that Violet would go without her dinner today.

After their meal, Mrs. Jackson spent a valuable half hour, when she should have been placing her weekly order with Fortnum & Mason on the telephone, looking for Violet. She searched the house while the family and their guests were gathered in the dining room for their luncheon, but there was no sign of the girl. She checked the kitchen courtyard, and sent Dick off to the kitchen gardens and the stable block. But when he came back to report that there was no sign of Violet, she decided that she would wait before she made a fuss about Violet's apparent disappearance—something she did not forgive herself for later on that day.

She became aware that the tenor of the afternoon had changed when Theo Cartwright arrived at the scullery door as they were cleaning up after upstairs luncheon. She heard his voice quite distinctly demanding to speak to Lord Montfort on a matter of great importance. He sounded so agitated that it caused Mrs. Jackson her first tremor of real anxiety about the missing housemaid. She sent for Mr. Hollyoak, who was enjoying forty winks in his pantry, to speak to the gamekeeper.

Whatever it was that Theo told Mr. Hollyoak, it was bad news of the worst sort, Mrs. Jackson grasped, as she watched the butler shrug himself into his morning coat and make for the scullery door with more haste than he usually employed. Convinced that Theo's waxy white face and agitated manner had something to do with Violet's disappearance, she hovered by the butler's pantry, waiting for Mr. Hollyoak to return. Her inner panic and horror knew no bounds when twenty-two minutes later he reappeared and told her that Theo had found a dead man hanging from his gibbet.

"Did he say who it was?" She had asked the butler this question a half-dozen times until she could tell by the set of his shoulders that she should not say another word on the matter.

"You are worried about Violet, aren't you?" She heard kindly concern in his voice and nodded her head.

"I want to send Dick to the village to see if she's with her father," she said.

"Not yet, Mrs. Jackson. A man has been killed on the estate, a missing housemaid is of no consequence right now. We will wait until his lordship returns to the house and then we'll see."

She had patiently waited in suppressed anxiety as she watched the kitchen clock and was almost worn to a frazzle when two hours later Lord Montfort returned to the house and Mr. Hollyoak came down the stairs and called her into his pantry.

"Strictly between us, Mrs. Jackson, it was Mr. Teddy they

found in the wood. Hanged from the large gibbet there, murdered. It's unthinkable, isn't it?" Hollyoak prided himself in never betraying emotion, but she heard how shocked he was.

She felt the last remnants of her energy drop away from her, and the butler's pantry did a slow, lazy circle and dipped to the right around her. She tried to speak but her voice didn't rise to the occasion. She heard Mr. Hollyoak say, "Send Dick to the village, tell him to go to Mr. Simkins and ask after Violet. But on no account is he to run around the cottages looking for the girl if she is not with her dad. Not yet. But before you do that, Mrs. Jackson, please attend to the servants, they are running around like a bunch of schoolchildren."

"What will happen now, Mr. Hollyoak?" Finally she found her voice.

"Colonel Valentine is to head up an investigation into Mr. Teddy's murder. His sergeant will arrive shortly to talk to the servants. You had better put him in my pantry, he will need privacy." She noticed how resigned and tired the butler was despite his correct and impressive comportment. They were old comrades, they understood each other well. She saw that he was coping but it was a struggle.

When Mrs. Jackson walked into the servants' hall to find Dick, she was aware that the buzz of gossiping voices, from all the servants gathered there, shut off like water from a tap. She stood in the doorway and stared coldly about the room, catching the eye of major culprits. In her opinion there was no greater crime than gossip about the family, especially with outside valets and maids in the house, and she would be fierce in quelling all offenders.

As she marshaled the servants into concentrating on their duties, everything was thrown into further disarray with the arrival of Sergeant Hawkins, who had come as part of the police investigation into Mr. Teddy's murder. She met him at the foot of the back stairs on his arrival and noticed with a sigh of resignation that he was a well-set-up, handsome man in his early thirties, with a glossy black mustache. This was all she needed, she thought. The sergeant would no doubt set the maids twittering through the servants' hall, adding significantly to the already considerable excitement of the afternoon and her own mounting unease and irritation.

"Good afternoon, Sergeant," she said as she walked him firmly toward the butler's pantry, aware of the female heads poking out of scullery, larder, and pantry doorways. "I am Mrs. Jackson, Iyntwood's housekeeper. I have arranged accommodation for you and your constable overnight in the stable block. The hallboy Dick Wilson will take you over when you are ready to turn in.

"In the meantime, you are free to use Mr. Hollyoak's pantry for your interviews. We might have to move you if things go on too long. As you can see, it's cramped digs down here."

She led him back to the butler's pantry and made sure that he understood he was not to smoke. She was pleased to see that he appeared to be a respectful man, which was a point in his favor, despite his flashy looks.

Mrs. Jackson had strong nerves and she rarely overreacted to bad news, but when Dick returned from the village to report that Jim Simkins had not seen Violet since his cup of tea with her at the house yesterday, she felt another ripple of acute alarm. She had convinced herself that Dick would come back to the house to reassure her that Violet was with her father.

Walking through the kitchen to check that preparations for the family's tea had not been forgotten in the desperate pursuit of information and gossip, she found the footman, John, holding forth self-importantly to a group of kitchen maids.

"She lost her temper really badly, never seen anything like it. First she threw a rock at him then she called him a pig and that he should get out, no one wanted him here."

"John." Her voice cut across the kitchen and the footman spun around. "What are you talking about? How many times do I have to tell you? There is to be no gossip. Now come with me, please, we are going to use the Royal Doulton for tea and I can't reach the top shelf."

John meekly followed her to the china pantry.

"Who were you talking about just now?" she asked, pushing the door of the china pantry closed for greater privacy.

"Miss Lucinda—she had quite a falling-out with Mr. Teddy on the terrace last night just before dinner. She was in a right old state, I could see and hear her through the terrace door."

"You are setting such a bad example, young man; this is not the sort of comportment I expect from a second footman. You never discuss our guests' behavior, do you understand me?"

"But should I tell the sergeant what I saw, Mrs. Jackson?"

She recognized he had a point. Who held the higher authority now? Herself and Mr. Hollyoak, or the policeman sitting in the butler's pantry?

"You don't volunteer information to the sergeant unless he specifically asks you. Is that clear?" She held her stern look until, thoroughly crushed, he said it was.

She grimly patrolled belowstairs until she felt sure she had suppressed the hysterical need for gossip that had prevailed ever since Sergeant Hawkins's arrival. She was aided in this by the massive effort it took to produce dinner for sixteen people in the dining room.

This respite gave Mrs. Jackson a few moments for some quiet introspection, and she took herself off to her parlor to ponder the unsolved instance of the missing Violet. She was sensible enough not to blame herself entirely for Violet's departure, but she certainly believed herself accountable for not knowing what had made Violet so unhappy in the first place that she had, in Mrs. Thwaite's parlance, gone and done a bunk.

She felt personally affronted by the third housemaid's abrupt and completely unjustifiable departure. She had been impressed with Violet from the moment the young girl had come to work at the house. Violet was deft about her work, and quick to understand the importance of detail, but with enough intelligence to comprehend how the house worked as a whole. Mrs. Jackson thought she had identified some of the qualities in Violet that were necessary for her perhaps to become a candidate for the post of housekeeper when Mrs. Jackson retired. The girl's unannounced departure was a slap in the face, and after Mrs. Jackson had recovered from the realization that Violet had actually bolted, she felt not only embarrassed that one of her girls had run off but personally and deeply hurt. Underneath this was the worry that a village girl with no life experience had left the security and safety of the house.

She pondered the possible reasons for Violet's running off and came up with nothing. The usual whys and wherefores connected to runaway housemaids were well known. They either were in the family way or had gone off with a "follower." Sometimes they were thieves who had been set up by gangs of housebreakers, trained to recognize lucrative hauls and courageous enough to open the door for the real work to be done in the night. All of these were highly unlikely in Mrs. Jackson's view, as far as Violet was concerned. She knew herself to be an intelligent woman with a practical cast of mind; she relied on reason to give her answers and very rarely wasted time on conjecture. Beyond that, she was incapable of venturing. She washed her face and hands and went back downstairs to the servants' hall. She knew that it was time she informed Violet's employers that she was no longer in the house.

Chapter Nine

Since the news of Teddy's death and the discovery of Lucinda's baffling disappearance, Clementine's nerves were so finely tuned that her skin felt too tight, every sound jarred, and it was hard to concentrate. Standing in the morning room with Hollyoak and Mrs. Jackson as they explained Violet's unaccountable disappearance from the house, she experienced such a wave of disbelief and incredulity that it took her several minutes to gather her wits enough to respond to the news.

No matter what question she asked, the butler and her housekeeper merely repeated their original asseverations. They didn't know where Violet was and no one downstairs could remember having seen her since midday. She had made them take her through it all twice, interrupting continually with more questions they were unable to answer. She was quick to notice that Hollyoak, always detached and unperturbed, after ten minutes of interrogation was now thoroughly perturbed. She watched his face almost quiver as if some human emotion was trying to break through the impassive mask of his composure, and he nearly lifted a hand to smooth his hair in a gesture she knew was an indication that he was discomfited and un-sure. There was a distinct whiff of reproach in the air when, utterly exasperated with him, she turned to her housekeeper for greater illumination.

Unlike the butler, Mrs. Jackson upheld iron self-possession and did not rush to smooth troubled waters. She repeated her side of the story calmly, no matter how often she was inter-rupted. Suddenly, hearing the sharpness in her voice, Clemen-tine appreciated that she was being a bully and felt ashamed of herself. It would have been impossible for Mrs. Jackson to know exactly when Violet had gone missing, she told herself. It had probably been quite busy belowstairs this morning. She listened to her housekeeper explain that last night Violet had been in-structed to clean and make-up the single guests' rooms this morning, which were in a wing on the other side of the house. Lucinda's and Teddy's rooms had not been made up, but as they were not there to complain, this had not served as an alert. The rooms occupied by Oscar, Ellis, and Harry were not made up either, but Clementine thought it was doubtful that they had even noticed. She knew that the rest of the servants would have been rushed off their feet this morning, putting the house in order after the ball: taking up early-morning trays, preparing breakfast for the dining room, and accomplishing a hundred other chores. With so many people staying in the house, visit-ing valets and maids would have been coming and going be-tween the servants' hall and the upstairs bedrooms, adding tremendously to the demands on her servants. With the addi-tion of her guests' servants there would have been more than thirty people milling around in the servants' hall for most of the day. It was fair to understand that Violet's absence would have been hard to detect until they had all taken their allotted places for their midday meal.

But after the news of Teddy's death, Clementine didn't feel particularly fair-minded. She offered no reassurance that all would be well, that Violet would no doubt be found, because nothing looked to her as if all would be well again. Neither did she rush to acknowledge to the butler and her housekeeper the stress the servants had been under for days on end. In fact, she stared at them coldly. They had let her down, her face told them, even if her tone didn't. She did not wish to be burdened any more than she already was.

When Hollyoak told her that despite's Dick's search of the village there was no trace of Violet, Clementine stifled a chirrup of annoyance. How could they have been so careless as to send up an alarm? Now the whole village would be thrumming with speculation and conjecture! God only knew what they were all saying. It didn't take much to set the village gossips alight, and Teddy's death would have certainly done that. Now the disappearance of a girl from the village who had barely worked at the house for two months would be like petrol on the flames.

She turned away from her butler and housekeeper and walked to the window to stare bleakly at the rain falling relentlessly from a wall of gray cloud. Her well-regulated, orderly household had disintegrated, replaced by violence and chaos. Within days the Iyntwood murder would be the sensation of the week, which meant newspaper scandal and gossip for months. She turned back to them with a helpless what-are-we-to-do-now expression on her face.

"Was Violet unhappy here, did she run away do you think?"

she asked Mrs. Jackson, but it was Hollyoak who answered, no doubt to save face for his fellow servant.

"She was a very grateful young woman, m'lady," he said diplomatically, "for the opportunity." Clementine harrumphed until he looked down.

"Well, I had better tell Lord Montfort and Colonel Valentine. Where is Colonel Valentine now, by the way?"

"He is with Lady Harriet and Mr. Lambert-Lambert upstairs in Miss Lucinda's room, m'lady."

"Very well then. Hollyoak, will you please ask Lord Montfort to come to me here; and, Jackson, we are going to have to plan menus for the next few days. I will send for you later this evening when I have the time." She heard herself and disliked her schoolmistressy and hectoring tone, so she quickly added as they left the room that she was sure Violet would be found. After all, she could not have gone far. She noticed the relief on their faces as Hollyoak closed the door.

Grateful to be alone for the first time today, Clementine sat down and stared blankly at the wall as she forced her thoughts into order. Teddy had been murdered, Lucinda had left the house, and Violet had run away. Her mind, while bleakly accepting these facts, would not oblige to venture beyond this understanding. So she sat with questions chattering through her head in a ceaseless, noisy torrent.

She jumped as her husband entered the room but managed to keep her voice level when she told him that Violet Simkins was missing. She was grateful for his stoicism as he received the news. After this nerve-racking day, her husband's sangfroid was admirable and Clementine was grateful for his ability to deal better the worse things became.

"I'm having difficulty keeping up with all of this," he said quietly. "They are sure, are they, that Violet hasn't hidden herself away for a quiet nap somewhere?" Obviously this was what her husband craved at this moment, she thought.

"No, darling, I'm afraid not. No quiet naps for anyone today."

Clementine trudged up the graceful, oval sweep of the staircase with her husband. Their footsteps, loud on marble steps, matched the rhythm of her inner interrogations. She struggled for answers but there were none to be had.

She found herself wondering if she might recall this time without the frozen confusion she felt at this moment. The relentless events of this bizarre day had had rather a numbing effect and she was prepared for anything when they swung open the door to Lucinda's room and entered unnoticed by its occupants.

Her gaze swept over the pretty room, elegantly furnished in soft tones of warm white and rose, well lit by a double pair of windows. The bed was crowned with a rose and cream tester, and there was a small satinwood Hepplewhite writing table by one of the windows. She took in the activities of the occupants with detached interest. Colonel Valentine was going through the drawers of the writing table; Gilbert Lambert-Lambert, standing in the center of the room with his hands on his hips, was frowning at the carpet; and her dear friend was head and shoulders into a large wardrobe that took up the west wall. Lady Harriet's muffled voice floated out to her.

"I don't know what she brought with her . . . her costume from last night is here . . . an evening dress . . . and a rather nice afternoon dress she bought from Lucile. She certainly hasn't left the house . . ." Lady Harriet stepped back from the wardrobe and sat down on a silk damask chair, looking expectantly at Clementine as if asking for help in understanding the unpredictability of the young.

Clementine stepped aside to allow Constable Dixon into the room and watched as he rather self-consciously announced that the young lady's motorcar was not in the wash-down. She felt a surge of relief. Lucinda had obviously decided to leave the house early and, with the atrocious manners of a modern girl who had been spoiled all her life, had decided that a formal leave taking was unnecessary.

"Well, there you are!" Gilbert Lambert-Lambert looked triumphant. "She has undoubtedly popped over to Vanbridge for luncheon; she's a good friend of Barbara." Gilbert turned to his wife. "It would have been nice if she'd said something, Harriet." His voice was testy and pompous and Clementine felt active dislike at his lack of sensitivity.

Harriet gave her an I'm-so-terribly-sorry look for her daughter's inexcusable manners.

But Clementine was interested to see that Valentine, after conferring further with his constable, did not acknowledge the jaunt to Vanbridge.

"Lucinda's motorcar apparently went very early this morning. A stable lad saw it at half past six when he was pumping water for the horses, and when he left the yard an hour later he noticed it had gone. That would mean your daughter possibly left the house after half past six and before half past seven, or at least her motorcar did; a bit early to drive over to Vanbridge for luncheon."

"Well of course there's a sensible explanation for all of this. Perhaps Lucinda was called up to town . . . or back to Girton . . ."

Gilbert Lambert-Lambert folded his arms and stared Valentine down.

Arrogant ass, thought Clementine. *Why would he antagonize the colonel?*

"Just because her motorcar is not at the wash-down does not necessarily mean Lucinda drove it away," Valentine pointed out and turned back to the desk, leaving them all time to adjust to this new thought as he searched through desk drawers. "There seems to be nothing here that belongs to Lucinda. Does she keep a diary?"

"Yes, she did." It was Gilbert who spoke, and Clementine heard his voice falter. "Yes, she does . . ."

"Well, there is no diary here, no letters or any personal papers. I don't know about you, but I usually leave my diary behind when I'm invited to luncheon and plan to return for tea." Colonel Valentine closed a drawer and opened another.

Lady Harriet crossed to the bed and rummaged among the pillows. "Her nightdress is here." Her voice was defensive as she bent down and looked under the bed. "And so are her slippers. Her hairbrush, tooth powder, and brush are here, too." She pointed to the washbasin, and then with faltering conviction: "I'm quite sure she'll drive up at any moment. Perhaps she had a puncture and has been detained."

"Possible of course, but not likely," Valentine replied, causing Clementine to feel even more annoyance. Why were these men being so insensitive to Harriet? Of course everyone blamed mothers when daughters misbehaved.

"You are surely not suggesting that Lucinda had anything to do with Teddy's death?" Harriet was now extremely worried. Clementine heard her friend's voice tight with anxiety and felt a wave of irritation. *Well done, Colonel,* she thought. *That's the way to do it, frighten the girl's mother out of her wits with mere speculation.*

"Your daughter's relationship with Teddy was close. I mean, she was a close friend?" Valentine asked.

"They were childhood friends, nothing more." Harriet's voice was low and she averted her face from them all.

"Any bad feeling—?" Valentine continued.

"I hardly think so, there was nothing they held in common," Gilbert cut in before Valentine could suggest anything improper. Clementine noticed the testy edge in his voice. He evidently resented what he felt were Valentine's insinuations.

"They did not get along then?" Valentine asked, and Clementine realized that the more evasive Gilbert became, the more Valentine pushed.

This was too quick for Gilbert's comfort. "They held nothing in common," he said, and his voice was ice. "Teddy Mallory was a complete reprobate. Lucinda is an intelligent and educated young woman. I'm sorry, but there it is." She saw him glance apologetically at her husband.

Clementine realized that Gilbert Lambert-Lambert was shaken out of his usual self-importance, as he did not often display the slight chip she knew he nurtured. She had always suspected that it was his humble beginnings that made Gilbert rather a touchy individual. Self-made men usually were, in her opinion. He had built his considerable fortune from his boot-and-shoe manufactory in Northampton and obviously believed he was tolerated within the group because of his marriage to Lady Harriet. It was all rubbish really, Clementine thought, remembering how penniless Lord Squareforth had been when his daughter had married Gilbert. Thanks to Gilbert's financial support, Squareforth had become a prominent and powerful man in the government. But she knew these things did matter, especially if you were the parvenu and without pedigree. She had heard somewhere last night that Gilbert had actually considered forking out fifty thousand pounds to buy a peerage, an innovation of David Lloyd George, the Chancellor of the Exchequer, who in her husband's opinion was himself a rapacious upstart unworthy of his post. She came back to earth as she heard Gilbert bark at Valentine.

"I simply don't understand how you could conceive there could be a connection between the two incidents. Our daughter left the house this morning. Since then, Teddy Mallory, a perfect lout of a boy, has been found dead. I am assuming he was murdered, though you refuse to reveal this fact. There can be no correlation between the two events."

She listened to Valentine's reply, as he spaced out his words. "No one seems to know where Lucinda is, so she is missing from the house at a very critical time. When we locate her, *then* we can eliminate her from any involvement in Mr. Mallory's death, either as its perpetrator, or perhaps as another victim."

Aghast at such tactlessness, Clementine was not surprised to see Lady Harriet's shoulders slump forward in despair as she openly wept, and Gilbert's confidence in his daughter's appointment for luncheon somewhere else melt away.

As Harriet's sobs became more desperate and Gilbert relinquished his commanding position on center stage, Clementine crossed the room to her friend and helped her to sit down in a chair. She stood between Harriet and Valentine, as if to protect her from any more cruel revelations. She was also relieved when her husband took this lull in the Lambert-Lambert storm to inform Valentine that one of the housemaids had been missing for most of the day. *Privacy is obviously a thing of the past,* she thought rather sadly. *Here we all are blurting out our dreadful little scraps of news.*

It was as if Teddy's murder was to be upstaged by a series of inexplicable and seemingly unrelated events that, because of his ugly death, now took on darker significance, she thought. And as if in confirmation she heard Valentine say, "If either of these two young women"—a snort of disgust from Gilbert as his daughter's actions were linked to those of a common maid— "do not make their whereabouts known within the next . . ." he looked at his waistcoat watch, "well, by breakfast time tomorrow morning, then we will have to organize a search for them."

Chapter Ten

Clementine came downstairs for dinner early. She had taken care over her appearance and had chosen her dress thoughtfully; it was part of her resolution not to let the side down, it was important to keep up appearances at times like these. Her friends gathered together in miserable little huddles throughout the room were a far more introspective and reserved group this evening, compared to the convivial get-together of the preceding night. When she had last seen them during tea, which now felt like years ago, they had known only that Teddy had been killed apparently somewhere on the estate.

Rather cynically, it struck her that within minutes of spending time with their valets and maids they were all now fully apprised with the known facts of Teddy's last days: his gambling club, his cheating, his expulsion, and how he had been killed. It didn't matter what the colonel had said about not discussing among themselves what had happened and how often the servants had been told not to gossip. Clementine accepted that human nature always prevailed.

Her mind went to Lucinda's abrupt departure. No doubt this had caused some ripples among them all, too. She felt almost resentful that her husband's nephew had been murdered so brutally on the morning following her ball, ensuring his death received maximum attention. She looked around the room at the composed and impassive faces of their friends—all determined not to be seen to gossip, or to give further rise to speculation—going to considerable trouble to exhibit behavior that was normal and everyday. She fervently wished they would all go home.

Hollyoak announced that dinner was ready and they all went into the dining room. She was aware that conversation around her came in short, sharp artificial bursts, with long periods of hesitant silence. She knew there were few among them who genuinely approved of Teddy, if they thought of him at all when he was alive. He had always been a difficult boy, never quite ready to join in, always at odds with his surroundings.

Her greatest concern was for her husband. He had spent the hour before dinner at the dower house with his mother, and Clementine could only imagine how wearing her mother-in-law's frantic questions and continual need for reassurance had been for him. She remembered that the dowager Lady Montfort had been particularly susceptible to Teddy. She had enjoyed his short, infrequent visits, had been proud of his good looks, his superficial brand of charm, and his willingness to pay attention to her for tips and injections of cash into his bank account. The poor woman's emotional devastation would have been exhausting and Clementine could see that her husband was coping because he must, but she felt sorrow for the burden he was carrying.

Glancing around the table as she carried on a stilted conversation with Lord Booth on her right, she noticed Oscar Barclay staring rather queasily at the turtle soup on his plate. Ralph had told her that Oscar had spent a good deal of time before dinner closeted in the study with Colonel Valentine. When he had joined them in the red room before dinner she had noticed immediately that he was pale and withdrawn. How many whiskey and sodas had the silly boy had before dinner, she wondered, and how much involvement had Oscar had in Teddy's gambling club at Oxford?

Sir Wilfred Shackleton, sitting on her left, was gulping down his turtle soup and looking extremely pleased with himself. Why on earth was that? What an odd individual Wilfred was, so hard to fathom at the best of times. This evening he seemed the only one among them who was actually enjoying his dinner.

Her eyes wandered around the table and came to rest on Gertrude, calmly eating tiny spoonfuls of soup and listening passively to Jack Ambrose, who was looking irritable and cantankerous, evidently still suffering from the overindulgence of the night before. Certainly Gertrude was subdued, everyone was, but her lovely ivory skin had a slightly yellow cast to it and her large green eyes were red and tired. Too much champagne and not enough sleep, perhaps? No, there was something else going on there; things were not right with her friend and had not been since before dinner last night. Clementine decided to seek her out later this evening.

She thought of the search tomorrow and shuddered and then with renewed determination turned to Sir Wilfred and made him walk her through his plans for the hunting season and whether or not he planned to take on Lord Booth's mare. It was a game she played to distract herself and a prelude to turning back to Lord Booth on her right and finding out if he actually intended to sell the mare to Sir Wilfred in the first place, or whether he was simply enjoying the power of having a horse so talented in the field she was coveted by everyone.

At the end of dinner, when Clementine stood up from the table to invite her friends to join her for coffee in the music room, there was an audible sigh of relief all around as the women rose from the table to leave the men to their port.

To help alleviate the strain of searching for safe topics of conversation, and to cover stilted small talk and yawning silences, she asked Pansy Booth if she would play for them. Pansy was an accurate if not particularly expressive pianist and Clementine hoped Agatha did not insist on having Blanche sing. Pansy's performance alone would provide a pleasant distraction; Blanche's singing would be a punishment no one deserved. An evening of music would provide cover until they could escape to the privacy of their rooms and lay their weary heads down for the night.

As Pansy launched herself bravely into a complicated and, to Clementine's ear, only slightly muddled étude, she wandered over to Gertrude, who was sitting on a sofa as far away from the piano as she could get. She was again struck by how wan her friend looked despite the studied lack of concern on her pretty, slightly triangular catlike face.

"Clemmy darling," Gertrude greeted her friend as she turned her head for the footman to light her cigarette. "How are things? Everyone's bearing up quite wonderfully, considering . . ." She laughed, as if Clementine's stage murder for drawing room entertainment had perhaps been a little excessive. Clementine was grateful for Gertrude's determined lightheartedness when all about her was gravity and gloom.

Fortified by her dinner, the brandy she was now enjoying instead of coffee, and her absolute acceptance that her house was in complete chaos had had a singularly strengthening effect on Clementine. Her mind was now working quite nicely. She took comfort from Gertrude's offhand remark, calculated to reassure her that all was not lost and that her friends were still gathered loyally around her. But she knew Gertrude well enough to understand that her friend was at her most elusive; Gertrude was signaling that she was off-limits. There were to be no revelations for Clementine—confided fears and trepidations were taboo.

Gertrude's greatest physical attraction lay in her lustrous pearly skin and her fine silver-gilt hair, giving her a rather opalescent quality, a lustrous sheen of sensual beauty. She gave the impression of complete immobility, and until one knew her well, it was easy to imagine her more at ease reclining in a drawing room, browsing through a book, or seated under a shady tree, contemplating the far horizon with detached indifference. But Clementine knew that Gertrude was a deceptively active woman, able to ride across country for hours and competently at ease on the most athletic horse. She had taken up tennis last summer, playing with powerful and wiry strength. Clementine did not forget that Gertrude was also adept at keeping her cards close; she rarely revealed her thoughts. Neither did she welcome other women's close confidences, as she never wished to be the subject of theirs. The recounting of light, amusing gossip, however, was a skill, the pastime of drawing rooms and gentle strolls in the garden with friends, and a pastime practiced by Gertrude with adroit ease. "What an exhausting day it's been." Clementine matched her friend's manner, fully conscious that Gertrude had been distant since her arrival in her house and had avoided any opportunity for private talk with her.

"Mmm . . . can't wait to bolt for my room, darling—in common with all of us, except that bloody Agatha." Gertrude laughed and flicked ash. "Look at us: scared to death of what old Val is going to dig up and who he is going to talk to. Talk about a blunderer. Is he up to the job do you think, bit of an old fogey really isn't he?"

"I suppose so."

But Gertrude had made an important point. What would Valentine dig up? An image of the boathouse garden flew into Clementine's mind and a horrid understanding began to assemble itself. The garden abutted the orchard, which ended abruptly at a corner by the back drive in front of the old carriage house.

Any visiting chauffeur could have heard Harry's loud, angry voice and taken a curious peek through the light screen of trees at the edge of the drive, to be rewarded with the sight of a violent quarrel between the two cousins. What would the police make of her son's reason for his fight with Teddy?

It was all she could do to keep her seat. She was half out of it, as if there were something she could do physically to prevent the catastrophe of Harry's arrest for his cousin's murder. Her escalating panic made her clumsy and she knocked over the heavy crystal glass on the table. "Oh, blast and damn." She never swore.

As John picked up pieces of broken glass and wiped spilled brandy, she made a decision.

She would not let an incompetent police inquiry land her son as their favorite suspect. It simply would not happen.

She looked up and saw Gertrude's cool green eyes watching her. With supreme self-control she adopted her earlier lighthearted tone and returned to their conversation.

"If you are to have a murder investigation going on in your house, Gertrude, better for it to be headed up by someone who understands the importance of good manners, rather than by some clod from Market Wingley who eats his peas with his knife." They both laughed. "Anyway, Valentine is not really an old fogey, just trying not to step on too many toes."

"I am sure he won't be cluttering your house up for long, Clemmy. You heard of course that there was some sort of stranger loitering about the village for the last couple of days?" Gertrude fixed a feline gaze on her friend's face.

Now this was more like it, Clementine thought. Here was something to hope for after this desperate day. She leaned toward her friend, and Gertrude laughed outright, acknowledging what a boon some wandering outsider would be for all of them.

"Well exactly, looks like it won't be such a big mystery after all."

Despite Gertrude's laconic Belgravia drawl and her studied insouciance, a manner Clementine recognized of old and one always adopted by her friend when she was disconcerted, Clementine knew enough not to be fooled by her outward show of indifference. She looked for other signs that Gertrude was rattled: those pretty gooseberry-green eyes of hers were far too watchful, her lovely jawline far too tense. *Why*, she asked herself, *does it matter to Gertrude that suspicion be cast outside the house?*

"Where did you get *this* information from?" Clementine asked, careful to keep her tone playful, as if she did not quite believe what she was hearing; there had been so much chitchat.

"Well, I always make sure I spend any time with my maid profitably. She overheard the handsome Sergeant Hawkins giving some instructions to his constable. Seems like your gamekeeper saw someone and so did your gardener—a stranger to the area wandering around the village, apparently. Considering what a little thug young Teddy was, there were probably no end to his grubby involvements . . . possibilities are endless where that boy was concerned. So there you are, darling, probably all sewn up by tomorrow."

Clementine kept her reply noncommittal.

"Well, that would be nice. Anything about Lucinda on the servants' grapevine?" She knew it was expected of her to ask.

Gertrude carefully blew a thin stream of smoke into the air, turned her head, and gave Clementine a tiny wink. "Ah Lucinda, now there's a dark horse if ever I saw one. The Lambert-Lambert family are in for some suprises there, I think. Not the jolly nice little girls that we are, Clemmy, you can be sure of that." Gertrude turned as John walked toward them with more coffee.

"Want to come for a ride tomorrow morning?" Clementine hoped that perhaps after a nice long gallop Gertrude might relax enough to confide her own concerns, but she was to be disappointed.

"Can't, darling, got a half past ten with old Val, but Constance will, won't you, darling?" she asked as Constance Ambrose plumped herself down on their sofa.

Clementine nodded absentmindedly, beckoned to John, and told him to ask Mrs. Jackson to come straight up to her sitting room when they were finished with their coffee after dinner. There was a lot to plan for.

Chapter Eleven

Mrs. Jackson had learned over the years that although Lady Montfort possessed many strong qualities, the art of remaining detached in the midst of calamity was not one of them. She played a pretty good game, did Lady Montfort, but the appearance of self-possession did not fool Mrs. Jackson. Her ladyship was not, by nature or inclination, blessed with an inner tranquility and she was a consummate doer, some might even say an interferer. Lady Montfort's response to the missing third housemaid had been evidence of that already. As she stood in Lady Montfort's sitting room she carefully took in all the little telltale signs that her ladyship's inner motor was positively racing. She was sitting bolt upright, for one thing, her back rigid, her hands clasped tightly in her lap, and she had that awfully bright, overattentive expression on her face.

"Jackson, what a terrible day. How is everyone coping?" To give her credit, Lady Montfort was certainly doing a good job of managing her inner turmoil. Her "everyone" of course referred to belowstairs.

"In spite of it all, very well, m'lady." Her response was cautious. After the harrowing interview with Lady Montfort that afternoon, she would hold on to the lifeline of business as usual until she managed to gauge which way the wind was blowing this evening.

"Visiting servants not causing any problems? Gossip, that kind of thing?"

She assured Lady Montfort that the visiting servants were old friends, respectful of the situation and doing everything they could to help out. She held in her hand menus for the next couple of days: beef consommé, followed by veal cutlets, dauphinoise potatoes, and garden peas, and then apple tart for tomorrow's luncheon. She handed over a menu to Lady Montfort as she went on to explain that another storm was on the way, so Cook had planned something warming for dinner. She took a moment to go through the menu and when she had finished she looked inquiringly at Lady Montfort, who had barely glanced at the lists in her hand.

So food was not what this meeting was about then, thought Mrs. Jackson, and sure enough, Lady Montfort asked about Violet. Was there any news?

Mrs. Jackson had spent a good deal of thought on Violet's disappearance and had prepared an answer for Lady Montfort that she hoped would go some way to mollifying her ladyship until she had the time to find out what Violet's running off was really all about.

"I believe that we . . . I . . . underestimated Violet, m'lady." This cost Mrs. Jackson a good deal, as she was still very annoyed with herself for having made assumptions where Violet was concerned. "I thought she had settled into a comfortable routine in the house, well that was certainly my impression. Now it seems I was wrong. According to Mary, who shared a room with Violet, she was homesick. I feel entirely responsible for not being aware . . ." Here she stopped to allow Lady Montfort to take in this information.

"But *you* said she was so willing, that she worked hard and got on with everyone." The poor woman sounded almost plaintive. There was a slight wobble in her voice.

"Yes, m'lady, but I was possibly mistaken in taking this to mean that all was well. Mr. Simkins is sending word to Ticksby, to his sister; he thinks that Violet has probably gone to her."

"Ticksby is miles away. How could she get there?"

"By train, or the Blue Coach I expect, m'lady, or perhaps she got a lift with a carter. Her aunt will send to us when she turns up. It can be the only explanation . . ."

She fully understood that it was out of the question for Lady Montfort to speak of her greatest fear, that Mr. Teddy's murder might have involved either or both of the missing girls. Until the young women were found, one way or another, she knew there would be an undercurrent of suspicion, doubt, and fear throughout the coming days. The Talbots and their servants must not react or become overemotional. Good manners and self-discipline were all they had to fall back on at times like these. She hoped they would all prevail and not lose their heads. These valuable thoughts were not ones she presumed to share with Lady Montfort, however.

"I simply don't understand this generation at all, Jackson. Their behavior is outrageous. Lucinda Lambert-Lambert left my house this morning at some frightful hour . . . without a good-bye to either her mother or to me. What do you make of that?"

If Mrs. Jackson was surprised that her opinion had been asked for, she didn't show it as she answered that Miss Lucinda, always an independent young woman, was probably quite safe and off about her business.

Mrs. Jackson could see that underneath her locked-down self-control Lady Montfort was beginning to unravel again and did what she could to bolster her. She reassured her that all would come clear in time, hoping that this would be enough to help her ladyship accept that before resolution there was often a state of flux.

"Yes, of course you are right, Jackson, there is some simple explanation and we must not jump to conclusions, very right and sensible.

"What have you heard about this stranger in the area? Another one of those village rumors do you think?" Lady Montfort was holding on to her handkerchief for dear life.

This was the first Mrs. Jackson had heard of a stranger, but she was not surprised. She wondered who could have started this particular tale, and was informed immediately by Lady Montfort. Theo Cartwright and one of the gardeners had evidently seen a strange man hanging about the village yesterday afternoon. Mrs. Jackson agreed that it was possibly just a rumor.

"You are doing the flowers again tomorrow, aren't you, Jackson?" Lady Montfort had a way of shifting from one topic to another with lightning speed. Mrs. Jackson said that she was, and was completely unprepared for what followed.

"Good, then please find out exactly which gardener saw this man and what he actually did see. I want the details."

Considerably taken aback, Mrs. Jackson was more than surprised at the impropriety of what Lady Montfort was asking her to do. It was completely out of character, and not only that, she thought, feeling quite trapped and resentful, it put her in an awful spot. Theo was employed by the Talbots, so why wouldn't Lady Montfort ask him directly herself? But Mrs. Jackson was an astute judge of situation and character and knew very well that Lady Montfort must not break caste and go dredging through the servants' hall and the estate for gossip, especially now. What was the expression Lady Montfort's father, with his Indian background, had used? That's right, a subedar: a noncommissioned officer in the Indian army who was above the other ranks. Lady Montfort needed a subedar, someone she could trust to sound out the troops and report back on morale and behavior. Mrs. Jackson was being asked to report on the lower servants, and the very thought of it was distasteful to her.

A long silence settled between them. Mrs. Jackson decided it was up to Lady Montfort to continue. She had nothing to say at this point. She watched Lady Montfort ball up her handkerchief and toss it to one side. Minutes passed. Mrs. Jackson continued to stand quietly, her gaze fixed on the fine Persian carpet. How well she knew its pattern. Then Lady Montfort impatiently burst into speech.

"Yes, you're right, Jackson, it is not fair or right of me to ask, it's just that you get on so well with Mr. Thrower."

A thought occurred to Mrs. Jackson and she lifted her eyes from the central medallion of the carpet and looked up at Lady Montfort as directly as she felt was acceptable, given the unusual circumstances of their conversation. "Is it his confirmation of the stranger's whereabouts you need, or is there something else troubling you, m'lady?"

Well of course there was, she thought as she watched Lady Montfort's shoulders come down several inches, as she almost collapsed in on herself. It was probably too direct a question, and she was ready to be put in her place for asking it. But here again Lady Montfort surprised her.

"Would you describe Harry as a needlessly violent boy, given to thrashings and beatings, and all of that?"

Lord Haversham? What could the Talbots' son and heir have to do with all this? She had known Lord Haversham since he was two and she had a soft spot for him. She remembered him as a sunny-tempered child growing up: loving and respectful to his mother, his sisters, and his nanny. He was to her mind a gentleman of the old school—a pearl, a gem. She was stirred to respond quite emphatically.

"Never, m'lady, I have only seen him lose his temper once and that was with that awful boy who tried to push Lady Althea out of the treehouse when she was eight. If anyone deserved a thrashing, that Boswell boy most certainly did."

She watched Lady Montfort stand up and wander over to the window, looking out into the dark night, her drawn face clearly reflected in the glass.

"Well, I have seen him lose his temper, Jackson, for the first time, and it was rather a shock." Lady Montfort drew back from the window and closed the curtains. She then proceeded to unburden herself about what she had seen by the boathouse, in what Mrs. Jackson saw as an act of courage and trust because what she revealed put Lord Haversham in a very bad position indeed. And then she went on to tell her about the awful business of Teddy and Harry's dog.

"Now what do you have to say to that?" Lady Montfort asked when she had related the whole story.

"M'lady, I have known Lord Haversham for most of his life. He is a staunch supporter of the underdog, so to speak. Kindness itself to animals and the village children; cruelty of any kind upsets him. And he can't abide a bully."

"Yes, Jackson, we all know this, of course we do. But the police don't know Lord Haversham. Colonel Valentine only knows him slightly. And if this fight was seen or heard by any of the visiting servants, say the chauffeurs, and they related it to the police . . . do you get my drift?"

Of course she did. If the police were told about the fight, Lord Haversham's part in it could be thoroughly misinterpreted, since twelve hours later his cousin had been brutally killed. The sense of dread that had been with her all day intensified at the direction this conversation was taking, but she owed it to her ladyship to be straight.

"Yes, m'lady, I understand. They could put a completely different interpretation on things."

"Yes, Jackson, and that would be bad. There is so much going on in this house, I can't keep it all straight. And I must if I am to be of any use at all in the coming days. Have you seen or heard anything? Anything at all that is unusual . . . ?"

Mrs. Jackson did not answer for a moment. She sensed all sorts of dangers ahead, but Lord Haversham's fight with Mr. Mallory reminded her of something else, and against her better judgment she made a cautious foray into no-man's-land.

"Miss Lucinda and Mr. Teddy apparently had an argument on the terrace before dinner last night. John saw it all; he said Miss Lucinda was quite angry." What on earth was she thinking? She should never admit that the footman would presume to report on the family's behavior. *This is what happens,* she told herself grimly, *when you step out of line.*

"Ah yes, that was probably my fault. I asked him to take her out for some fresh air, perhaps not a particularly good idea. But she was absolutely fine during dinner and at the ball. I saw her myself. Did John say what it was they were arguing about?" Lady Montfort reached for a glass on the table by her elbow and took a sip.

It occurred to Mrs. Jackson that Lady Montfort had already

broken with convention by discussing private family business and now she was waiting for her housekeeper join her.

For the first time in her many years of service to the Talbot family, Mrs. Jackson actually reported something she had heard or knew directly without coating it to sound acceptable. *All right, Edith,* she said to herself, *tell her and get it over with.*

"John said he heard her call Mr. Teddy a pig and that no one wanted him here, and then she threw something at him . . . but before that he had heard Mr. Teddy refer to the Derby and the woman who—"

"Oh yes, the Derby, what a tragedy: some woman threw herself under the king's horse, poor deranged creature. I suspect Lucinda is one of those new-thinking young women. It is a pity she has sympathy for the Women's Social and Political Union, because that is not the way to go about getting votes for women. The Pankhursts just put everyone's backs up."

Mrs. Jackson managed her long working day by conserving her energy, not squandering it, and now she listened to her ladyship run through all her conscious thoughts since Teddy's murder had been announced. She spilled them out to her in an incoherent, tumbled torrent. She was like a woman in a confessional, Mrs. Jackson thought, unstoppable. It was exhausting to listen to and she was more than a little alarmed that so much information about Mr. Teddy was being blurted out to her.

". . . Just don't see Lucinda murdering a childhood friend and then running off, so I am sure what John saw was just a little tiff. Teddy had a way of getting under people's skin, it amused him. But we should not ignore it; it might lead us to something more important." Lady Montfort finally came to a halt.

Lead us to something . . . lead us to what? Mrs. Jackson felt unease turn to anxiety.

"Oscar worries me. What do you make of him?" Lady Montfort was bowling bouncers, and out of habit Mrs. Jackson resorted to a defensive position.

"He's probably just coming to terms with the shock of it all." She gave one of her bland stock answers, of which she possessed a million.

Lady Montfort ranged about her sitting room; she straightened up books, rearranged flowers, and then finally came back to her chair and sat down.

"But I am sure he was involved with this gambling club of Teddy's. I must find out more about that. In fact I must find out a good deal more about all Teddy's little goings-on.

"That is why, Jackson, I would like you to find out absolutely everything you can about this stranger. Talk to Mr. Thrower, Theo Cartwright, and Fred Golightly at the Goat and Fiddle if you have to. You might even find out what the sergeant knows. The servants may have been told not to gossip, but they will. Don't shake your head, Jackson, human nature always find a way. So please gather as much information as you can." Lady Montfort picked up her notebook and pencil. She did not look directly at her housekeeper, which was a good thing because Mrs. Jackson was quite sure her face reflected how frankly appalled she was.

"Think about everything that happened in this house from the moment everyone arrived, until Sunday morning. Anything that crops up in conversation, pounce on it. It could be something extremely useful."

Mrs. Jackson watched her jot down a note or two and waited, mesmerized by the flow of information. In not ten minutes Lady Montfort had broken several unspoken precepts that existed between upper servants and those they worked for. She had revealed far too much about her family, had confided personal opinions of those staying in her house, and had openly requested her to spy on those whom she worked with and who reported to her. Mrs. Jackson was so aghast at the idea that she resolved the best thing to do was to say nothing.

Lady Montfort put her notebook down and looked at her housekeeper with such an imploring expression on her tired, tense face that it quite caused Mrs. Jackson to step outside of what convention demanded of their relationship. Her ladyship, poor woman, was quite drained, the housekeeper thought; she had lost that gleam that was always a vital part of her and she was fretting that her son might mistakenly be implicated in this awful mess. What choice did she really have but to comply with Lady Montfort's wishes? Mrs. Jackson absolutely believed it was her job to ensure the family's comfort and protect their interests. What harm could it do if she reported her observations to Lady Montfort?

Her silence made Lady Montfort nervous and she began to talk again.

"Of course I have to use my eyes and ears too. Some of my friends are definitely exhibiting some very odd and self-protective behavior and there must be a reason. We need to have our wits about us in the coming days. I don't just mean giving everyone nice comforting dinners to warm up their tummies on chilly nights. There is a murderer running around in the woods and we should do everything we can to find out who he is." She ended melodramatically, and Mrs. Jackson suddenly felt immensely tired.

Chapter Twelve

After the alarms of the preceding day, when it seemed that barely an hour had passed without evidence of some new calamity, Mrs. Jackson was thankful that Monday morning was business as usual belowstairs.

Her startling conversation with Lady Montfort the night before had caused a disjointed night's sleep. She had been asked to do something that was personally repugnant to her, that had offended her sense of dignity, and did not sit right with her strong sense of propriety. But it was after all her job to help the family in whatever way she could, and there had been nothing illegal in Lady Montfort's suggestion. After hours of tossing and turning, Mrs. Jackson had reluctantly resigned to do her very best and it was only then that she turned over in her bed and fell into an exhausted sleep.

The next morning, remembering Lady Montfort's suggestion that any trivial or innocent event that had happened on the day preceding the murder might throw light on the events surrounding it, she dutifully tuned in to the whispered conversations of those around her as they went about their daily tasks. Her natural attentiveness sharpened into observance.

The morning was a particularly lovely one and she took some time to sit in the kitchen courtyard to enjoy the sun, now burning brightly in the sky, giving lie to the falling barometer.

Sunshine makes us all kindlier folk, she thought, as she allowed herself a moment to consider that perhaps she had made a bit too much of Lady Montfort's request. *So much better to take things as they come.* To help reinforce her new understanding, she was interrupted from this reverie by Bill Craddock from the kitchen garden. He had trundled up with his handcart of fresh vegetables for the day's luncheon and dinner. Mindful that she was on a quest for information, she opened her ledger and appeared to be engrossed in the daily accounts as she watched Iris come out to inspect Bill's load of vegetables. In Mrs. Jackson's opinion, old Bill was a chronic gossip and, for all his sixty years, a flirt. He liked to pass time with the kitchen maids and would go to any lengths to get their attention.

"Good morning to you, Miss Iris." His cracked old voice was thick with dialect, and to Mrs. Jackson's critical eye he almost bridled as he began to share his gossip. "That Sergeant Hawkins, you say? Oh yes, he were up early this morning, almost as early as me. I saw Mr. Makepeace on the way over here and he told me." Bill looked over his shoulder and Iris and the kitchen maids closed in. He lowered his voice, but it was still loud enough for Mrs. Jackson to hear. "He told me that the sergeant went over the dray, inch by inch, while they was mucking out the stalls. Took his time he did, ever so thorough he was. Then he asked Mr. Makepeace to start her up and drive her out into the daylight, for a closer look-see. Even, Mr. Makepeace told me, of the wheels theyselves and whyfor he didn't know, seeing as how they was all covered in mud."

Mrs. Jackson repressed a huff of irritation. The silly old man was puffed up with self-importance as he recounted his news, causing a flurry of excitement among the kitchen maids. They had only just become aware that she was sitting quietly under the mulberry tree, her account book open on her knee.

Her first instinct was to stand up and order everyone back to work and to give Bill a scolding for his gossip. But, mindful of her new role, she ostentatiously turned away to watch the kitchen cat stretch in the sun.

How elegant cats were, she thought as she watched the cat extend her forepaws and sink her claws deep into the coir doormat, pulling back to elongate her spine, her tail curled up and over toward her back, like the handle of a pitcher. The cat jumped up onto the windowsill and, half concealed by a branch from the mulberry tree, settled down to wash herself. Dick Wilson came out of the scullery door with an enamel pail. He swung his arm back, dashing soapy gray water onto the flagstones. He was usually well coordinated, but the backward movement of his right hand on the pail handle was awkward and the water hit the ground too near his feet. She saw him skip backward to avoid getting his shoes wet. The cat, alarmed by his abrupt movement and the splash on the stones so near her window, jumped off her sill, hissed at him for alarming her, and ran up the tree. Dick paused to laugh up at the cat. He moved his disordered hair from his forehead and, turning, caught sight of Mrs. Jackson sitting nearby. He lifted his hand again to his forehead in the time-honored countryman's salute of both deference and polite acknowledgment. She nodded to him and went back to her thoughts. But something had caught her attention. When Dick had swung his pail back to his side, she noticed that the knuckles on his right hand were red and swollen, the skin abraded and broken. *Footmen in training take care of their hands,* she thought. She must find out how the hallboy had so badly injured his.

Well, she said to herself, *all this sitting about can be very profitable.* She stood up and smoothed her skirt and then her hair. Half an hour in the courtyard and her information had increased immeasurably. Now it was time to organize flowers for the house. She sincerely hoped Mr. Thrower would be around to help her and not one of the under-gardeners.

On her arrival in the kitchen garden, the first person she saw was Mr. Stafford. He strolled out from behind the forcing house, and when he saw her he stopped and lifted his hat in greeting to her with his customary good humor. His unexpected appearance was so discomfiting that she had to look away for a moment before she turned to greet him.

"Moss, Mr. Stafford?" She indicated the slice of dense, brilliant green he was holding, the rich black earth it grew in so damply compressed that it barely left a trace on his open palm.

"Yes, that's right. Look at this beautiful shade of green." He turned his palm and she saw that the emerald moss was thick and flawless, dense as velvet. "Beautiful underplanting in shade gardens, if it doesn't dry up. I think it would work well among the Hellebore under the trees in the sunken garden, against the wall. There will be enough water from the spring, but I need . . ." Here he lost her, as he happily described soil conditions while she wondered how she could bring their conversation around to the dray. In the end she decided that being straightforward was the best way and made her feel less of a spy.

"Do you happen to know if the dray is still locked up in the old carriage house, Mr. Stafford? I mean, has the sergeant finished with it yet? We need to use it for bringing up more vegetables and fruit from the gardens for the rest of the week. The handcart doesn't hold enough and I don't want to bother the dairy for one of the wagons."

"Well, I think the best person to ask about the dray is Sergeant Hawkins, seeing as he is the one who gave orders for it to be locked up in the carriage house. The dray is part of his investigation now."

"I will, of course," she answered. "but I just wondered . . ."

"What I knew? Not much I'm afraid, but the sergeant did find Mr. Teddy's evening shoe in the back of the storage box in the dray. Which leads all of us to suspect," he smiled at her and she could have sworn he winked his eye, "that Mr. Teddy was locked in that storage box and taken up to Crow Wood that way. Oh, I am sorry, Mrs. Jackson; I didn't mean to . . . It doesn't bear thinking about, does it? That poor lad being kept in a box like that; course he might have already been dead."

Momentarily taken aback at finding herself so swiftly precipitated into a conversation on what she would have been considered a forbidden topic yesterday, and surprised at how quickly Stafford had guessed what she was up to and how much he was willing to share, Mrs. Jackson could think of nothing to say at all. She must have looked disapproving, she thought, because Stafford hastened to explain that Mr. Teddy's being put in the storage box had been Makepeace's theory, not his. Makepeace, she thought, seemed to have a very strong opinion of what had been going on. Should she talk to him? No, she decided not, the head groom was a man's man.

It suddenly occurred to her that outside in the open, away from the hushed, protective shelter of the house, an act of intentional violence resulting in the death of a young man had been committed. Here, she thought, where they all lived, a murder committed by someone they all knew. For the first time the reality of what had taken place hit home hard, and her stomach felt sick and heavy.

She managed to nod, she hoped in encouragement, and Stafford went on to say that Mr. Teddy's being carted about in the storage box of the dray had been all the talk at the Goat and Fiddle last night. The pub had been packed with villagers and farm laborers; it must have been the busiest night of the decade for Fred Golightly.

"Someone had given Mr. Teddy quite a beating before he was killed—gave him a right punch on the nose. I didn't know he was so disliked, did you?" Mr. Stafford asked.

This was awful news, not what she had hoped to hear at all. She tried not to show her concern or any reaction. But the information served to push her out of her earlier reticence with Mr. Stafford and to overcome her reserve with him. She risked a question of her own.

"Wasn't there a stranger hanging around in the village on the day of the . . . the day of the ball?"

Stafford's glance was shrewd and Mrs. Jackson tried not to let his knowing look fluster her, but he answered her willingly enough.

"Yes, there was, Mrs. Jackson. I saw him myself, walking from the direction of Cryer's Breach railway station toward the village. He was on Dodder Lane when I spotted him at about three o'clock. Then Theo Cartwright saw him later on hanging around the back of the pub at about five o'clock or thereabouts. Sounded like the same man and he looked just like a Londoner: cheap, flashy clothes; pasty and unhealthy-looking."

"Not from around here, then?"

"No, didn't look like a local man or a countryman either. There are a lot of men wandering the country these days look-

ing for work, but this one certainly wasn't a tramp. Fred Golightly said that Mr. Teddy came to the pub that afternoon, about
the same time as Theo saw the stranger hanging around the
back."

"Did Mr. Teddy meet with this stranger, then?" Mrs. Jackson's
question was out before she could stop herself.

Stafford put his hands in his pockets, tilted back his head, and
laughed at her question.

"No, it didn't seem that way. Fred said Mr. Teddy came into
the pub, looked around as if he was hoping to see someone he
knew. Then he left and drove around the back of the pub. Fred
saw him sitting in his motorcar, as if he was waiting there for
someone. Next he knew, Mr. Teddy had driven off.

"Not very popular was he, Mr. Teddy? The locals don't seem
to have much time for him."

Mrs. Jackson was certainly not going to let her information
exchange with Mr. Stafford lure her that far. His straightforward, easy way of talking, pleasant as it might sometimes be,
also reminded her that she had a position to uphold. She fell
back on platitudes: what a dreadful thing Mr. Teddy's death had
been, and how distressing it was for the family. She didn't want
to snub Stafford and preclude any opportunity for more information, so she was careful to keep her tone regretful and not
reproving, and then, circumspect as always, she changed the
subject.

"I am hoping the rain hasn't ruined all the flowers. Are the
irises open?" She was surprised how much more relaxed she felt
with Mr. Stafford after their little gossip about Teddy's murder.

"We'll have to check with Mr. Thrower. The peonies are still
looking good, which is a miracle considering the heavy rain-
fall, and we have plenty of roses that are opening up from the

bud—they withstood the storm pretty well. Good Lord, look at the time." He had pulled a watch out of his waistcoat pocket. "Getting on for nine o'clock and Colonel Valentine wants all the estate staff and the villagers assembled outside the stables in fifteen minutes. We've got to go and look for that nice little girl who worked up at the house, and the other young lady. What a business it's been."

It had been a business indeed and suddenly Mrs. Jackson felt rather swamped by everything she knew and what she had just learned. The thought of choosing flowers seemed ridiculously trivial. She looked up and understood that Mr. Stafford was aware of her hesitation.

"It must be difficult for you right now. So much has happened, it must be hard to take it all in," he said, and she was struck by how kind and concerned his voice was.

Her reluctance to discuss family business was deeply ingrained, but she found it quite easy to answer this sympathetic man.

"Colonel Valentine is talking to the family, and Sergeant Hawkins is talking to the servants. Everyone visiting the house will stay over for another three days. And it's all rather awful; there is an atmosphere of excitement in the servants' hall, the wrong kind of excitement." It wasn't very interesting stuff, she thought, in comparison with what he had told her, but it was a long speech for her.

He looked concerned as he bent down and put the piece of moss neatly back into the place he had cut it from, a slice from the cake of rich, wet earth. When he straightened he looked at her carefully in his direct way, and she found it a little unnerving but quite agreeable to be so noticed.

"Keep your wits about you, Mrs. Jackson. That young man

was murdered in a nasty way. Now two girls are missing, it's all linked you can be sure. Something bad is happening here, so be on the alert." He brought his right hand up and gave her an ironic salute, since he was neither estate worker nor villager, and started to walk in the direction of the stable. He hadn't gone three paces before he turned back to her again, his eyes squinting in the sun's glare. She thought for a moment he was going to tell her something of importance, his expression was so grave, but all he said was:

"Mr. Thrower won't be joining the search. So he will be able to help you with the flowers."

Chapter Thirteen

Clementine felt stifled and restless when she awoke that morning, and as the day was quite beautiful, she thought that if Colonel Valentine wanted to interview her then he would just have to wait until she had come back from her ride. Taking out her mare for a nice long gallop would invigorate her and help restore a sense of proportion.

Constance Ambrose had sent word to her that she had awakened with a slight headache and did not care to ride that morning, and Ralph had rushed off to his breakfast so he could meet with his agent, Archie Pommeroy, before he joined the hunt for the missing girls later that morning. She would ride alone. She rang for Pettigrew to help her dress in her riding habit.

As Clementine approached the stable block she heard its occupants snorting as they searched through the straw bedding of their stalls for leftover morning oats, and she stopped to enjoy the mingled scents of hay, horse, and saddle leather lifting up out of the stables to meet the cool morning air.

When she turned the corner into the stable yard she was thrilled to find her son examining the right front shoe of his horse. As he called his good-morning to her, she asked him who he was riding out with.

"No one, Mother, I'm all yours," he said as he dropped his horse's hoof, lifted the saddle flap, and tightened the girth. She watched his groom, Davey, give him a leg-up onto his tall bay gelding and felt almost happy at the thought of a ride on her favorite mare, with her son for company.

Clementine's pretty gray mare, Catch, was led out into the yard. She bent her head and rubbed her cheek against the mare's soft, delicate muzzle, and then led her over to the mounting block. As she settled herself on her horse's back and organized her riding habit, she asked the head groom, "How is she this morning Tom?" as Catch pinned her ears at Harry's dignified hunter.

"She's in a sweet and listening mood, your la'ship." Tom Makepeace touched his cap to her. "Took her out yesterday and she was a lamb." The mare snaked her neck at Harry's horse and Clementine heard her teeth click.

"Little witch, she's full of herself." Clementine laughed and felt almost lighthearted. "Come on then, Harry, let's be off," she cried out to her son as she trotted around him on her excited mare, who insisted on being the first to leave the yard. In the sunlight atop Catch, she felt normalcy and even optimism return as the two of them clattered out of the yard and up the lane in the direction of the home farm.

"Not that way, Mother," Harry said as she turned her mare into the home-farm lane. "Let's give that blasted wood a miss for a few weeks. If we go left up the cart track we can pick our way round the back of the dower house, come out by Feltham's field, and take our gallop across the top there." He slowed his bay to a walk and she fell in beside him, careful not to let her mare's nose poke ahead and cause rivalry.

They walked their horses through the gate and onto the cart track and then broke into a trot and Clementine could almost feel her liver thanking her for exercise. They rode in silence through the pasture where a herd of cows slowly turned to watch them, their heavy, bovine jaws working steadily as they tore up rich mouthfuls of lush green grass.

Grateful to be away from her house, she inhaled the soft scents of the day: rain-drenched earth warming in the sun, the sweet crushed grass under their horses' hooves, pollen and meadow flowers. A blissful morning, she thought as she looked out across the pasture and into the shady beech woods at its edge. She almost felt normal again.

Harry urged his bay forward and Clementine's mare broke into a canter before she was asked and off they went. She heard herself laugh as Catch exuberantly kicked out at a patch of dandelions, sending seed heads flying into the sunlit air.

She felt like a new woman when they returned more than an hour later, her face flushed with the effort of their long gallop. They turned down the lane past the dower house and fell into a slow walk. As they passed the turnoff for the home farm she saw Mr. Jenkins and his farm laborers walking up the lane, no doubt on their way to the stable block to join the search party assembling there. She lifted her hand in greeting.

"Wish I could go out with them, but I can't," said Harry. "Valentine wants to see me later this morning, before he and Oscar leave for Oxford."

Clementine was instantly alert. "Why are they off to Oxford? Surely Valentine doesn't believe Oscar had anything to do with Teddy's gambling club?"

She turned in her saddle and noticed that Harry was looking particularly derisive as he answered her: "Well quite, anyone who knows Oscar knows he never plays cards. It's pathetic really. And even if Oscar and Teddy were as thick as thieves, I just don't see Oscar running an illegal club."

Clementine thought this rather an unfortunate aphorism considering that Teddy had in actual fact been a thief and privately wondered that even if Oscar didn't play cards, perhaps he had something to do with the organization of the gambling club and the systematic cheating that had taken place. She rather liked Oscar, and had often puzzled over his friendship with her husband's nephew. She asked her son if he knew why Oscar had to go to Oxford.

"Only thing he said was that he had some papers of Teddy's and that he had to go with Valentine up to Christ Church so he could hand them over. He didn't *say* anything more, but I could tell he was all shaky and anxious about it. You know Oscar, he gets keyed up about little things, it's just how he is."

"I don't think that going up to Oxford with Valentine as part of a murder investigation is a little thing. Oscar looked almost ill last night at dinner."

"Well that's an understatement. He was Teddy closest . . . only friend at Oxford. Poor chap's quite sick with nerves, and then of course he had quite a few too many last night . . . so he is probably feeling pretty low this morning. Now he's got to spend the entire afternoon with Valentine, what a thought." Obviously Harry, like Gertrude Waterford, held Morris Valentine in low esteem.

She sat deep into her saddle as Catch decided to be melodramatic about an old wheelbarrow leaning up against the post of the gate. When she had the mare walking obediently alongside Harry again, she asked if he thought Valentine suspected that Oscar had something to do with Teddy's death.

Her question made Harry turn toward her. He considered and then said, "Well, Oscar seems to think that Valentine might suspect him. Apparently he does not have what Valentine calls an alibi from the end of the ball until early the following morning."

Clementine digested this sizable crumb and then cautiously asked her son if he had an alibi.

"Yes, Mother, I do, actually." He turned in his saddle to look at her and smiled. "Do you?"

"Is that what Colonel Valentine is asking everyone?" she persisted.

"Yes, that's what he is asking. He says, 'Do come on in, Lord Haversham, and take a chair,' all very friendly. Then all of a sudden it's, 'How much time did you spend with Teddy, were you close, did you get on with your cousin, what do you know about his card club, did you play?' And just as you are adjusting to that, it's a wallop: 'I need to know where you were from the end of the ball till breakfast the following morning. Who were you with, will they vouch for you?' You have to give the right answers of course; it's like being back at Eton, but not as intimidating."

"Did you give Valentine the right answers, Harry?"

He gave her the smile he had used since he was a boy when he was asking too many questions of her. She felt hugely irritated by it.

How infuriating he could be, she thought. *Why was he so flippant about something so terribly important?* His unselfconscious charm could be very disarming, but it worked only with mothers, nannies, and young women. She was quite sure that someone like Valentine wouldn't be taken in by it.

Inwardly fuming over the inconsequential attitudes of the

young, she became aware that he had slowed his horse to a halt, turned its nose toward her mare, and was now looking at her very seriously indeed. Surprised by the rapid switch from playfulness to gravity, she drew her mare up and looked back at him expectantly. He was evidently going to tell her something significant. He was watching her intently, as if trying to decide how best to put what he had to say. She held her breath and her inner tension communicated itself to Catch; the mare danced up and down on the spot and then started to back up.

"Mother, I rather need your help . . ." Harry said and waited as she brought her mare back under control. *Oh God,* she thought, *what is he going to tell me?* She composed herself for the inevitable.

When he had finished explaining his situation, she became so alarmed that it was hard for her to let him finish. She had to force herself to be silent until he was done.

"So you see, Mama," he said as he wound up, "I really need you in my corner. Will you help me?" His disarming smile had gone, and his face was as grave and serious as it had been when he was a boy and had brought home a sack of mongrel puppies, rescued from the village pond, and had come looking for her as an ally. But this request was far more calamitous than hand-raising mutts.

She finally found her voice: "A flyer? You want to become a flyer? I'm not even sure I understand what that means. It has to do with those blasted aeroplanes, doesn't it? We all know they are death traps." She felt the tension of the last few days return and had to hold her breath when she saw the look of incredulous dismay on his face. She waited until she was quite sure her next words would not sound angry. She breathed evenly as she waited for calm, for patience.

"We are in the middle of a murder inquiry, Harry, and you are in a very precarious position indeed. How could you possibly bring up a thing like this? Of course your father will object to your flying. Most strongly I hope." She had managed the first part quite well, but heard her voice beginning to rise. *Breathe,* she said to herself, *calm down before you continue.*

"Harry, you have a duty." She waved her whip around her at the stables, the horse pastures, and the great beyond that stretched all around them, acre upon acre of farms, fields, and woodland. "And it's all this . . ." She pointed her arm down the valley. Productive, bountiful, arable Talbot land stretched for miles, representing the Talbots' responsibility to hundreds of families: tenant farmers, estate workers, and neighboring landowners who made up their agrarian world.

But Harry had grown up with "all this" and apparently, unlike his father, he was not as impressed with his duty to it as he should be; she could tell by the look of polite patience on his face.

"Yes, I know that, Mother, but it will be years until I inherit. I need something useful to do . . ."

"Of course you do, Harry, and it's taking your place as a member of parliament for the county. That's your job, until you inherit. That is what people like us do: we take our place in government, and we are responsible for the land we inherit." She reined in her frustration and her nervous mare. *And you can't do that with a broken neck,* she said to herself.

"Yes, Mother, I am completely aware of my duty, and completely prepared to do it. But I can also join Tom Sopwith and that is what I want to do this summer. He is the best aeroplane designer this country has, and we both believe flight is a big part of the future."

As they walked their horses back to the stable she asked herself in despair why children were such a challenge when they grew up.

Clementine's interview with Colonel Valentine was set for a little later that afternoon. As she waited for her turn to come, she had plenty of time to prepare her thoughts as she idled away the afternoon with her friends.

After luncheon she had settled down to play bridge with Olive, Gertrude, and Sir Wilfred, who had already paid their visits to the morning room. Gertrude seemed a good deal more relaxed since her interview with Colonel Valentine, she thought. Clementine watched her play with her usual effortless skill, interjecting the occasional amusing observation, doing her best to keep the occasion lighthearted. She was grateful that her friend was holding the social fort because she had never felt so anxious and miserable in her life.

She knew she was playing badly, unlike Olive, a serious and competitive player who bent to her work with the relentless focus of an addict. Her partner, Sir Wilfred, was inattentive and his concentration for the game erratic. Between them they put up such a poor show that Olive got quite tetchy and reproached her husband for drumming his fingers on the table and scowled when Clementine had to be reminded that it was her play.

Instead of concentrating on her hand, she glanced over at Sir Wilfred. What an odd duck the man was, she thought. His interests in life were focused only in two distinct and separate areas. He did something very important on the board of the White Star shipping line, and when he was not directing the efforts of others, he spent as much of his winter as he could on his archaeological dig in Egypt, of which he was apparently the sole financial contributor, and where, she had no doubt, he continued to direct the efforts of others. She had always found him a desiccated and rather self-absorbed specimen, who relinquished all responsibility for social intercourse on whoever he was with at the time, making him an exhausting person to be seated next to at dinner, unless you were a shipping magnate or an Egyptologist.

She found Olive, on the other hand, practical, pleasant, and socially adept. She enjoyed her company and her fund of wicked and often very funny stories about her arch nemesis, the ambitious and ruthless Lady Constance Gwladys, the Marchioness of Ripon, who had successfully competed with Olive for Sir Thomas Beecham's wandering attentions.

Clementine idly wondered how her dear friend Harriet was holding up. She knew Lady Harriet and Gilbert Lambert-Lambert were keeping each other company as they made or waited for telephone calls from butlers at their various houses, in their quest to locate their elusive daughter. Clementine had made the study available to them to be handy for the telephone room, where they repaired to shout instructions to servants at their house in London and their country houses in Derbyshire and Leicestershire.

After luncheon, when she was walking through the hall she heard their voices raised in accusation or argument behind the closed door of the stuffy telephone room. She had almost laughed when she heard Gilbert's voice shouting, "How many bloody times do I have to telephone the house? It's harder to be put through to damn Nanny than to Herbert Asquith." Gilbert's overbearing and humorless pomposity had evaporated overnight, she thought with compassion, for although she often found him hard to take, she was immensely fond of his wife.

She looked at the clock on the chimneypiece. Surely more than ten minutes had passed. Sir Hugo Waterford was keeping his appointment with Valentine and she was "up next." Such was her preoccupation that she was barely aware of the cards she held in her hand. She muttered, "Two, no trump," without really thinking, causing her partner to suck air over his teeth and to sigh with relief when the footman John arrived to curtail their game. It was time to keep her appointment with Colonel Valentine.

Having mentally rehearsed several different tactics for her meeting throughout her bridge game, Clementine was rather surprised that she was given very little opportunity to ask her carefully phrased questions. Apparently their talk was meant for Colonel Valentine to do all the questioning and for her to supply the answers. This was a new experience for her, but once she got the hang of it, she was quite happy to play along. She supplied information about Teddy, his friends, and his possible enemies and past indiscretions, and when Valentine was satisfied they moved on to Teddy's arrival at Iyntwood and any conversations that Clementine might have had with him that could be useful information to Valentine's inquiry into his death.

She happily told him that she had greeted Teddy on his arrival, when he seemed as usual, before she had gone out to spend the hours before tea with her garden architect. *Goodness me, there is nothing to this,* she thought. *It's going to be easier than I had imagined.*

"And did you perhaps see Teddy later on that afternoon when

you returned to the house? What time was that, by the way?" Throughout his interview Valentine had been excessively courteous, careful not to offend any sensibilities; she thought his manner quite delightful.

"Yes, I did see him . . . must have been about four o'clock. I was on my way to the house to change for tea. I saw him only from a distance." This was almost true, she convinced herself.

"Was he with anyone?" he asked, and Clementine noticed that after each question he tended to incline his head sideways and open his eyes a little wider, rather like one of the Labradors when a biscuit was in view.

Having not paid proper attention, she found that they had wandered into a sticky area and it was here she told her first fib: "I can't honestly remember if he was with anyone, isn't that silly of me? I just sort of noticed him; he was walking towards the orchard." *What a plausible liar I have become,* she thought with a thrill of horror at how easy it was to dissemble. "Of course I saw him throughout the evening, and I have tried to remember the last time I noticed him. I think it was in the ballroom when we were dancing the Lancers. You were there, Colonel Valentine, what time was that?"

"At about quarter past one o'clock, I saw you, too. I think it was actually the Dashing White Sergeant, my hip remembers it well." Colonel Valentine gave her a regretful smile, no doubt, she thought, to encourage her to believe that he was a harmless old dog whose dancing days were pretty much over. Clementine in turn hoped that her inaccuracy would in some way build up a picture in Valentine's mind that poor Lady Montfort was getting to that time of life when her memory was unreliable. *Watch yourself,* she instructed, *don't be lulled into a false sense of security.*

"Know of any discord between Teddy and anyone staying at the house?" he asked. And it was here that she knowingly told her second lie, or what came close to it.

"Teddy was such a complicated young man, often secretive and rather self-centered. I do not think he got on particularly well with anyone." She was again surprised at how smoothly this came out.

"Quite, I understand that. No quarrel that you know of . . . with anyone?"

She felt a moment of real fear. Did Valentine know of Harry's falling out with his cousin?

"No quarrels of any kind, Colonel," she replied, compounding her second white lie into a whopper. Her heart raced and she felt a huge wave of heat wash over her face and neck. *Now I've done it,* she thought. *I have blushed like a blasted housemaid after breaking a teacup.* She looked at him out of the corner of her eye. He was engrossed in his notebook, thank God.

He then asked her what time she had retired for the night, if her maid had been with her, and what time Pettigrew had left her and then awakened her in the morning. He was punctiliously correct in how he phrased these particular questions. He didn't actually refer to her bedroom at all. In fact, afterward she wondered if he had even said the word *retired.* Somehow they had managed that part by implication alone.

When it seemed that he was finished with his questions, Clementine decided it was time to reciprocate and swiftly asked if the colonel had heard from the coroner and when he thought it would be possible for them to release poor Teddy's body so that she might talk to his mother, when she arrived in a few days' time, about funeral arrangements.

"Probably by the end of the week," she was told.

She innocently followed this one up with what time he thought Teddy had died. She infused enough sadness into her tone to make her question one of concern rather than a desperate need of facts. It struck her as she asked this that in Valentine's view she no doubt lacked all feminine decorum with this ugly question. Men like Valentine so hated it when women asked the sort of questions that it was acceptable only for men to ask. But she had surprised him into answering that Teddy had died between three and six o'clock on Sunday morning.

Clementine heaved an immense mental sigh of relief as she left the morning room. As soon as she closed the door behind her she almost felt triumphant and could not imagine why anyone thought that Valentine wasn't up to the job. He had been careful not to offend, but he had certainly been searching with his questions. Of course, he had not asked her if she had an alibi, which she found a little strange. Perhaps this was a question he felt he need not ask of her; after all, she obviously had no motive to kill her husband's nephew. She felt she had handled her untruths very well indeed, which made her feel a little like a whited sepulcher, and she hoped that she was not tempting fate to intervene and even out the score.

Outside in the hall she found Oscar drooping by the radiator as he waited to set off for Oxford with Valentine. She noticed that his appearance was rather distressing. He was extremely pale and his eyes were so wretchedly tired that Clementine was immediately concerned for him.

"Oscar dear, what are you doing here?" she asked as she crossed the hall toward him.

"Good afternoon, Lady Montfort. I am going to Oxford with Colonel Valentine . . ." He paused and muttered, "Just to help him tie up some loose ends about Teddy's business."

Clementine rather approved of Oscar, another boyhood friend of her children. He was always deferential and his manners were quite beautiful. There was a genuine sweetness to him that she found charming. He often took the time to chat about this and that, unlike Harry and Ellis, who were always intent on their own pursuits. She was saddened to see him looking so desolate and thought that of all of them, he was possibly the only one who was genuinely grieving for Teddy.

"This must be especially hard for you, Oscar. I am so sorry about what happened." She grasped his lower arm in sympathy genuinely felt.

To her immense astonishment, she saw tears spring into his eyes. He dashed them away and nodded, too overcome to speak. She gave him some breathing room. It was awful to see him so unhappy.

"He was the greatest friend anyone could have . . ." he muttered at last, looking down at his feet. "I simply can't believe he has gone. I can't believe . . . what happened to him." A small, tight sob almost broke, but after a few moments of struggling Oscar managed to get himself back on track.

Clementine was horrified. She felt terrible that she had helped to unravel the poor boy so thoroughly just before his meeting with Valentine. It really wouldn't do, she thought, for him to fall apart quite so easily in the middle of a murder inquiry. "All will heal in time, Oscar," she said, careful not to overdo it and precipitate another bout of anguish. "All this will fade and you will remember him as he was." She patted his shoulder briskly and sought to change the subject to help him pull himself back together.

She fell back on the national love of Bradshaw train timetables and the best roads to take between towns, and asked him if he was driving up or going by train. He cleared his throat and managed to get out that Valentine was driving them up.

"Ah good, then you will be back in time for dinner, and I'll see you then, Oscar." She said this in a rallying tone, hoping to infuse him with a little more backbone than he appeared to have.

He looked at her directly as he said that he really hoped she did see him for dinner. She shivered slightly as it struck her that Oscar had completely accepted he was Colonel Valentine's favorite suspect for Teddy's murder.

So much for Gertrude's convenient stranger, she thought as she walked across the hall and went out through the terrace door. Walking briskly to the bottom of the lawn, she looked across the valley to the hills beyond as if hoping to see her husband. What a long, long day it had been: it was only four o'clock now and it would be hours yet before the search party returned. More than anything she wished to ride out and join him, but that would never do. Instead, she must return to the house and change her dress for tea so that she might brave the rest of the afternoon in the company of her closest friends.

Chapter Fourteen

Lord Montfort rode out earlier that morning with the search party for Lucinda Lambert-Lambert and Violet Simkins, joining more than three hundred men from his estate, nearby farms, and the surrounding villages. He found the activity similar to beating for a local shoot, but it covered a far greater distance and many of the men had brought along their wives and older children. Knowing what was expected of him, Lord Montfort had laid on a good supper for the searchers with local publicans for the end of the day.

After the inertia of the past two days, he was grateful for the opportunity to leave his house and take an active part in the day as they searched hedgerows, copses, ditches, country lanes, meadows, fields, pastures, and woods, and the barns and outbuildings of small holdings and large farms. After the downpour of the preceding night, the air was heavy with evaporation. Overhead, clouds formed and broke, and on the horizon the sky concentrated into a thick, dark metallic gray line to meet the earth's heavy green.

Lord Montfort's hunter, Bruno, towered over the tall June meadow grass, eager to canter every lane and mown pasture.

At their heels were his three yellow Labradors, ready to enjoy to the fullest extent the freedom offered on this summer day. They romped through fields and undergrowth, their large rumps disappearing into tall grass, and their enthusiastic faces peering up from ditches, with the flowers of Queen Anne's lace adorning their ears. Lord Montfort was an uncomplicated man: a day spent on his horse with his dogs for company was a good one, even this day.

The day wore on and by four o'clock his energy and that of his horse and the dogs began to fade. He separated from his group, rode up to the brow of the hill, and came to a halt under the canopy of Saint Simon's Wood, not fifteen miles as the crow flies from Haversham, and halted in the shade of a beech hanger. He took off his hat and let the breeze cool his head. The dogs collapsed in an ungainly pile around Bruno's legs, ears pulled back, huge mouths wide and tongues lolling. The sound of their heavy panting completely drowned the birdsong and made Lord Montfort feel hot and thirsty.

He looked around him and considered his lot. This wood had once been part of an ancient oak forest that had stretched from the base of the Pennine Gap in an unbroken bulwark to the south downs of England. Before his family had even come into existence, six hundred years ago, the forest had no boundary or purpose other than to cloak England with a habitat for wolves, bear, deer, and boar, providing wild game for the royal hunt and for the occasional outlaw seeking shelter and a bit of poaching. It occurred to Lord Montfort that he would have loved to be alive at that time, when the words *petrol, cotton mill,* and *slag heap* were unknown. His wife always told him that he had been born two hundred years too late.

The Talbot family had been active in century after century

of British civilization. They had certainly contributed to finding a use for the old forest. The oaks had been felled for timber and had lived on, for a time, in the country's cathedrals, churches, fortresses, ships, and great houses. Talbot ships in the eighteenth century had made his family tremendously wealthy and influential.

He turned in his saddle to look over his shoulder. Saint Simon's Wood came to an abrupt end on an escarpment of land jutting southward, and at its base were the domesticated fields and pastures of the Talbots' land. It was flanked by gentler, rounded hills, and beyond that by another long ridge that lay almost on the boundary of the two counties.

Lord Montfort, perched on the highest point in several miles, gazed down on the years of human endeavor that had created his properties. He saw the straggling line of men working their way through fields and into small stands of trees, toward the road to Market Wingley that cut his estates into two almost-equal halves. Fields green with young wheat and barley stood brightly, segregated by dark beech and hawthorn hedgerows. To the south, cumulus clouds moved gently northward. Between billows of rounded clouds the sky was a transparent aquatint of northern blue.

If Lord Montfort were to indulge himself in a sense of loss for what had been and what might come, this would be the moment, as he looked down on his family's hard-won, carefully tended agricultural land. The Talbots had been country men throughout the ages. Their fortunes, however great or small, depending on the time in which they had prevailed, had been returned over and over into the land. The people who had worked hard to drain, hedge, ditch, plow, and reap had raised large families on the estates and lands of the Talbots. This was all Lord

Montfort had ever known, a still-feudal way of life that had struggled into a new age and a progressive century. As head of the Talbot family he was bound to the people who lived and worked for him, no matter what came, and he earnestly believed that they were still bound to him. He was also astute enough to know that this orderly life was doomed to change completely within the century; he was an antiquated old relic, as his son had so often said.

All that day he had searched the country for the two girls. But it was Violet Simkins who had predominated in his thoughts as he paced the countryside on Bruno's strong back. He wasn't terribly sure what Violet looked like, but in his mind he saw a young girl, frightened and injured, waiting to be found, and who depended on him for her existence. Because of Teddy's terrible death, he had been most anxious that they might find her badly hurt, perhaps even dead. As the day wore on, he realized he had been dreaming. His hope of finding her was just that, and bore no reality to what had happened at Iyntwood in the last two days, and to the changing world he lived in. Violet, like her more sophisticated counterpart, Lucinda, had certainly disappeared from Iyntwood, but for her own reasons, and ones that he couldn't begin to understand. Now all that remained was for him to walk his tired horse back to the village and let Jim Simkins know that they had been unable to find his only child.

The search wound down as Lord Montfort and the Haversham men tramped to their village. They were too many to cram into the Goat and Fiddle, so they grouped themselves outside, filling their tankards from the keg. Lord Montfort was pleased to discover that Fred Golightly and his wife had spent the day cooking up large, generous pots of a rich beef stew with dumplings, all costs to be absorbed by him. As the men gathered to eat, Lord Montfort walked his horse over the green toward the church and the one-room schoolhouse behind it.

Jim Simkins lived in a small two-up-and-two-down cottage next to the schoolhouse. There was a light in the lower window, and Lord Montfort slid off his horse and tapped on the door. It was not closed fast. It swung open as if Jim had known someone would drop by and had made sure that he would hear their knock or call. The older man walked across the brick floor of the kitchen and pulled the door open wide. Lord Montfort was stunned by the change in the man's appearance. It looked as if he had lost height in just a few days: his body seemed to have folded in on itself. Jim straightened up as he saw who his visitor was, nodded his hello, and extended a welcoming hand into his cottage.

"Jim, I am most terribly sorry . . . we have not been successful." He closed a mollifying hand on the older man's shoulder; it was stick thin, the skin hot under the fabric of Jim's rough wool coat.

"Well, your lordship, I didn't think somehow it would be. But I thank you for your time, thank everyone for their time. I know you have done all you can." They stood awkwardly for a moment before Jim took hold of the door and swung it back.

"Would you come in for a moment?" The room was stuffy and although clean and tidy had an airless atmosphere. Lord Montfort looked over at Bruno, who wanted his stable, oats, and hay, and was grinding away at his bit and tossing his head, ears pinned at the unwarranted stop that was far from home. Feeling that it would be unsympathetic to leave too quickly, Lord Montfort sat himself down outside under the cottage window on a small bench and gestured to Jim to join him. The two men sat in the quiet of the evening; the clouds were banked up on the horizon, but the sky was still clear, and the coming night was cool.

"Coming in to rain again, you can smell it in the air," Jim said, and Lord Montfort nodded.

"Yes, the barometer was falling when I left the house this morning, and it looks like another rainstorm . . ." He stopped. He didn't want to remind Jim that somewhere out there without a roof over her head was his only child.

Together they watched early stars come out. Lord Montfort listened to the hedgerow creatures scurrying about their nightly routines in the hawthorn and eglantine hedge by the lane. *The hunter and the hunted,* he thought. He watched the bats as they flapped in the upper canopy of the elm trees. A flock of crows flew noisily across the lane to roost in the trees at the edge of Deansfield.

"And the other young lady, Miss Lucinda—anyone know where she's got to?" Jim asked.

"We haven't heard directly from her. We are hoping that none of this is linked . . ."

"I'm sure it's not, just a set of coincidences. I expect Violet will turn up, word will get out and someone will have seen her. She might even be with her aunt over in Ticksby. It's hard to understand the young sometimes."

Jim was a gentle man, if not a gentleman. There was not a shade of blame or reproach in his voice, Lord Montfort realized, grateful for the man's dignity. He had always had time for Jim Simkins, a philosopher and natural scholar much liked and respected in the village though he didn't quite fit in. He'd heard somewhere that in his youth Jim had left the village but had never been the same since he had worked as a housepainter in Market Wingley when he was a lad. The Reverend Bottomley-

Jones had told him that Jim was already sick and broken down by town life and had returned to the village with his only child. And with some strange ideas about a new philanthropic and collective social order—a socialist, some of the villagers said. Lord Montfort thought that if Jim was a socialist he was a remarkably quiet one. There was nothing of a Keir Hardie about this man. He lived quietly in his cottage with his books and his thoughts, tending his garden and rambling through the countryside. Ten years ago, at Lord Montfort's suggestion and with his backing, he had started the village school. He taught the children how to read and write and do their sums when they could be spared from their work on the land. He had thought Jim a good teacher; he had a gentle authority and was a kindly schoolmaster, determined to do what he could for the country children and always happy to find a bright spark among them whom he could bring on. He knew the challenges Jim faced, as the children rarely stayed on a regular basis, often pulled away from their studies for haymaking, harvesting, or seasonal planting.

Lord Montfort kept Jim company for a little longer, until he was summoned by his horse, snorting and stamping for his saddle and bridle to be off.

"Well, Jim, you know we are still on the lookout for her. If you hear anything, or if you need anything, please let me know."

"Thank you, my lord." Jim turned and almost shuffled into the house. His health had never been good, but Lord Montfort was concerned to see how thin and frail he had become in so short a time. It was known that Jim had trouble with his lungs, had been nursing his condition for years. Now the shock of Violet's disappearance had broken the last reserves of his health. Lord Montfort led Bruno up the lane to a stile, climbed up onto his back, and trotted back to the village, and the heaviness he had felt in his chest since the death of his nephew deepened.

He looked up as a large barn owl dropped out of an oak tree, its great round head turned to fix Lord Montfort briefly with an accusing stare before it leveled out on powerful wings to glide silently ahead of him down the lane. In the twilight of the evening its feathers gleamed silver-white against the dark hawthorn. If he had been a Roman he would have taken the owl's appearance as a very bad omen indeed. *But you're not a Roman*, he told himself, *all you need is a decent dinner.*

Outside the public house, he let his horse drink at the trough. The dogs hadn't moved from the group of men enjoying their supper at the wood tables against the timbered frame of the building, but now two of them wandered up and sank their muzzles into the water alongside the horse. For Lord Montfort it was a companionable moment; on any other evening, at any other time, this would have been a peaceful end to the day.

He walked his horse over to the crowd of men who were gathered around a keg of ale. He handed Bruno's reins to a young boy standing on the edge of the group and loosened the horse's girth before he joined the crowd at the pub door. He allowed himself to be welcomed by those who worked for him, reassured by the closeness of men he had known for years.

"Been a long day, my lord, and a pity we didn't find the young misses."

"Sure to turn up though, your lordship, young people being what they are these days."

"Thank you, Dawkins, I'm sure you're right."

"Know I am, my lord. That Violet's a good girl, she ain't in no trouble, you can be sure."

Lord Montfort was grateful for their cheerful determination

to be optimistic; he was conscious of their respect and knew they only wished him well. He spent a little while with them outside, drank a tankard of ale, thanked them for their help, and apologized for taking them away from their work at one of the busiest times of the year. Then he climbed back on his impatient horse and made his way home. As Bruno clattered up the village street, the gossip, which had been fueled by the first tankard of ale and quelled by his arrival, flared up with greater relish and he was glad that he was not around to hear it.

Chapter Fifteen

Belowstairs at Iyntwood, there was no respite from a grueling schedule that was beginning to take its toll on Mrs. Jackson's beleaguered staff. With the additional visiting personal maids and valets swelling their numbers, she felt as if their world had been condensed into an obstacle race without a finish line. With Violet's disappearance, the housemaids Agnes and Elsie were shorthanded, and very early that morning Mrs. Jackson and Dick had helped them ready the reception rooms before returning belowstairs to help with the breakfast trays.

As soon as guests and family gathered on the ground floor of the house later that morning, Agnes, Iris, and Dick—once again helped by Mrs. Jackson—worked through the guest wing and the family's bedrooms. They were exhausted at the end of the morning and Mrs. Jackson was grateful for the particularly delicious dinner Iris had prepared for the downstairs midday meal: shepherd's pie, followed by a nice jam roly-poly pudding with custard.

Mrs. Jackson knew that a good meal and an opportunity to relax from the labors of the day often produced a surfeit of idle chatter among the lower servants. So when Mary and Myrtle had cleaned up the kitchen after the family's luncheon, and Iris joined them for Mable Thwaite's instructions for tea and dinner, the housekeeper went into her stillroom across the corridor from the kitchen and kept the door open. She quite easily heard the housemaids and the kitchen servants chewing over the events of the morning. Myrtle had been talking to one of the gardeners who had delivered fruit and vegetables for the family's dinner; in the village they had still not heard from Mr. Simkin's sister over at Ticksby if Violet had gone to her.

"How's that search going on?" Iris White asked for the fifth time that day.

"Not very well, my girl, because if they'd found them, it would be all over. Anyway, you hope they don't find them, because they wouldn't be alive if they did." Only Mable Thwaite could be this callous, thought Mrs. Jackson as she leaned a little farther toward the open door of the stillroom.

"How could you say such a thing?" Iris was shocked.

"Because Violet is a local girl, not from the town." Mrs. Thwaite snorted in contempt. "And she knows the country round here like the back of her hand. So she's not lost. And we all know that Miss Lucinda went off in her motorcar."

"Well, it's poor little Vi I'm worried about—"

"Well don't be, she's done a bunk. Mr. Hollyoak had better start counting the silver."

As soon as she judged the kitchen staff was breaking for their afternoon tea, Mrs. Jackson washed her hands and joined them in the kitchen.

"The strawberry jam is ready, so you can make scones for upstairs tea, Mrs. Thwaite. Mr. Brown brought some clotted cream up from the dairy early this morning."

"Good. Lady Montfort enjoys a nice scone at teatime, poor thing. She must be worried sick. Have a cup, Mrs. Jackson?"

"Yes indeed, thank you. How is everyone coming through for you with all this extra work, Mrs. Thwaite?" Mrs. Jackson put a sugar lump into her cup and stirred lightly.

"Well trained every one of them, my girls have certainly pulled *their* weight." Here of course was a little gibe. Mrs. Jackson almost laughed. Evidently all of the cook's *kitchen* maids were present, correct, and doing their bit for King and Country.

"I think the food for the ball was a success, but it's all been forgotten because of that dreadful murder."

Mrs. Jackson nodded in agreement. Of course, Mrs. Thwaite's greatest remorse was that her sensational food had been completely eclipsed by Teddy's murder.

"Course, we're all tired and distracted so it will be a few days before everything is back to normal. It's poor Mr. Hollyoak I feel so sorry for. Nowhere to go because that blinkin' sergeant is in his pantry, nosing around and asking questions as if anyone in this house had a reason to off Mr. Teddy." Mable Thwaite lowered her voice. "Of course, the biggest strain is having all these extras here, cluttering up the place when they should have all gone home. That's what's tiring everyone out." She drank her hot tea rapidly, taking little sips as her eyes darted back and forth across the kitchen and the girls working around the large, scrubbed table. "Oh yes, it's quite clear of course that the one that done *him* in is that stranger wandering around the place. That's why the colonel's dashed off up to London."

"Oxford I thought, with Mr. Barclay."

Mrs. Thwaite clapped her hand to her mouth and shook her head. "I am so sorry, Mrs. Jackson, I meant to tell you. Mr. Barclay will be back in time for dinner. Colonel Valentine telephoned his sergeant, who just now told Mr. Hollyoak there had been a change in plans. Colonel Valentine has left Oxford and is on his way to London to talk to Scotland Yard."

"Oh, I see. Please keep that information to yourself, Mrs. Thwaite. Will Colonel Valentine return tonight?"

"No, he's spending the night in town. I expect he'll return tomorrow when he's done." Mrs. Thwaite let out a gusty sigh. She poured them both another cup of tea, and Mrs. Jackson felt almost companionable in her role of confidante.

"Let's hope that the colonel has got everything sewn up and they can all go home." Mrs. Thwaite jerked her head sideways.

Mrs. Jackson nodded. She heard the racket coming out of the servants' hall as visiting valets and maids took their tea. "Very hard on our people, Mrs. Thwaite," she agreed.

"It certainly is. They are being pushed out of their own servants' hall by that bunch of stuck-up visiting ladies' maids and valets. Full of themselves they are, so la-di-da, and," she added with so much contempt that Mrs. Jackson laughed, "they never stop their tittle-tattle: it's gossip, gossip, gossip from morning to night."

"Quite shocking of them, Mrs. Thwaite. Now a word about tomorrow: there are still some tables that need to be moved from the music room back down to the library and the smoking room. James and John are run off their feet, and I think Dick can manage with a handcart." It was important that she observe protocol as Dick was primarily under Mrs. Thwaite's supervision, and even though Mrs. Thwaite reported directly to Mrs. Jackson, the housekeeper did not presume to instruct the kitchen staff directly. Having finished her tea, she had her notebook out and was working her way down a list of jobs that still remained undone since the ball, as she waited to be informed.

"Sorry, Mrs. Jackson, Dick can't do any heavy lifting at the moment, because he's injured his right hand. Crushed it bringing down a full churn of ice cream from the anteroom at the end of the ball. Why he didn't ask for help I don't know. Just struggled down the servants' stairs and mashed it up against the wall getting round the landing corner. Stupid boy." Mrs. Thwaite drained her tea in one gulp and set her cup on its saucer.

"Oh really? Then I'll just have to manage with a gardener's boy and Dick's direction then." Mrs. Jackson made a little note in pencil as she mentally filed away this information.

"Right you are then, Mrs. Jackson. Now I've got to get back to it . . . they'll be wanting their tea up there before you know it." She heaved herself to her feet, straightened up her cap, and took a deep breath before issuing the first of her instructions.

Mrs. Jackson went off to check that the footmen had lit the fires in the long drawing room and the red room and that the housemaids had tidied the guests' bedrooms before the changing bell rang. Then she shut herself in her parlor to work on her household accounts for her meeting with Mr. Hollyoak tomorrow morning. In the quiet of her room, she went methodically about her task with half a mind, as she ran over her own movements late on the night of the ball.

On Sunday morning, overtired but far from ready to turn in, Mrs. Jackson had been in the laundry room, washing two linen napkins that had been stained with red wine. When she was finished, she switched off the laundry-room light and walked the length of the servants' hall corridor to the back stairs. Out of habit, she checked rooms as she passed. There was a quiet orderliness in the spare and silent workrooms that Mrs. Jackson particularly enjoyed. She pottered about, tidying-up things left out and generally imposing order on small evidences of chaos, inevitable when everyone worked at full stretch.

Quite suddenly she had felt tired; it must have been getting on for four o'clock, and she reminded herself that she had to be up at seven. She decided to call it a day and trudged up the stairs to her own quarters by the second-floor back stairs. As she pushed open the door to the second-floor landing, she had been aware that the heavy green baize door at the entrance to the servants' stairs off the ground floor of the house had closed; it had a way of swinging to with an exaggerated creak no matter how often the hinges were oiled.

As Mrs. Jackson hesitated in the doorway, she held the door slightly ajar for a moment, and heard footsteps, light and quick, coming up the stairwell. Then complete fatigue overcame her and she stepped back, letting the door swing to, catching out of the corner of her eye a flash of black and white starting up the next flight to the maids' quarters on the third floor.

Mrs. Jackson could have checked whether it was Agnes or Elsie coming back from working in the anteroom, but she was done with her day and eager to get her shoes off and relax in her bed with a book until she nodded off to sleep.

She had made the assumption at the time that it was either Agnes or Elsie, but now that she came to think of it, who was it running up the stairs so lightly? The first housemaid, Agnes, and the second housemaid, Elsie, attired in their best black uniforms, had been stationed in the south anteroom attached to the ballroom, where they had kept the footmen supplied with ice cream and champagne throughout the night.

But now she knew that it could not have been either of these two girls returning from their work to their attic bedrooms.

Elsie was heavy on her feet and Agnes, a deliberate and methodical worker, proceeded everywhere at a frustratingly slow pace. The footsteps Mrs. Jackson had heard were those of a slightly built figure and neither Agnes nor Elsie could be described as petite. And if it had been either Agnes or Elsie returning at the end of the night's work, she would have walked across the terrace to the kitchen yard, come through the scullery door, and had a cup of cocoa belowstairs before going up to her room on the attic floor for the night. It was doubtful that either of them would have presumed to walk through the ground floor of the house to the use the back stairs by the dining room.

Mrs. Jackson's subconscious had done its job, and now she stopped what she was doing and concentrated hard. Whoever had started up the stairs immediately after her had joined the back stairs from the ground floor of the house and not the servants' hall. So who could that be? Mrs. Jackson worked a process of elimination. All the kitchen maids wore gray dresses, so it could not have been any of them, and they had all been in bed anyway. There were only three housemaids who wore black dresses after four o'clock in the afternoon: Agnes, Elsie, and Violet. Violet had been asleep in bed at ten so that she could be up early to help put the house in order. Agnes and Elsie would not use the main floor of the house to get to the back stairs. Lady Montfort's personal maid, Miss Pettigrew, wore black, and was slight in form and about the same height as Violet, but her room was on the far side of the house on the servants' floor above Lady Montfort's room. All the visiting ladies' maids would have been in the guests' rooms on the second floor of the house and with no need to use the servants' hall stairs, as they had their own set of stairs from their attic bedrooms to the guest bedrooms and then on down to the servants' hall at its far end.

Black and white, Mrs. Jackson thought, *black and white,* and for one terrible moment she wondered if she might have seen a valet or a footman. No, they had sounded like a young woman's footsteps, light and quick, not those of a man. Though of course there were men who were light on their feet.

Surely it had to be Violet. What on earth was she doing coming in from the main house at that hour of the night? What was she doing out of bed at all? Mrs. Jackson was suddenly aware, with a little startle of surprise, that Mr. Hollyoak and she had assumed they knew where everyone had been on the night of the murder. They believed the lower servants were obeying orders. Violet should have been upstairs in her bedroom with Mary, in bed and asleep by ten, not running about the house. Of course it was Violet, she thought, Violet going up to her room to change before she ran away. She had not been asleep in bed. The housekeeper wondered who else had been out of line on Saturday night.

Chapter Sixteen

Clementine had spent a wretched afternoon waiting for her husband's return from the search for the missing girls. When he finally came into her sitting room, he bent to kiss her on his arrival but said nothing, and Clementine took one look at his tired face and knew the two girls had not been found.

She dismissed Pettigrew and sat down next to her husband. The quiet minutes ticked by and she took comfort in the simple pleasure of their being alone together. Unlike many of their friends', theirs had been a happy marriage. Yes, she thought, they were well suited for the long haul of bringing up a family of children, often encumbered by an irritable mother-in-law, peevish spinster sisters, and shoddy nephews; an estate that required ever more attention; and the villages and the county that would always depend on what the Talbots would unstintingly give. All these loves, loyalties, and responsibilities levied their natural toll. Clementine knew they had been lucky in their marriage; she was reminded of it whenever they spent time with their friends. But she also recognized that it was a success because they had always found the willingness and desire to extend the largest kindness to each other first. Their duty was to their family and their position, but their friendship was important to them both, and they placed each other first in their busy, overburdened lives. She laid her head on her husband's shoulder and waited for him to tell her about his day.

"I had to drop in and see how Mother was doing." He sounded all in, as anyone would be, Clementine thought, having spent an hour with the dowager countess at the end of a long day. How heavenly it would be to have a quiet dinner and then settle down with a book, just the two of them.

He went on to tell her that Lady Booth was keeping the dowager company in her bereavement. Grateful that a strong corrosive such as Agatha was so readily willing to provide a distraction to his mother's often unappeasable demands, Clementine listened for reproach in her husband's voice. Finding none, she suffered only a momentary pang of self-inflicted guilt at having fallen in her duty. She promised him she would go to the dower house tomorrow to pay her respects.

"Darling, I think you have enough on your plate. She understands your duty is to our guests. Strangely enough, she was remarkably sympathetic, even offered to put up Valentine until this was all over." Clementine was thankful that her husband understood his mother so thoroughly. She couldn't imagine how difficult it would be if Ralph were one of those men who suffered from an excess of mother worship.

"She has heard from Verity, though." Here Clementine brightened up and lifted her head from his shoulder.

"Christina will be arriving in Paris from the South of France tomorrow, and when she has had some time to recover from that journey, will continue on here. Verity is coming with her. Of course, Mother will have Christina stay with her at Haversham Hall . . ." There was no need for him to reassure her that her sister-in-law, Christina, would not be staying with them. Clementine knew exactly how Christina's visit with her mother would play out. They would be overjoyed to see each other; inseparable for the first three days of their time together, before the inevitable falling out. Then it would be petulant accusations and tearful misunderstandings, imagined slights and misery to anyone unlucky enough to be with them at the time. It was a scenario that replayed itself whenever the two of them got together. She didn't share these wicked thoughts but allowed herself a moment as she remembered her last meeting with her sister-in-law.

Christina Mallory had lived on the Riviera ever since the death of King Edward and rarely came to England these days unless she had to. It was rumored that Christina, a member of the then Marlborough set, had been one of the old king's favorite companions, perhaps not as popular as Mrs. Keppel, Clementine suspected, but nonetheless a woman of consequence in his circle of intimate friends and many mistresses. The last time Clementine had had to spend time with Christina's set, they had still behaved as if the now-dead king had just left the room and would return at any moment. Their style was almost passé: champagne for breakfast; expensive, overbred racehorses; baccarat until dawn; twelve-course dinners; and, as the years wore on, wealthy businessmen advisers and compliant husbands who looked the other way. Yes, Clementine thought, Christina moved in a different sphere entirely to that of her elder brother.

But a visit from Verity was another thing entirely. Clementine had hoped their daughter would accompany her aunt to Iyntwood and now she saw her arrival as a ray on the horizon. She wondered how long Verity would stay with them.

Her husband broke into this pleasant daydream: "I saw Sergeant Hawkins just before I came upstairs. Please don't mention this to anyone, but there were papers belonging to Teddy at Christ Church—Oscar Barclay had them, apparently—that clearly indicate he was involved in something other than his gambling club. Another dubious business venture I am quite sure, and no doubt illegal. No, please don't ask me what, because I have no idea. But I am thinking that perhaps this whatever-it-is might have backfired on him and be a possible reason for his murder. Valentine will be returning tomorrow. I am hoping this business will resolve itself in a day or two. Thank God Valentine has things sewn up. Anything on Lucinda, by the way?"

Clementine recalled the desperate afternoon that Gilbert and Harriet had spent shouting down the telephone. "No, nothing at all, and I think Gilbert and Harriet are at their wits' end. They have heard nothing from any of their houses, from Lucinda's friends, or from Girton. It's quite awful." She felt his hand close around hers and they were silent for a moment.

"Yes, it is. The whole thing is awful," he answered, and then finally he got to the part of his day that she knew had caused him so much distress.

"I dropped in on Mr. Simkins at the end of the search to tell him we had not found her."

Clementine straightened up. Jim Simkins had been at the back of her mind all day. She knew the maid's disappearance had sorely contributed to her husband's belief that he had somehow failed in his responsibility to Violet and her father. Whatever had caused her to run, she had run from their house.

"Poor Mr. Simkins. How is he?" she asked. She felt the same weight of guilt she suspected he felt, as she thought of Violet's troubled and fearful father waiting for news of his daughter's whereabouts.

"He took the news with dignity, but of course he is much shaken. He looks desperately ill. I think the shock of Violet's disappearance has brought him very low. I hope to God we find out where she has got to soon."

"I'll telephone Dr. Carter first thing in the morning and ask him to go round to Mr. Simkins's cottage." Then, with one of her usual swift changes of tack: "Has anyone asked the station-master if he saw Violet?"

"No one has seen her, Clemmy, no one in the village, Cryer's Breach, or Little Buffenden. It's as if she has just vanished."

"Like Lucinda," Clementine added incautiously, and was immediately corrected.

"No, I don't think so at all. Lucinda decided to go and went. There's a difference." And there was a difference in her husband's tone of voice, too. He disapproved of young women who were independent and unmannerly and Lucinda in his view was both. "We must sit tight and wait for Valentine to complete his investigation, and then we will see." He stood up and put on his tailcoat, then reached out a hand to help his wife to her feet. When she was standing in front of him he put his arms carefully around her so as not to rumple Pettigrew's efforts and gave her a kiss.

"But, Ralph, I don't want to sit tight and wait to see what Valentine turns up. This inactivity is so frustrating." She knew she was overtired and that her voice was almost as petulant as that of Christina Mallory.

"Now, Clemmy, please don't be obstinate about this, and don't interfere. There is a logical process and it has to be followed."

"I am logical!"

"Yes, you are, of course you are, but you have a slight tendency to get too involved. It's that wretchedly unconventional upbringing of yours. What a wayward and headstrong girl you are underneath your nice party manners. Please, tell me you are not going to interfere."

"I wouldn't dream of interfering in Valentine's business; to the contrary, I think he is a splendid man and he's doing his very best."

Obedience did not come naturally to Clementine Talbot. Her pedigree, perhaps not as old as her husband's but equally august, was Anglo-Indian: Clementine's father, Sir Nigel Badham Thornhill, the governor general for Madras, and her mother were eccentric enough to have kept their only daughter with them in India when it was usual to send children back to England until they were older. As a result, her childhood had differed hugely from those of her cousins, reared in the prosaic Anglican safety of the British Isles.

On her return to England with her mother when she was eighteen, Clementine was considered a bit of an oddity in a homeland completely alien to her. English society, always so reticent about someone they have not grown up with, rarely rushes to welcome outsiders with open arms, no matter how well connected. During her first, and only, season, she was the most observed debutante of the year. Society matrons reluctantly extended invitations, judging her to be independent and unbowed. Her contemporaries fell into two distinct groups: the young men who lined up to dance with her every night and found her enchanting and original, and her paler and plainer female companions who found her too outlandish and strange.

She knew that society had found it surprising when the careful, prudent, and immensely rich Ralph Talbot, Earl of Montfort, the natural choice for ambitious mothers, had asked Clementine to marry him.

"Well, she's got some fitting-in to do," they had probably said to one another as they shook their heads. And Clementine, if she had heard them, would have been the first to agree. Life in the county as the wife of a territorial peer was a far cry from the palaces and durbars of a distant and sadly missed subcontinent.

Fortunately, Clementine was a sensitive girl. She was astute enough to understand how important it was at least to assume the patina of repressive decorum required by ladies of the English landed classes, and plucky enough to jump in and learn to swim in choppy seas. But there it ended. Assuming a veneer of compliance was one thing, but Clementine's natural independence of spirit, accepted entirely by her husband, had emerged as the years of their marriage had passed and her popularity had become well established. At this moment, Clementine's Indian childhood asserted itself, and instead of dread and anxiety, she felt a surge of energy and determination. Of course she would not run to Valentine with her ideas and interfere, as her husband had called it. There was no need for that at all. But she would take the opportunity to seek out Oscar and find out exactly what had happened up at Oxford and what papers he had given to Valentine. Then she would meet with Mrs. Jackson and between them they would have some information that would help them understand a little more than they had yesterday.

Evening set into night and a strong wind blew up from the southwest. As Clementine and her guests seated themselves to dinner, the storm that had been expected all day broke and rain beat against the windows, making everyone shiver, despite the heavy, drawn curtains. She was relieved that Valentine's search for Teddy's murderer now appeared to have moved from Oxford to London, it had had a pronounced effect on their friends' morale for the better.

Her cook had certainly rallied her efforts to the occasion and dinner was of the usual high standard happily anticipated at Iyntwood. The pièce de résistance of the evening, and a perfect choice for such a cold, cheerless night, were exquisite little steak and kidney pies, a favorite of her husband's. Tender glazed piecrust, molded with flowers and ivy leaves, covering succulent meat in dark, rich, wine-based gravy, thickened with beurre manie: each perfect little pie was placed before her guests. Accompanied by a galantine of potato and leek, and some of Lord Montfort's best Château Lafite, the result was magic. For the first time since the night of the ball, Clementine found she had an appetite for her dinner. Looking down the table toward her husband, she saw him laughing quite flirtatiously with poor old Agatha Booth, and as her gaze traveled up the table she was pleased to see that good humor and a sense of well-being were almost restored.

Good food always lifts the spirits, she thought as talk turned away from the present coal miners' strike, the vicious tactics of the Labor Member of Parliament, Keir Hardie, and possible war with Germany, to lighter and more amusing topics.

Course after course was presented, accompanied by more delectable wines. Although Clementine loved good food, she was not, unlike Agatha, a hearty eater. Nonetheless, she always followed the fashion set by the late king, who had been devoted to the delights of the table; eight courses were a necessity when one was entertaining, twelve when he had been a guest in the house. She took a little bite of a spectacular Charlotte russe and was not surprised as they ate their pudding that talk should turn to the Ballets Russes, which would open very shortly in London for its third season.

Clementine and her friends were avid admirers of the superbly agile and athletic dancer who seemed to possess the gift of being able to fly—Vaslav Nijinsky. Jack Ambrose had met him two years ago, when he had first performed in London for the coronation. Nijinsky, who spoke little English and bad French, was undoubtedly a strange sort of individual, Jack was happy to inform them. Clementine leaned forward as Jack addressed the table at large.

"More Gypsy than human, incredible athleticism, never seen anything like it. The man is immensely fit and fearfully strong, even for such a slight fella. He wears these ridiculous outfits when he dances, of course, makes you wonder really. I asked him how he achieved that kind of leap, it's almost inhuman in its height and strength." Jack put down his wineglass to better demonstrate with his right arm the speed, strength, and height with which Nijinsky had moved, and Clementine and her friends burst out laughing. Jack's stories were emphatically told and often cruelly humorous.

"Luckily Diaghilev was hovering around and translated for me," Jack went on, pleased to have everyone's attention. "Nijinsky apparently had said, 'Well, I just jump and then stop in the air for a moment!' You see, he believes he has a relationship with the air! Of course we don't know how the cove really does it, but he *is* simply marvelous." There was another ripple of laughter at Colonel Ambrose's incredulity that he could actually enjoy ballet.

"How wonderful!" Harriet came out of her inner preoccupation. "Gilbert, I insist we go this season."

"Can't stand the ballet myself, all that mincing about in fluffy little skirts," said Sir Hugo rather predictably. Clementine knew he despised culture and kept himself firmly fixed in the company of real men, devoted to country sport. "Give me Nellie Melba singing Wagner any day."

It was doubtful, thought Clementine, that Hugo had ever been to a ballet. His presence at the opera was hardly believable. He was a man of fields and woods, dogs and horses, in contrast to his cosmopolitan and sophisticated wife, who was welcomed everywhere and spent most of her time in London.

"There isn't a scrap of mincing to be seen anywhere in the Ballets Russes," said Olive Shackleton. "I have not missed a season since the coronation. I went five times to *L'après-midi d'un faune* that year. It was a mesmerizing experience: the unbound, out-of-this-world glory of Nijinsky—he was like a pagan god." Clementine noticed little smiles among them at Olive's theatrical appreciation; they were all used to her rhapsodies. She remembered that Olive had told her that she was so swept away by elation and joy that she had almost been in tears during Nijinsky's solo performances. Not surprising really, she thought, considering what a dried-up old fusspot Sir Wilfred was.

Sir Hugo was still prepared to be unimpressed: "Friend of mine told me that Nijinsky is completely illiterate, spent his life as a Gypsy performing in a circus when Diaghilev discovered him. Actually he did more than just discover him; he's his manager and his, you know . . ." Sir Hugo stopped eating to sip wine, his eyebrows raised to communicate that he was being risqué. "They don't make any secret of it apparently, completely flagrant. It makes complete sense to me that a man who dances that effeminately should turn out to be a blasted pervert. They only get away with it because they are foreigners."

Everyone laughed, and Sir Hugo happily ate the last of his Charlotte russe and beamed around the table. Clementine was quick to note that his remark had shattered Lady Booth, who was sitting with her mouth in a small tight line, glaring in Sir Hugo's direction. Clementine found his remark a little outré considering that Pansy and Blanche were present, but nonetheless she marveled at how perfidious society often was. Oscar Wilde had been imprisoned not so very long ago for a "certain type of friendship," and now everyone in society was quite happy to have two men, who were not secretive about their relationship, sit down to dinner with them. Still laughing, she happened to glance down the table to where Oscar Barclay sat, quietly remote from all of them; he had barely taken a bite all evening and looked peaky and unwell. She had noticed his head whip around in Hugo's direction at his last remark with a look of distress and embarrassment on his face. He quickly glanced at everyone at the table for reaction, before he lowered his gaze and began pushing his pudding around on his plate. His cheeks were flushed and he looked quite wretched.

Oh dear, thought Clementine. *Dear, innocent Oscar. I should check up on him, poor boy.* And almost simultaneously she decided that a little talk with Mrs. Jackson would be a good idea, too. She turned to catch Hollyoak's eye.

Chapter Seventeen

Clementine had discovered that her guests were more forthcoming at the end of the day, when they had eaten a decent dinner accompanied by the splendid offerings from Lord Montfort's cellar, and she was not above taking advantage of that. When the men joined the women in the long drawing room after their port, Clementine made a detour from her usual round to Oscar who was sitting off in a corner reading a book. As she took a chair next to him she asked him how his day at Oxford had gone, as if he had run up for a day's punting on the river with friends. She did not want to cause him to lose the tentative hold he seemed to have on himself. He smiled his bravest smile and told her things had gone better.

"Good, Oscar, I'm glad to hear it. So, Valentine was pleased with the papers you gave him?"

"Yes, he seemed to be," he said and fell silent.

Clementine remembered that Oscar had always been rather a sad sort, even before all this awfulness had happened. He was an only child; his mother had died when he was a baby and his father, rather disinterested in being a father in the first place, had turned Oscar over to a spinster sister, who had devoted endless stifling years to his upbringing, which had resulted in a restricted, forlorn childhood of the sort that only a pious Victorian spinster could be expected to provide.

She noticed that he had a book in his hand. "What do you have there? Ah, Forster. I loved *A Room with a View*. What's this one, *Howards End* . . . is it good?" She was making small talk and was not prepared for the considered thought that Oscar gave to her question.

"Oh yes, it is a very good book indeed, the best Forster has written so far. I love the character of Mrs. Wilcox, at ease with who she is and accepting of those around her; transcending the vulgarity of her husband and children and their striving, narrow, unforgiving view of life. Mrs. Wilcox is at her happiest in the country in her old family house, Howards End. To me she represents the old England: sadly destined to be swallowed up by our restless, rootless, modern world." Catching her look of surprise and mistaking it, he went on to explain, "We are so preoccupied with progress, rushing forward to the future that I think we might lose our ability to connect with each other on the fundamental level of being simply human. But perhaps I'm feeling a bit gloomy this evening, that's just my take on it." He laughed, completely at ease with her.

Oscar rarely presumed to take up one's time with his opinions. This unsolicited critique of a writer he obviously admired struck Clementine as both earnest and sincere.

"Then I will read it," she said, quite enchanted by his description and by what he had revealed of himself. She wondered how a young man as sensitive and thoughtful as Oscar could have been close friends with someone like Teddy, who rarely connected with anyone on a simple, straightforward level unless it was to make things work to his advantage.

There was a natural pause at this point, and since they could not be overheard, Clementine decided to ask him about his trip to Oxford. She was so unaffectedly forthright that Oscar did not appear to feel threatened by her questions.

"Actually, Teddy kept some papers in my strongbox. I am not too sure what they were. Most of them were diagrams, or drawings, and I barely glanced at them. They looked rather like rough architectural drawings, not to scale, more in sketch form. They had symbols in some of the rectangles and squares: ticks, arrows, and numbers. It was all rather meaningless to me. But the colonel was pleased with them; he put them in his document case along with a bundle of old invitation cards Teddy had locked away in his desk. That was it really."

"Did he say what he planned to do with them?"

"Not really. He told me he was off to London, would spent the night with his sister, and come back here tomorrow. I understood that he had an appointment with the Metropolitan Police and he was eager to get up to town."

Oscar paused in the lackluster recounting of his day, but Clementine sensed that he had kept something back about his time with Valentine. "You told me you had no alibi; is that a problem?"

"I hope not, I really do. Colonel Valentine told me I was free to come back to Iyntwood, but that he was going on up to London to Scotland Yard. I have to wait for him here for when he returns tomorrow."

"Well, that sounds like a remarkably good outcome to your day. If he suspected you, wouldn't he have taken you with him on to Scotland Yard?" She kept her tone bright, hopeful.

"I suppose so . . ." His voice tailed off and sorrow threatened to return.

TESSA ARLEN

Clementine did her best; she carefully turned the topic to other books they had read, in an effort to take him out of himself a little. He seemed so bereft and solitary and she felt tremendous sympathy for his plight. She wondered if his lonely childhood and his distant, disinterested father still weighed heavily on the boy. She also wondered what significance Teddy's papers had held for Colonel Valentine.

When Mrs. Jackson was summoned to Lady Montfort's sitting room for their evening meeting she was curious as to the form the conversation would take. She was prepared with menus for the next few days, as she knew that this was how their talk would begin, and she was right. After she had updated Lady Montfort on the state of the storeroom and larders and which bedroom Lady Verity de Lamballe would occupy when she arrived, Lady Montfort opened up her little notebook and asked her housekeeper to take a seat.

"It is so late, Jackson, you must be exhausted."

It was half past eleven and Mrs. Jackson had been up since six o'clock. She was yearning with an almost frantic need for the quiet of her quarters, the opportunity to stretch out full-length on her bed, and listen to the only sound in the room, that of her own even, unhurried breath.

"Please make yourself comfortable so we can get to the business of what is happening in the house."

In inviting her housekeeper to sit down in her presence, Lady Montfort had made a mere hop, skip, and a jump of breaching the abyss that separated her upstairs world from Mrs. Jackson's downstairs existence. Mrs. Jackson had never sat in Lady Montfort's presence before, and it did not come naturally to do so

162

now. In fact, it made her feel extremely tense and self-conscious. However, she perched on the very edge of the chair, gazed down at her hands folded in her lap, and waited for Lady Montfort to begin. And there was no doubt that Lady Montfort understood her unease, because she decided to go first with sharing information, which came to Mrs. Jackson's ear rather like an announcement.

"Colonel Valentine went up to London to consult with Scotland Yard this afternoon after he left Oxford. According to Oscar Barclay, he had in his possession some of Teddy's papers that provide a new possibility in this business, and that have nothing to do with gambling clubs . . ." Lady Montfort proceeded to fill her in on the drawings that Oscar had described.

"Interesting, don't you think?"

Mrs. Jackson said, "Yes, m'lady, it was," because it was, and waited.

"I think these drawings and the colonel's meeting at Scotland Yard are a clue. At the moment I am taking it to mean that there is another party involved in Teddy's murder and one that is being taken seriously by the police." And then, by the way of nothing at all, only in that it had obviously come into her head, she added, "It was interesting today, Jackson, I noticed that whenever any of my friends came out of their interview with Colonel Valentine, that they appeared to be more relaxed than when they went in. I am not sure what to make of that." Lady Montfort spent a moment or two thinking on this further, then turned to her housekeeper, her eyebrows raised and a gentle inquiring look of interest on her lovely face.

Mrs. Jackson appreciated that it was her turn and she tried to be as businesslike as Lady Montfort.

"As you suggested, there was a stranger in the village, m'lady;

he was seen both by Mr. Stafford and Theo Cartwright. I spoke directly with Mr. Stafford and he told me that a strange man was last seen at the back of the Goat, by Theo. And around that time Mr. Teddy pulled up to the public house in his motorcar and went inside and took a look around, as if he expected to see someone he knew. Then afterwards Mr. Golightly went out to the pub yard at the back of the house and Mr. Teddy pulled his car in and waited there for a moment or two before driving off. Perhaps he was there to meet with the stranger."

"There you are, Jackson, it's obvious Teddy had some arrangement with this man, this stranger. Any other information on him?"

"Mr. Stafford said that he saw the stranger in Dodder Lane, walking from Cryer's Breach station at about half past three that afternoon. I looked up train times from London in the Bradshaw. Where the man was at that time would mean he had come in on the half past one express from Marylebone—there isn't a train in at that time from the Birmingham direction—and had then walked up from the station. The express doesn't make any stops so he would have come from London."

"Now that's what I call detective work, Jackson. Well done. Did Stafford say anything else?" Lady Montfort was scribbling away and then sat biting the tip of her pencil as she waited for more clues.

"Yes, he did. When Sergeant Hawkins inspected the dray he found a gentleman's evening shoe in the large storage box behind the driver's seat. It is commonly thought that Mr. Teddy had been tied up and put in the box. Apparently when his body was found in the wood it was missing a shoe. This might mean that the dray was used to take him up to the wood." This was another hugely long speech for Mrs. Jackson and she stopped here to see its effect on her ladyship. She was gratified to see that Lady Montfort looked impressed. She was nodding and writing and then she looked up and smiled at her housekeeper as she made a heavy, full stop at the end of what she had scribbled down.

Mrs. Jackson judged it was time to report on further Goat and Fiddle gossip and reluctantly told the part about Mr. Teddy's having been given a punch on the nose. Of course Lady Montfort didn't like this at all; she stared at her housekeeper blankly with her mouth open, rather like a landed cod fish, and said, "Oh, God," under her breath. And Mrs. Jackson, repentant at having caused pain, went on to explain that perhaps Lord Haversham was not the only one with a grudge against Mr. Teddy, and told her about Dick's swollen knuckles on his right hand.

"Yes, you're right, Jackson—if the police find out about their fight, a punch on the nose wouldn't necessarily implicate Harry, would it?" Lady Montfort seized on the opportunity to see this new information from all sides. "It could have been Dick I suppose, but highly unlikely as Dick is such a nice boy, and Teddy was not. Anyway, Dick was busy all evening, he didn't have time to give Teddy a punch, let alone take him off to the wood. Where was the dray during the ball, Jackson?"

"It was outside the north anteroom, in the service area for the ballroom, m'lady, same as always. Mrs. Thwaite had it stocked with food and ale for the musicians for when they took their breaks from playing."

"So Teddy might have been taken from the ball to the wood in the dray?"

"I suppose he might . . ." Mrs. Jackson was careful not to put forward any premise of her own that might lead them up the garden path. She was determined to report facts only and would not be drawn into giving an opinion. That is, until she was specifically asked.

"But how would that work, do you think?"

Oh, Lord, and here it is, she thought, and reluctantly continued.

"The dray was in the service area throughout the ball, m'lady. At the end of the night the musicians were driven to the stable block in the dray, where they spent the night, and the dray was left in the wash-down until early Sunday morning, when it was driven back to the home farm. Then, of course, after luncheon when Mr. Teddy was found, it was driven up to the wood to bring his body back. It was then locked up in the old carriage house. I think . . ." She hesitated to say what she thought, but Lady Montfort eagerly nodded for her to continue. "Maybe Mr. Teddy was met by whoever it was who killed him by the stable block; he overpowered him, tied him up, and took him up to Crow Wood."

"Why would the murderer have to put Mr. Teddy into the storage box do you think?" Lady Montfort asked.

"Because it was raining heavily—because of the storm?" Mrs. Jackson shook her head as she spoke. "No, he was going to hang him. If he'd punched him on the nose, and tied him up, why put him in the storage box? Not to keep him dry!" she added rather callously, since it was Lord Montfort's murdered nephew she was referring to.

Lady Montfort laughed. "Exactly, Jackson, not to keep him dry. I think he was put in that box to conceal him. He was tied up and put in the box as there might have been people around. But who would have seen him at the stable block at well after four in the morning? Everyone would have been tucked up for the night."

"Mr. Makepeace was there when the sergeant examined the dray. He said there was plenty of coiled rope under the seats. It was probably used to tie him up with."

"So this murderer knew where to find rope, knew there was a storage space in the dray. Would a stranger to the area know all of this?" Lady Montfort was busily jotting things down in her little book; she did some heavy underlining and then looked up. Mrs. Jackson saw the strain on her face and comprehended that Teddy's murder by the stranger was the ideal outcome, but her ladyship was not going to be lulled into a false sense of security.

She thought for a while and then pointed out, "But anyone would be able to see the storage box, it's large enough, and there is always plenty of rope visible in the dray." She closed her eyes as she tried to imagine how it would be. "It was dark. The rain was pouring down . . . he met Mr. Teddy by the stable block . . . he knocked him out, tied him up, and dragged him up onto the dray . . . perhaps he heard someone coming . . . he put him in the storage box and when it was all quiet, he drove up the lane to the home farm . . . but yes, you're right," she said as inspiration flashed. "How would anyone unfamiliar with the area know where the gibbet was, and if they did, how could they find it in the dark? I am not sure that anyone unfamiliar with the estate could find it in the daylight, let alone in the middle of a storm."

"That's absolutely right, Jackson. It would have to be someone familiar with the estate, someone who has been here many times—"

"Someone who had been at one of his lordship's shooting parties, m'lady. That could mean any of the estate workers or your friends who have come over for one of his lordship's shoots."

In her enthusiasm Mrs. Jackson had interrupted Lady Montfort and was horrified at her disrespectful manners.

But Lady Montfort hadn't even noticed. She was running out of steam and her voice was suddenly tired. Mrs. Jackson could tell she was circling back to home, returning to the idea that her son might be in danger as a suspect.

"Yes, friends or family . . . you see we are back to where we started, Jackson. No matter what Teddy was up to with strangers from London, it is unlikely that he was taken to his death by someone who did not know the estate. Unless Teddy arranged to meet the stranger by the gibbet . . . No, then the dray would not have been used, and it seems that was how he was taken to the wood.

"And that is why when Colonel Valentine comes back tomorrow his investigation here will not be over. That is, unless he plans to arrest one of us for Teddy's murder." Lady Montfort sat back in her chair with her eyes fixed on her housekeeper. She had hoped that the stranger was going to save them, and with determination she summoned her concentration again.

Mrs. Jackson had never seen her ladyship so single-minded and intent, and it came to her in that moment that in less than fifteen minutes they had spanned the dark hours of Sunday morning clearly enough for them to make sense of what might have happened. She sat back in her chair, quite confident that between them they could make sense of this puzzle.

"Then we have to be a step ahead of him, m'lady," she said.

"Yes, Jackson, we do. So, it's back to punches on the nose, motives, missing alibis, and how Teddy was put into the dray. And whilst we are at it, what has happened to the two missing young women?"

Chapter Eighteen

It was a perfectly lovely afternoon with no possibility of rain to spoil it, which did much to alleviate the tension at Iyntwood as Clementine and her friends waited for Valentine's return from London. Determined to save her house party from a swift return to the doldrums, Clementine suggested that they spend the afternoon outside on the lawn. Lady Shackleton and Lady Waterford challenged Lord Montfort and Colonel Ambrose to a game of croquet, and Harry, not to be outdone, enlisted Oscar, Ellis, and Sir Hugo in a doubles lawn-tennis match, with Pansy and Blanche eagerly running up and down to retrieve balls.

Lawn games were probably not a fitting occupation for a house in mourning, or a house suspected of murdering one of its occupants, but the Iyntwood house party was doomed to be the center of scandal anyway, she thought, and activity soothed the nervous system and passed the time.

Clementine, who needed time to think, wandered back and forth between the two games, played within several hundred feet of each other, which gave her the opportunity to move about without having to engage in conversation. Croquet gave Lord Booth, whose preferred activity, other than smoking huge cigars, was to pontificate, a chance to do both as he stood directly among the players, getting frightfully in the way, she noticed.

She briefly joined Lady Harriet and Gilbert Lambert-Lambert, Sir Wilfred, Lady Booth, and Constance Ambrose, who had stationed themselves under the shade of the chestnut tree. Here they observed a strenuous game of tennis, with Lady Booth kindly amplifying the rules of the game and keeping score.

"Fifteen love . . . each," she said, happily inaccurate, and turned to fix Constance Ambrose with her eye, as Harry smashed a ball over the net to whip up off the grass out of Sir Hugo's reach. "And it's Sir Hugo still to give service. Though good heavens would you look at the perspiration, it simply isn't fair to have him up against Harry and Ellis this way. Oh dear, yes, well that would be his fault, two into the net. He does look tired. That means fifteen to him and Oscar and then thirty, or is it forty, to other side? Do you see how it goes, Constance? First one side, then the other—that's why it's called tennis!"

Constance didn't see, but Clementine guessed she would enjoy any sport that involved athletic men, balls, and a lot of speed. She smiled to herself, enjoying the idea that tennis observed the niceties of prep school: each politely taking it in turn, first one and then the other. *For heaven's sake,* she thought, *is that what happened to Teddy—was there more than one person involved in his death? Two people working together?* Clementine ranged back and forth between tennis and croquet under her sunshade, her mind taken up with a missing shoe, strong rope, storage boxes, and forked lightning.

Just as Sir Hugo and Oscar had managed to turn the game against Harry and Ellis, she looked up and across the lake saw Colonel Valentine's motorcar coming up the drive. He briefly appeared on the terrace and then, ignoring welcoming cries from the lawn, locked himself away in the uninterrupted quiet of the morning room, apparently—so Hollyoak informed her—to put together a report of his investigation thus far.

Clementine did not suspect that the colonel consciously set out to keep everyone in suspense. But since his return all lawn games had stopped, and when he stayed away from the group, pressure had started to build, reaching a tight-lipped, preoccupied politeness among them. And despite Clementine's efforts they stayed that way until Valentine strolled out to join them for tea, when they grouped themselves in a semicircle around him like so many rabbits gathered in front of a stoat. She watched her friends sip tea and nibble sandwiches and cake, chattering about things they didn't give a fig about, as they waited for Valentine to begin.

"I know you are all most concerned about events surrounding Mr. Mallory's tragic death," he opened up. No one spoke, and she was conscious that all eyes watched him finish his salmon and cucumber sandwich and sit back to address the now silent group.

"Based on my original findings, this investigation now falls under the purview of the Criminal Investigation Department of the Metropolitan Police, who are sending down one of their top men, Detective Chief Inspector Ewan, to help us through the last part of the inquiry. This is a formality only, as it would seem, from evidence I found at Oxford, that Mr. Mallory's involvement with an organization in London is the probable reason for his death." There was a pomposity about this lack of real information that was infuriating, thought Clementine. It was certainly received with a certain amount of pursed lips and fretful, furrowed brows among the tea drinkers on the lawn.

For heaven's sake, why would the Metropolitan Police be coming up to Iyntwood if their investigation was now down in London? Clementine struggled to be fair, and while she believed that Valentine had tried from the start to shield them as much as he could from the scandal of Teddy's death, the age of hushing up unattractive and embarrassing breaches of the law for the country's privileged classes was a thing of the past. Five or ten years ago Valentine could have protected them all from gossip and the public eye by exercising his position as the county's chief constable. But now, unable to wrap up the murder investigation satisfactorily with an arrest, he had most likely been obliged to go to a higher authority for help, and obviously the Metropolitan Police were not as impressed as he was by his "new evidence found at Oxford."

Clementine turned her head and caught her housekeeper's eye with an I-told-you-so look on her face. She had asked Mrs. Jackson to help out with tea today so that she would hear firsthand what Valentine had to say, and her housekeeper was standing within earshot under the shade of the chestnut tree, keeping water hot for tea and filling trays of sandwiches for the footmen.

Turning back to her friends, Clementine listened to the silence deepen into a yawning, wordless protest. *You could cut the atmosphere on the lawn with a cake knife*, she thought.

Her husband cleared his throat so that attention might be transferred away from Valentine.

"Thank you, Valentine, well done indeed, everything superbly taken care of. I'm sure Chief Inspector Ewan only needs to tighten up a few lose ends . . . not that there could be any!" He nodded his thanks to Valentine before continuing with what she knew troubled him the most.

"Christina will arrive tomorrow morning, with Verity, who

accompanied her from Paris. Christina will decide when the funeral will take place, of course, but more than likely it will be on Friday, as the coroner's office has given us the go-ahead."

Clementine observed her guests fuss with bread and butter, teacups, and newspapers, or turn to one another in scarcely concealed exasperation, obviously concerned with plans that were seriously awry for the rest of the week. Of course they were irritated, she thought, and by the look of it seriously worried, too. She watched Sir Wilfred get to his feet, almost furtively, and walk away from the group to stare intently into the woodland like a retriever waiting for the pheasant to break.

Lady Harriet and Gilbert Lambert-Lambert excused themselves, as they were expecting a telephone call from Miss Davis of Girton College momentarily. Clementine had noticed with particular interest that there had been no mention from Valentine of Lucinda's ill-timed disappearance or, come to that, of the missing maid. But then she remembered that Violet's absence had not been publicly revealed, though she had no doubt everyone had been informed of her disappearance via their servants.

She heard Agatha, beside her, take in a breath as she turned to Olive Shackleton and Constance Ambrose. "I admire Harriet's fortitude, I really do. I always say that quiet strength is the hallmark of good breeding. Unfortunately, this is exactly the price one pays for educating young girls as if they were boys. A very bad thing indeed for people of our background. Education has a particularly vulgarizing effect on a gentle mind. What on earth possessed them I simply don't know . . . it has quite ruined Lucinda."

Olive Shackleton straightened up in her chair and Clementine waited with anxiety for what was to come: "Good heavens,

Agatha, what a preposterous thought! We can't just write off education for women like that—it is precisely the lack of it that causes so many problems for women today."

Clementine had never seen Olive so impatient with Agatha's archaic snobbishness. *Captivity certainly speeds up the erosion of restrained, good manners,* she thought.

Lady Booth appeared happy to be appalled. "Olive, how could you say such a thing? Lucinda would never have done something as scandalous as this if she had been kept at home until she was married. She will single-handedly pull down the entire Squareforth family, and it is this obsessive quest for education and independence that is to blame." Lady Booth's voice sounded harsh and staccato as she drove home her point.

"I quite agree with you, Lady Booth," said Constance Ambrose. Well, of course she did, thought Clementine. For a woman whose entire preoccupation was focused on her wardrobe, and the attentions of very young men, Constance evidently believed that a woman's place was with her *lingère* and her dressmaker. Staying another two or three days meant she would probably miss a fitting at Lucile.

But Constance, she noticed, enthralled, was not finished. "Educating women is on the same par as socialism and both will destroy the country," she said, quoting her husband, who never picked up a book if he could help it. "Socialists and the women's movement are treasonous."

There, thought Clementine. *Now Constance can be quoted all over London as saying that Lucinda should be shot for treason because she went to Girton. Could this afternoon become any more disastrous?*

A row was happening before their very eyes. Clementine felt five parts alarm and five parts fascination as she watched what followed. There was a stunned silence as everyone frantically thought of something to say to change the direction of this dreadful exchange. Lord Booth rose to the occasion, clutching a cup and saucer in both hands as he got to his feet and glared at his wife. Clementine almost expected him to gnash his teeth and she watched with interest, as this was something she had never seen done before.

"What utter rot." He towered over Olive and Agatha, his dark eyes narrow as he frowned down at them. "I don't want to hear another damned word about women's education, their right to vote, and other rubbish. It is a most vulgar preoccupation. These young women have simply got to pull themselves together and get on with doing what they were bred to do: looking after their husbands and their families." He turned to address his daughters, who were cowering in their lawn chairs. "And if they don't have a family then they should concentrate their efforts on getting one, and leave the business of education and government to their fathers and husbands. My dear," Clementine saw him bend a horrid look of dislike upon his wife, "I am sure you think this absorbing topic has gone far enough." Looking thunderous, Lord Booth slammed down his cup and saucer and marched off to the house, leaving them sitting on the lawn with their mouths open in mingled amusement and horror.

Lady Booth, outraged at being publicly corrected, struggled to her feet, hampered by humiliation, rigid whalebone stays, and her fat little dog, who was struggling for air in her tight grip. She looked down at Olive Shackleton and said in a voice shaking with suppressed anger that set her hat feathers quivering, "Olive, perhaps you will forbear to discuss in public what you clearly don't understand, and by doing so cease to cause trouble. I have some letters to write before dinner." She stumped off up the lawn toward the retreating back of her husband, her short legs desperately trying to close the distance between them.

Mrs. Jackson, standing behind an array of tea paraphernalia and cake stands, was a silent spectator to the unraveling of the Talbots' house party. Trapped at Iyntwood, their guests suspected things were about to get a good deal nastier at the hands of a top man from Scotland Yard. Patience had come to an end and tempers were beginning to fray. She happened to glance over at Lady Waterford, who had been sitting thoughtfully quiet throughout the exchange, and noticed that her hands shook as she lifted her teacup to her lips. Mrs. Jackson's eyes swept over the rest of the group and assessed reactions.

Sir Wilfred was staring into the middle distance as if nothing had occurred at all, and Colonel Ambrose was glowering at Mrs. Ambrose. But Sir Hugo, as he lolled back in his lawn chair, was silently watching his wife in a peculiarly detached manner. His speculative stare was fixed on her face with an odd expression of amusement and inquiry, as if he were watching her struggle with the answer to a tricky question she did not have the answer to.

After a while Lady Waterford rose to her feet with the habitual poise that Mrs. Jackson had long admired in her. "Off for my afternoon stroll," she said as she adjusted the brim of her hat against the direct sun. Mrs. Jackson felt tremendous admiration for the woman's self-assurance, as she watched Lady Waterford walk across the lawn to the house, quickly enough to be ahead of the group as they got to their feet, and certainly quickly enough to pass Lady Booth plodding toward the terrace. But at no time, thought Mrs. Jackson, did she look as if she was racing Lord Booth as he gained the terrace door, where it appeared he paused as if waiting for Lady Waterford to catch up with him.

Chapter Nineteen

At the end of the afternoon and just before the dressing gong sounded, Mrs. Jackson came out of her parlor and was about to go belowstairs before dinner preparations reached their greatest pinnacle of activity, when Lady Waterford came though the green baize door from the second-floor servants' landing. As soon as Lady Waterford saw her, she came to an abrupt halt, and stood silent and motionless like a lovely but rather battered statue. Her arrival in this area of the house was remarkable in itself, but her appearance was so profoundly perplexing that it took Mrs. Jackson a moment or two to take it all in.

Having evidently covered the back stairs at quite a clip, Lady Waterford was out of breath, her silver-gold hair hung in tangles around her face, and her ivory shantung silk skirt was twisted at her waist, giving her a rather lopsided, unbalanced look. The skirt's back, now worn on Lady Waterford's right hip, had several ruinous grass stains. Her fine silk blouse with its intricate gathers and tucks had been ripped away at the sleeve.

It struck Mrs. Jackson in that moment that Lady Waterford looked exactly as if she had been pulled through a hedge backward, and she had the sense to avert her eyes. When she was sure that her face would not betray surprise, she risked a glance and was grateful to see that Lady Waterford was looking back at her with an expression of frozen dignity that forbade any comment whatsoever. A moment of silence hung between them. Then Lady Waterford asked her if she would be so kind as to bring her a cup of tea and while she was at it to send up her maid. She then proceeded past the housekeeper toward the guest wing as if nothing had happened at all.

In four minutes flat Mrs. Jackson accomplished three things: she ran downstairs and asked Agnes to find Lady Waterford's maid, instructed Iris to prepare a tray of tea to be taken up to Lady Waterford, and doubled back to Lady Montfort's room.

Lady Montfort had evidently just emerged from her bath, as she was wrapped in her dressing gown and staring out of her window down at the rose garden, evidently deep in thought, when Mrs. Jackson walked into her sitting room. If she was surprised to see her, thought Mrs. Jackson, she wasted no time in grasping that she had arrived on an errand of great importance.

Mrs. Jackson came straight to the point: "I have just seen Lady Waterford, m'lady. She has been placed in rather an awkward situation. And if I might be so bold, I think it would be a good idea if you went to her immediately."

"Yes, of course, Jackson." Clementine looked around for her slippers. "When you say awkward, what do you mean exactly?"

"Well, her appearance is rather disheveled; I would go so far as to say very disheveled," replied her housekeeper, with the vision of Lady Waterford's extraordinary appearance etched distinctly in her mind.

"Do you mean someone attacked her?" Lady Montfort turned, the better to judge her expression.

"M'lady, I think Lady Waterford needs your help. And I am sure she has something to tell you." Mrs. Jackson was concerned that, given some moments to collect herself, Lady Waterford would lock down before Lady Montfort got to her.

To her credit, her ladyship needed no further prompting. Mrs. Jackson watched her fairly fly down the wide corridor from her room and turn left at the top of the stairs to fly another one hundred feet to the guest wing. Mrs. Jackson had just rounded the second corner when she saw Lady Montfort knock on Lady Waterford's bedroom door, crack it open, and slide into the room, leaving the housekeeper to stand outside to wait for further revelations.

Clementine had always admired Gertrude Waterford's remote, cool beauty. It was well known that John Singer Sargent had been desperate to paint this lovely, enigmatic woman's portrait, but Lady Waterford had refused and he had had to make do with Madame Pierre Gautreau instead. Used to seeing her friend draped in a pose of careless but haughty elegance on a drawing room sofa, Gertrude's extremely raffish appearance brought her up short.

She looked as if she had returned from the sort of country house party that went in for high jinks and the wilder sort of lawn games in vogue with the younger married set. Clementine was not familiar with this type of house party, but she had certainly heard some outrageous stories: sliding down the stairs on tea trays, and playing games of hide-and-seek where soda siphons were used to hilarious effect, sprang to mind. Gertrude looked as if she had spent the afternoon taking part in a giddy romp of blindman's buff with her friends, had fallen on her bottom, and had then been dragged, whooping with laughter, across the lawn by one arm. That was of course except for Gertrude's palpable air of exhausted despair.

Clementine dismissed Gertrude's maid, who was standing helplessly by with a hairbrush. It was going to take some time to extricate the bits of twig and leaf from those tangles, thought Clementine.

"Ah, Clemmy, here you are." Gertrude's voice sounded flat and tired as she sat down at her dressing table and stared at herself in the looking glass without expression. "Bloody hell, what a ruffian I look." Clementine could not help but admire Gertrude's attempt to pass off her alarming appearance. Gertrude picked up a brush and began to brush her hair, her movements jerky and ineffectual.

"Gertrude, I am here to help you. But you have to tell me what on earth is going on." Ignoring the tea tray, Clementine went to the door and asked Mrs. Jackson to fetch brandy and two glasses. This was done with the speed of anticipation and she poured a generous amount into a glass and handed it to Gertrude. "Now, tell me what happened to you," she said, and to steady her nerves she took a sip of brandy.

Gertrude shook her head, knocked back her brandy in two quick swallows, and drew a long, deep, sighing breath. Then she turned back to the looking glass and began to pick garden debris from her hair. "I can't say anything Clementine; I am in no position to." Clementine saw her friend gathering herself together and before she could shut her out, she crossed the room and taking the brush from Gertrude began to gently untangle her hair. But her tone was uncompromising: "Who did this to you, Gertrude?"

Lady Waterford shook her head.

"Gertrude, you have to tell me what happened, so I can help you." She caught her friend's eye in the looking glass and held her gaze. "Tell me."

"Very well then." The last of Gertrude's resolve to soldier on alone evaporated. "I was being blackmailed by Teddy." Clementine continued to untangle, keeping her face passive. This explained all the tension of the past few days, but not Gertrude's appalling appearance.

"But you were not the only one Teddy was blackmailing, were you?" she said, lifting her eyes to look at her in the glass. She stood with the hairbrush in one hand and waited.

After what seemed an awfully long time, Gertrude finally said, "No, I am not alone, Clemmy, but I am horribly at risk. Teddy had a letter to me from someone I had an association with for several months. A very revealing letter."

Clementine decided to come straight to the point: "A letter from Lord Booth."

She was completely unprepared for the panic her statement caused. Gertrude almost bolted to her feet and her voice was very loud in the quiet room. "Oh dear God, then everyone knows!"

Clementine placed a firm hand on her friend's shoulder and gently pressed her back into her chair. "No, Gertrude. No one here is aware of the trouble you are in but me. And I didn't *know*, I guessed. But now you have confirmed it's Lord Booth."

Clementine did not particularly approve of Lord Booth. He was certainly a man who attracted female admiration, she thought. He had all the attributes of masculine magnetism with his thick, wavy, silver and black hair and a luxuriant mustache the kaiser would have envied. But she thought she recognized that under the engaging manners of flattering pursuit there was a quality of self-adoration that bordered on narcissism, which she found particularly unpleasant.

Gertrude, her secret out, allowed the floodgate to open: "Teddy was blackmailing both of us. He had Lord Booth's letter to me. Lord Booth was to meet with him on Saturday evening after dinner. Teddy didn't have the letter with him, but the little bastard actually quoted from it to Lord Booth. He wanted us to buy the letter from him; the sum he named was unbelievable. Then on Sunday we heard that Teddy had been found. Lord Booth managed a search of his room here, but couldn't find the letter. If it's discovered . . . well, there's our motive for murder."

Gertrude would not look at her or catch her eye in the looking-glass and her voice was low with shame as she said, "Lord Booth is not dealing with the situation well, as you saw this afternoon. He's on edge and he seems to have lost his nerve now that this policeman from London is coming here. I am terribly worried he's going to muff it all completely." Gertrude sank her head in her hands in such a tired and dispirited way that Clementine poured her another dash of brandy.

"Here, Gertrude, sip this one slowly." She handed the glass to her friend. "First of all, I think if the letter had been found you would have already heard from Colonel Valentine. So it might be safe to assume that Teddy had the letter hidden somewhere. Chances are it will remain hidden and no one will ever find it.

"Did you have an opportunity to talk to Teddy, before he . . . ?" Clementine had finished with the tangles and now sat down close to her friend, took a small sip of Gertrude's brandy, and gave her some time.

"Yes, I did. I could sense that things had not gone well between them, because Lord Booth was so preoccupied and snappish. I also thought that if I had the opportunity, I might persuade Teddy to come round." She colored a little; at least her ears were red and hot at the tips. "Later on that night, toward the end of the ball, I cornered Teddy on the terrace and took him off to the south pavilion. I asked him what I could do to get the letter back. I was prepared to do . . . well, anything at all. I made this clear to Teddy." She paused, the humiliation of what she was confessing apparent only in her bowed head.

"And?" prompted Clementine, as if offering yourself to your blackmailer was the usual way of settling things.

"And Teddy turned me down flat, laughed at me actually. He made it clear there were no alternatives. He told me how much he wanted for the letter. It was an outrageous amount. If we didn't come up with the money he would sell the letter to the *Daily Express*. Can you imagine? I knew exactly how poor Daisy Greville felt after she sent that stupid letter to Lady Beresford and Charles Beresford threatened to take Daisy to court. *I* can't be the woman who is used as an example of indiscretion to future generations of silly girls."

Gertrude continued to recount the details of her humiliation on the night of the ball: "Well, Teddy left and I sat there for a while before I went back to join everyone on the terrace. When I got there, I could see Teddy; he was looking frightfully smug and smoking a cigarette on the other side of the rose garden. I was already thinking how I could put up my half of the money."

Clementine took another sip of Gertrude's brandy and asked her what time that had been.

"About half past three, probably a little later, I am not completely sure. The next day I heard Teddy had been found." Gertrude looked at her empty glass, picked up her hairbrush, and began methodically to brush her hair.

Clementine said, "Sir Hugo—"

Gertrude rushed in with such emphasis that her voice was almost loud in the still room, "Must *never* know, *never*. It is not part of the understanding we have."

Clementine felt great sadness for her friend's lonely and vulnerable situation. She completely understood the rules of the game. The overriding consideration was that there must be absolutely no exposure of any misconduct. The unforgivable sin was to bring disgrace among them. And apparently as far as Gertrude was concerned, her husband would not be her ally, no matter what arrangements they had. Sir Hugo wouldn't divorce Gertrude if this all came out, but he would certainly make life difficult. She had seen that on the lawn this afternoon. Lord Houghton Lew had never spoken to his wife again, except in public, after her affair with Charlie Stampton became known.

Clementine asked her friend if she thought Lord Booth might have killed Teddy.

There was only a moment's hesitation before Gertrude answered quite plainly, "I wouldn't be surprised, Clemmy. He lost his temper in a very horrid way this afternoon: he actually . . ." Gertrude nearly broke down as the remembered shame and shock of the incident returned, "shook me . . . violently . . . threw me on the ground. His rage was devastating. Yes, I think he is capable of murder."

"Then keep away from him, Gertrude. There is nothing you can accomplish here at this point. Let's just pray the letter is never found. Are you planning on coming down to dinner?"

"Oh yes, Clemmy, of course I am. I have only an hour to get myself dressed but I must come down." She laughed. "Can't let anyone see I'm rattled."

* * *

Clementine walked slowly back to her room as the dressing gong sounded in the hall. Mrs. Jackson was waiting for her in her sitting room, and no doubt since they were both sharing information she was hoping for an explanation. If she updated her, she would be moving into forbidden territory in discussing her closest friend's business with her housekeeper.

But wasn't it a bit too late for that? she asked herself. Hadn't she made an agreement with Mrs. Jackson when she wanted her housekeeper to get information for her? Now they had reached a tipping point and she knew she must not be rash. She remembered that she had drunk nearly two glasses of brandy, which were now floating around in her stomach with nothing but half a cucumber sandwich and a bite of Victoria sponge cake to give it ballast. She fixed Mrs. Jackson with her eye rather sternly, as if the poor woman had already said, *Well, what's going on then with Lady Waterford, ay?* and told her housekeeper as accurately as she could what Lady Waterford had told her: intimate letters, blackmail, and sudden death. It was the stuff of penny dreadfuls, she thought.

"So you see, Jackson, things are looking pretty dire for Lady Waterford," she finished up.

From the look on her housekeeper's face, she obviously had not wanted to be taken into Lady Montfort's confidence. The rules that upper servants lived by were as rigid and unbending as those of her own class. In telling her housekeeper about the blackmail of Lord Booth and Lady Waterford she had crossed the line and had taken Mrs. Jackson with her, and they might survive with their respect for each other intact, if they were prudent.

"What happens now, m'lady?" Mrs. Jackson asked with her customary calm; she could have been referring to Lord Booth as a suspect for the murder or just as easily asking whether they should take their tea on the lawn or in the library. Clementine was reassured by her phlegmatic response.

"I am not too sure. Jackson. Let's both think things over for the next day or so. Perhaps we should let things percolate a little. Sir Arthur Conan Doyle told me, when he was writing *The Speckled Band,* that the introduction of new characters to the plot stirs things up a little, giving an opportunity for fresh clues to emerge. I think that is wise counsel and we should keep our eyes peeled and our wits about us." She reminded herself that this was actually the advice of an author and not a detective.

"Right, m'lady," said her housekeeper with such intention that Lady Montfort relaxed in the comfort that at least she had a true ally, even if poor Gertrude did not.

Chapter Twenty

Early the following morning, Lord Montfort was on his way from the small dining room to his study when Detective Chief Inspector Ewan arrived at Iyntwood, accompanied by his detective sergeant. Lord Montfort paused in the hall in time to observe the exchange between his butler and Chief Inspector Ewan as Hollyoak ushered the two men into the house.

Afterward he wished that he had taken the time to brief Hollyoak on the policeman's importance before his arrival, as Hollyoak's attitude to the chief inspector caused considerable resentment from the moment the man stepped over the imposing threshold of his house; regrettable for what was to follow.

Lord Montfort was fully aware that Hollyoak, like most butlers, was a far greater snob than anyone else he knew. Among his butler's many foibles on protocol and procedures, of which there were many, was his disapproval of incorrect attire for the country. The chief inspector was not in uniform, which was unfortunate, as it might have saved him from a thorough snubbing.

He had to admit that Ewan's brand-new lounge suit, a startling shade of royal blue in rather a busy check, with which he was wearing brown shoes, was an eyesore. But his butler was guilty of being patronizing and unpleasant to the chief inspector because of this innocent sartorial blunder.

"Perhaps I may take your hat, sir," Hollyoak said, his face registering the silent contempt he obviously felt, as he held out his hand for the policeman's hideous hat. He was ignored, Lord Montfort noted, although the sergeant hastily proffered his hat, as if to balance out his superior officer's bad manners in refusing his.

He hastily stepped forward to greet the policeman, hoping to prevent Hollyoak from doing any further damage, but it was too late. He could see that Chief Inspector Ewan felt thoroughly insulted by his butler's assessing glance as it took in the offensive brown bowler still clamped on the policeman's head, the acres of blue check, and the glaring ocher shoes. Ewan was looking rather touchy to say the least as he turned to Lord Montfort, preempting Hollyoak's announcement.

"And you must be the gentleman of the house," he declared as he cast an assessing glance over the dark wood paneling of the hall, on which hung generations of Talbots depicted in murky oils.

"Chief Inspector Ewan? I'm Ralph Talbot, Earl of Montfort." The chief inspector sighed, and his sigh spoke volumes.

As a country dweller Lord Montfort spent most of his day out on his estates. He enjoyed an easy communion with the land-based working-class men and women who served and worked for his family and rarely had anything to do with the urban professional classes, except for his doctor, his solicitor, and his man of business. But he was not unobservant or indifferent and gathered, from Ewan's deep sigh at the size and splendor of his house and his refusal to remove his hat in it, that he was the sort of man who disliked the idea of the landed class and their kind.

He probably believes we are all antediluvian members of a soon-to-be-bygone age, he thought as he took in Ewan's affronted air and reluctance to look him in the eye. Ewan was probably what Lord Booth often referred to in exasperation as a "new Englishman," one who did not knuckle down and get on with it under the old order, but more likely supported the union leader and labor politician, Keir Hardie. Lord Montfort, who would not have offered anything less than welcoming good manners to anyone who came to his house, resolved to speak to his butler about the importance of treating everyone who came through his front door as a guest, despite choice of attire and a tendency to suck their teeth.

To his relief, Colonel Valentine chose to arrive through the terrace door at this moment and Lord Montfort called out a greeting in the hope that Valentine would help ease the tension of Ewan's unfortunate beginning in his house. More introductions were made, and then, fully apprised of who was who, Lord Montfort led them all into the morning room, so that they could get the business of the day going. It was here that Ewan finally took off his hat, and put it down reverently on a small table out of the sun. Lord Montfort decided to take a seat in the corner to be out of the way and to allow Valentine to get on with building a smooth bridge for Ewan with the family.

"Just thought I'd pop over and say hullo, as I am sure you have some questions for me," Valentine opened up in his straightforward and forthright manner.

"Thank you, sir. Very kind, I'm sure. I have read your sergeant's notes on his interview with the servants; he did a very thorough job of it, sir, so I am only really interested in talking to the family and their guests. Evidence in this area seems rather sketchy to say the very least."

Lord Montfort felt they were off to an inauspicious start.

"There is also this question of how many guests there were at the ball. You did not mention how they left, or when they left."

"Lord Montfort's guests started to leave the ball at about half past three on Sunday morning; the last of them had left by four o'clock. Most of them came together and left that way. Friends in the county had house parties and they put up Lord Montfort's guests who live further afield. That is how it usually works."

Valentine was clearly taken aback by Ewan's rather uncivil tone, but he forged ahead, determined to be helpful. "The time of death was between three and six o'clock on Sunday morning. Mr. Mallory had been seen by both a footman and Lady Waterford, who was staying at the house, at a quarter to four in the morning in the rose garden. So it was not too difficult to establish that from the end of the ball at four o'clock when the family and their guests retired for the night, everyone in the house was in the clear at that time. Valets and maids confirmed that family and guests were settled in their rooms for the night between four and a quarter past five, where they stayed until they rang for their tea later that morning."

"So you have said in your report, sir, but what about after they had gone to bed?" Ewan asked with exaggerated patience. "This leaves forty-five minutes to an hour unaccounted for by everyone staying in the house, except of course the servants." There was a supercilious expression on Ewan's face as he made this last observation, as if Valentine had missed the point, and Lord Montfort watched Valentine struggle for patience as Ewan drove that point home.

"You see, sir, this is why I need to interview everyone who

was staying in this house and at Haversham Hall again, to find out where they were and who they were with in those critical moments on Sunday morning. Then there is the matter of this young woman, Miss Lambert, who left the house at an unknown hour and now can't be found, and I believe a young maid has run off and no one knows where she is. You did not address in your report what steps were being taken . . ."

Lord Montfort thought Ewan sounded rather triumphant and understood why Valentine stared down his nose at the man standing before him.

"If a gentleman says he was asleep in his bed, you have his word on it; I can assure you of that at least, Chief Inspector. I have uncovered no motive whatsoever for anyone working or staying as a guest in this house to have murdered Mr. Mallory. Or have the time to get up, dress, walk to Crow Wood, and murder Mr. Mallory before six o'clock. It would take you at least thirty-five minutes in daylight to walk from the house to the wood. That is if you knew where the gibbet is located inside the wood. The night in question was obscured by heavy cloud and hammering with rain. It would have been tough going to achieve the wood and hang the victim from the gibbet all in the space of an hour, even if you had previously arranged to meet him at the stable block." Valentine had all Lord Montfort's sympathy. Ewan was barely listening to him. *He's treating Valentine like an amateur,* he thought, as the policeman nodded impatiently and started in before Valentine could say another word.

"In the Criminal Investigation Department we first of all establish how the murder was done and then bring in motive to back up proof. We address how, when, where, why, and who. Now it seems we have got the when and the where, and as soon as I have worked out *how* Mr. Mallory was taken to his death,

I will know *who* murdered him and *why* he did it. Which brings me back to my point: so far as I can make out, Mr. Mallory was last seen at a quarter to four in the rose garden."

"In my interviews no one saw Mr. Mallory after a quarter to four on Sunday morning. He was in the rose garden, and—"

"And the dray was in the service area by the ballroom."

Valentine, having recovered himself, now pounced. "I recommend you read my report and then visit the rose garden. The butler will show you the way. Mr. Mallory could not have been knocked unconscious, tied up, and stowed away in the dray before the end of the ball. The rose garden and the service area where the dray was parked are separated by a ten-foot-tall yew hedge that is four feet wide, which completely encloses the rose garden. It would be like trying to leave a room by walking through the wall. If anyone had forcibly taken Mr. Mallory to the dray from the rose garden, everyone on the terrace would have seen this happen. I was there, Chief Inspector, I can tell you Mr. Mallory was not taken before the end of the ball. He had to have agreed to meet his murderer either by the dray in the service area before four o'clock, which would have meant walking through the ballroom and the rest of the house through crowds of people who would have noticed him, out of the front door, and along the north walk to the service area. Or he met him by the stable block, which is the more likely of the two."

Lord Montfort saw that Ewan was now even more irate than he had been before Valentine arrived. He wondered why the two men could not pool their information, rather than butt heads in this ridiculous conflict. Ewan, having apparently not listened to Colonel Valentine, started a fresh tack.

"Well then, Colonel Valentine, sir, to me the answer is clear.

Someone from the house left their room after having retired for the night. They walked to the stable block to meet Mr. Mallory, where they overpowered him, knocked him unconscious, tied and gagged him and stowed him in the dray, and then drove up to the wood.

"When I arrived I took the opportunity to time the walk from the stable area to the house as fifteen minutes. All perfectly doable, sir. I can't imagine why you have not questioned the guests about this time."

It occurred to Lord Montfort that they were all in for a harrowing day at the hands of Ewan and his search for ironclad alibis. He heard Valentine sigh as he made as if to get up from his chair and then sat back down as he reached hopefully for a solution.

"Just one more thing, Chief Inspector. The drawings I found in Mr. Mallory's room and brought to Commander Eastman at Scotland Yard—surely they throw some light on events in Mr. Mallory's life before he . . ."

"Yes, sir, I am sure they do. But my job is to investigate the facts and the evidence here in the house, among Mr. Mallory's close friends and family. The contents of Mr. Mallory's personal letters and documents are under a separate investigation; as soon as they have information for me I will be notified. And if you are presenting this strange man from London as Mr. Mallory's murderer and the gibbet is so hard to find in the wood, how would a complete stranger have been able to take Mr. Mallory there against his will? I am afraid I must cross-question everyone staying in this house again."

Lord Montfort saw that Ewan was frustrated with what he obviously felt was Valentine's lack of efficiency as his voice sounded terse and impatient. He came to the conclusion that

Scotland Yard's top detective had a first-class chip on his shoulder and it would be wise not to provoke him further. Hoping to help both men save face, as they were now on their feet, and facing each other in the standard posture of individuals protecting their turf, he left his corner and came forward.

"How can I help you, Chief Inspector?" he asked courteously, determined not to make anything more difficult than it was apparently going to become.

"Thank you, Lord Montfort. Since you are here, there is a question you can answer for me. Would you please tell me where you were on Sunday morning between three and six?"

Lord Montfort noticed Ewan's glance at Valentine as if to say, *This is how we do things in the Metropolitan Police Force.*

"Certainly, Chief Inspector," he answered willingly. "I was with my guests until they left at the end of the ball and our house party retired for the night. That would have been getting on for half past four or thereabouts. I can't be sure of the precise time, I'm afraid. Then I went to bed. Actually my valet would know what time that would be." If his manner was a little vague, he did not mean it to be.

"And you went to bed at that time in your own room?" Ewan demanded, turning away to see if his sergeant was writing everything down.

"Well, Chief Inspector, this is my house; of course I was asleep in my own room!" He was rather taken aback by the man's impudence.

"If you spent the remainder of the night alone in your room, then you don't have an alibi who can vouch for your whereabouts until six o'clock on Sunday morning."

"An alibi? I have just told you, Chief Inspector, I was asleep in my bed." He was beginning to feel confused.

"When your valet left you in your room, you could have dressed, left the house, and murdered your nephew at any time between half past four and six o'clock in the morning. There would be plenty of time for you to accomplish this, Lord Montfort."

Lord Montfort stood quite still with his brows down, in complete silence. The sergeant scribbled away frantically behind him on the window seat. Still he did not speak and, aware that Valentine was standing in the window, fuming, was careful not to look in his direction.

"I understand Mr. Mallory had run up considerable debts both in London and among friends, and had been expelled from Oxford for extortion. You are his guardian so he must have been a liability both to your bank account and your family's reputation. It would be understandable—"

"Not to me, Chief Inspector." Irate and perplexed, Lord Montfort could not quite take in that within minutes of arriving in his house, this police officer was accusing him of murder.

"Lord Montfort, until you can produce an alibi for the time in question, you are naturally a suspect. This is an official police investigation."

"It is also an investigation that touches my personal life, Chief Inspector Ewan, and an intrusion. I would appreciate a little more courtesy." His voice was cold.

"I beg pardon if I have offended you, but I cannot be clearer than I have. You are either a suspect or not, based on the facts available. Your household has been placed in a serious situation with very serious consequences. Is there anything else you would like to say?"

Lord Montfort glanced over at Valentine, who was standing

with his hands in his pockets, shifting small change, outraged on the earl's behalf.

"My valet left me in my room between half past four to five o'clock. Check the exact time with him if you wish. From then until ten o'clock in the morning I was with my wife in her room. I understand the necessity of your questions but I find your manner impertinent and needlessly invasive."

"In which case I apologize and thank you, Lord Montfort, for providing yourself with an alibi. I need trouble you no further."

"I sincerely hope you do not intend to corroborate what I have just told you with Lady Montfort."

"I am afraid that I must, Lord Montfort."

"Then I hope you will take care with your manners when you do so, Chief Inspector."

"I will do my utmost to phrase my question to the countess very carefully indeed, Lord Montfort."

Having been thoroughly and unnecessarily insulted, Lord Montfort recognized quite sadly that Ewan was oblivious of how rude he had been.

He left the room, convinced that the world he had known had changed quite drastically for the worse, and felt only deep embarrassment for his friends. They would all be put through the same wretched experience. He was not a prude about his friends' personal lives. He had never been interested in any woman other than his wife from the day he had met her. But he was a realist, and without wishing to know the details, he knew that this was not the case with most of the people he knew. Ewan's probing and prying would be acutely awkward for at least half of his guests, of that he had no doubt. He hoped that Mrs. Thwaite had a decent luncheon organized, because they were all going to need it. He went into his study and rang for his butler.

"What is planned for luncheon, Hollyoak?"

"I believe we are to have roast chicken with foie gras stuffing and *pommes sarladaise* with truffles and garden peas, my lord. A cold consommé to begin and an apricot tart with cream for pudding."

"Good, then bring up some Pavillon Blanc du Château Margaux, the 1910 will do, and make sure you bring plenty of it. Now where is Lady Montfort?"

"On the south lawn, your lordship. Lord Haversham and Mr. Ellis are giving the ladies an archery lesson."

Off Lord Montfort went, still bemused at the state of the world he now inhabited, to find his wife. As he drew near he was impressed to see that she had just sent an arrow straight into the middle of the butt, standing quite eighty feet distant. Her son cheered and Harriet Lambert-Lambert reached out and gave Clementine a little pat, as Constance and Olive let out peals of laughter.

"Clemmy, Harry must have been giving you lessons on the quiet. You are usually hopeless. Come on, Harry, show us how to hit the target!" There was more laughter, and Lord Montfort decided that the kindest thing he could do was to let them enjoy their few minutes of simple pleasure, because the top man from Scotland Yard was certainly going to wipe some smiles off a few faces by this afternoon.

Chapter Twenty-one

In spite of Ewan's impertinent manner when she met with him and his determination that she divulge whom she had slept with on the night of the ball, which she found both provocative and intriguing, Clementine was in good spirits that afternoon. Apart from Ewan's arrival at Iyntwood, which was having a profoundly dismal effect on their friends, the second thing of great moment that had happened that day, anticipated by her family with interest if not with absolute enthusiasm, was the arrival of Teddy's mother at Haversham Hall.

Hollyoak had informed her that Mrs. Mallory had arrived on the half-past-eleven express train from Marylebone, accompanied by the Talbot s' eldest, married daughter, Lady Verity de Lamballe. Lady Verity would stop for luncheon with her grandmother at Haversham Hall and then in the early afternoon drive over to Iyntwood. Her arrival was anticipated by her parents with the greatest of pleasure. Verity was outgoing with a sunny disposition and was a huge favorite of everyone. Her lively presence would provide a distraction from the dreaded horrors of the policeman from London, Clementine thought, and it would be delightful to spend time with her daughter again.

After an enjoyable afternoon with Verity, Lord and Lady Montfort were expected at the dower house for tea to pay their respects to Christina Mallory. At half past four her husband was waiting for her in the hall when she came down the stairs, pulling on her gloves and adjusting her hat. Together they walked outside to the pony and chaise and with Lord Montfort driving off they went into a dripping afternoon with a sullen gray south horizon and intermittent bursts of bright sky and sunshine as clouds moved overhead. The trees sparkled in the changing light, showering tiny crystal drops on them as they bowled through the park. They jogged along the narrow lane, under a high overarching roof of green boughs full of shadowy light, like the nave of a great gothic cathedral.

All too soon the tall iron gates of Haversham Hall appeared on their left, and the pony picked up his pace as they turned into the gravel drive. On either side, towering rhododendrons, in the last of their garish flower, formed a high bank, obscuring a perfect view of the park.

Clementine was a proponent of the charming and comfortable country house. She had never liked Haversham Hall; it was a house full of dusty carpets, looming ceilings, and an overabundance of stained glass. Built in 1840, at the height of England's philistine years as far as architecture was concerned, Clementine found the house unwelcoming and ugly: stuffy and airless in summer, drafty and cold in winter.

Her husband helped her down from the snug rustic comfort of the pony chaise and the vast doors swung open to reveal Stevens, the dowager's elderly butler, bowing deeply to both of them, as if they had arrived at the Court of Saint James. The hall was a cavernous and echoing chamber large enough for a tennis court, with a double staircase in a deep, brownish red marble that always reminded her of raw liver. Huge stained-glass windows cut out any opportunity for light, making the hall as welcoming as a tomb. The echo and bone-chilling cold made Clementine feel depressed and hopeless the moment she arrived. Whatever the weather, she always dressed in her warmest clothes and rarely surrendered her coat to the butler on arrival. In winter she wore woolen undergarments. Preceding them through the echoing hallway, Stevens took them to the east drawing room, where the dowager had chosen to take her tea.

Clementine, used to the warm, well-lit rooms of her house, shivered. She noticed a sad little heap of logs trying its best in a baronial fireplace big enough to roast an ox in. Because the house was in mourning, the heavy green-velvet curtains were drawn tightly across the windows, shutting out all natural daylight. Some ugly lamps had been lit—there was no electricity in Haversham Hall. She huddled her fur collar farther up around her neck and chose to believe that up in the shadowy heights there was a ceiling somewhere, presently obscured from view by the gloom.

Crossing the room, she went over to her mother-in-law, Sylvia, the Dowager Countess of Montfort, sitting behind a battery of tarnished Georgian silver, pouring tea. She was a diminutive woman. Her slight figure and her fluting, high-pitched voice gave her the deceptive appearance of a fragile girl even though, Clementine had calculated, she must be well into her seventies. Clementine knew she did not have her mother-in-law's approval and had accurately guessed that the dowager considered her a brash arriviste from the outer edges of the empire, where she had grown up surrounded by pagan gods, rabid dogs, dirt, disease, and failing drains. Well, at least she had the last part right, thought Clementine.

That she was aware of her mother-in-law's opinion of her and did nothing to try to offset it said much for her self-assurance. She had done her time, endured a million corrections, ignored a thousand snubs, and moved serenely on. Clementine's was indeed the patience of a woman, if not bred to the muddy-English-manor born, one who had brought to her position more élan and generosity of spirit than the Talbots had seen in centuries. It was this thought that gave her comfort as she arrived before the dowager.

Clementine always maintained scrupulously good manners toward her mama-in-law and kept any opinion that might irk or cause ruffled feathers carefully under wraps. Privately she thought the dowager was a cold and selfish woman, ungenerous and reluctant with even the smallest of considerations. Coming as she did from one of the most venerable families in the country put the dowager above such trivialities as welcoming her guests with carefully prepared food in warm and welcoming rooms.

Looking about her, she was happy to see the Reverend Bottomley-Jones sitting in the corner of a huge Victorian wing chair, sipping a cup of lukewarm tea and nibbling a dry cucumber sandwich already curling at the edges. He was one of her favorites, a man of sly wit, great erudition, and small stature. Mr. Bottomley-Jones was talking to Morris Valentine on his left; and on his right, taking up an entire sofa, the one closest to the fire, like someone from a stage play fifteen years earlier, in a welter of silk shawls, little bags, back-dated copies of *The Tatler,* and pages from the *Times Court Circular,* was Christina Mallory. She was dressed in the deepest and blackest of black. And next to Christina, as close to her as she could get, but not upon the sofa, was Lady Booth, also dressed in full mourning and clutching her little dog on her lap.

Clementine watched her husband cross an acre of carpet in a pattern of snaking vines in murky browns and jaundiced yellow to bow over his mother's hand, and then go straight to his sister, who was watching him with tearful and somewhat resentful eyes. He inquired after her journey as he joined her on the sofa, where he devoted his time to her for the rest of their visit. Her responses to his solicitous questions were inaudible to Clementine, but were said with a little smile of effort and a tremor in her voice.

Aha, she thought, *Christina is playing the brave little woman for now. At least she will behave herself in front of Valentine and Bottomley-Jones.* Clementine walked over to her sister-in-law to offer her condolences and sympathy. But Christina, having used up her limited supply of manners on her brother, found that there was little to say to her. Clementine's mother-in-law followed this up by presenting a cheek that felt like lightly floured uncooked dough for her kiss.

The niceties observed the, dowager countess waved her hand at her teapots and inquired, "Indiah or Chinah?"

Clementine wished ardently that she lived in either and took refuge next to the Reverend Bottomley-Jones.

It seemed at this point that all social exchange had been exhausted. Thank God for Lady Booth, who could always be relied upon to maintain an uninterruptable flow of observations on the manners and habits of others. The afternoon trundled forward, creaking and groaning under the solemn weight of the occasion. Clementine settled in for a nice cozy chat with Mr. Bottomley-Jones, assuring him that of course they would be happy to donate new bellows for the church organ and that she would get together with Mrs. Clemson to finalize details for the summer fete, an annual event held on Iyntwood's south lawn by the lake every August. All proceeds went to the cottage hospital.

As she chatted with Mr. Bottomley-Jones she turned her head a little to take in Lady Booth's conversation with Christina. Her only child had been murdered not less than a week ago and she had been in the country only twenty-four hours, but Clementine was amazed to observe that she was already quite caught up with all the London gossip. Lady Strathdevon had become a Theosophist, overnight, and had recently squandered hundreds of pounds on some post-Impressionist paintings that were so violent in both color and content that her husband had banned them from the house; Lady Constance Lytton had disgraced herself again with her suffragette friends and Emily Lutyens, when everything was going so well for poor Edwin with his architectural plans for New Delhi; and the Marchioness of Quakestone had been seen twice with Sir Thomas Beecham in front of the Strand entrance to the Savoy Hotel and a further three times leaving from the service entrance at the side of the building.

Clementine glanced at Mr. Bottomley-Jones and smiled as she noticed that his eyes were as round as the saucer he was slopping his tea into, as he listened in to this choice array of cosmopolitan tittle-tattle.

He caught her eye and asked whether she thought "Lead, Kindly Light" and "I Dwelleth in the House of the Lord" were hymns better suited to the occasion of Teddy's funeral as selected by his grandmother. Receiving her compliant nod, he turned to the dowager and Lord Montfort to help make the final choice, leaving Clementine in the company of Colonel Valentine and free to eavesdrop on Agatha and Christina's conversation.

"How are you doing up at the house with this awful fellow from London? This policeman . . . what's his name?" Christina was ready to talk about the new investigation into her son's death, and Clementine sat farther forward in her chair.

"Ewan, and he is quite awful, a *new Englishman* if ever there was one. No respect, dreadful manners, and simply no idea how to behave. You would not believe what he has subjected us to. Of course we had no choice, as you can imagine." Agatha put her little dog on the floor so it could lap some cool tea from a bowl at her feet.

"Agatha, of course you have a choice, never put up with that sort of rubbish . . . But what did he do?"

"Do? Why, nothing at all. It is what he *required* that was so unspeakable: an *alibi,* as he called it, from everyone in the house as to where they were on the Sunday morning from three until six o'clock, when of course we were all in our beds, sound asleep. Can you imagine? Nanny said that she heard everyone was *somewhere else* after we all retired at the end of the ball. You know what I mean. It's quite outrageous. I would never have thought for one moment . . ." Lady Booth searched for the right phrase.

". . . That Ralph's house parties were so sophisticated? I would have thought their set far too stodgy. Oh I'm sorry, Agatha, I don't mean to offend, but you take my meaning, don't you?"

Clementine, avidly listening in, guessed that Lady Booth would never believe that anything improper might go on in a house she had agreed to stay in for a Saturday-to-Monday house party, but like all prudes she loved to hear what those with lesser morals had been up to. It was what made her such a merciless gossip.

A little prod from Christina: "Come on, Agatha, what else did Nanny tell you?"

"Well, all right then. Who do you think Constance Ambrose said she was with on the night of the ball after lights out?"

"Do I know Constance Ambrose?" Christina was pleased at the possibility of a cosmopolitan soufflé as an alternative to the provincial suet pudding of gossip to be had at Haversham Hall.

"Yes, of course you do. She married Jack Ambrose, the third son of the Duke of Denver, he was . . ."

"Ah yes, I remember now . . . Jack Ambrose's a bit of a stick-in-the-mud. Isn't Constance much younger and quite pretty?"

"Yes, if you like strident coloring . . . She is the daughter of Viscount Slitherton."

"Ah yes, *that* Constance. Agatha, I can assure you *that* Constance is very attracted to assignation. So what did Nanny say about Constance Ambrose?"

"Nanny said Constance's maid was being very tricky after her interview with the police sergeant, dropping hints and so forth, you know how they do. But what it boiled down to was that Constance told her maid, 'I spent the night with that crusty old bachelor, the Badger.' Sounds to me like a bunch of twaddle; the only bachelors staying at the house were Harry and his set, so she can't have meant them. I just ignored it. After all, Constance is not particularly bright . . . like most of the Slithertons."

"I am sure there is more to it than that. I think you are taking what the maid said too literally. It's code for something." Christina would be happy to mull over those words minutely for the next three days, a morsel to provide a distraction.

Clementine, listening quite closely to this exchange, didn't need three days. She knew precisely whom Constance had meant by a "crusty old bachelor" and understood quite sadly that she had lost her most favorite suspect for Teddy's murder. She glanced over at the Reverend Bottomley-Jones, who, having secured a list of hymns from the dowager and relying on his years and status as a man of the cloth, had drifted off to sleep, his cup and saucer clasped askew on his tummy and a slightly conspiratorial smile on his mouth.

Later that night, after dinner, Mrs. Jackson had detailed John to look after the younger guests who had wandered off to the music room with the Victrola to practice the fox-trot, which was all the rage in London this season. The young gentlemen were permitted to drink whiskey, Mrs. Jackson had told John, but the young ladies might only have lemonade. She was aware from her corner of the servants' hall that John had returned for more lemonade and to report that Pansy and Blanch were having the time of their lives now that the mesmerizing Miss Lucinda was no longer staying in the house. They were dancing, he said, and dancing quite nicely in the arms of either Lord Haversham or Mr. Oscar, as their brother, Mr. Ellis, good-naturedly changed gramophone records.

"It's a wonderful dance, the fox-trot. Look, I've been watching them, it's quite easy really." John pulled Mary to her feet and demonstrated the dance with her, singing the lyrics as he trundled her around the room:

Oh ma honey, oh ma honey,
Better hurry and let's meander.

He executed a perfect feather step and then a reverse. Mrs. Jackson, looking up from her mending, thought it a charming exhibition. John was agile and light on his feet, and Mary had no trouble following his lead. She smiled to herself and threaded a darning needle with gray yarn. The servants' hall felt almost normal again.

"They have two records, this one and the 'Alabama Slide.' It's called ragtime and it's wonderful to dance to." John swung Mary to a seat by the table, and turned to laugh at his fascinated audience. "Those two young ladies are having the time of their lives. They're both in love with Lord Haversham and Mr. Oscar, though they're certainly wasting their time on Mr. Oscar Barclay." John allowed his right wrist to flop down as he did a neat little spin in his patent- leather slippers. Mary burst out laughing and was promptly told off by Mrs. Thwaite.

"I want none of that in front of my girls, John, d'you hear me? It was dreadful what you just implied . . . Mr. Barclay is a lovely young gentleman; he's almost as nice a young man as our Lord Haversham is." Having scolded the footman, Mrs. Thwaite now encouraged him with loud laughter.

Mrs. Jackson looked up from the stocking she was darning to pay more attention.

"He certainly *is* a lovely young gentleman," said John, who had become a little more urbane and worldly under the influence of visiting valets who saw a good deal more of life than he did. "He's a right old chip off the block is Mrs. Oscar."

John, left arm pointing upward, twirled his silver tray on his finger and stuck his right hip out sharply, head coyly on one side, causing the girls to shriek. Mrs. Jackson looked up and saw Mrs. Thwaite give John a shove, roaring with laugher and swatting at him with a tea towel.

He went sideways, his feet rapidly two-stepping for balance as he flipped his tray up and neatly caught it, which caused even more of an uproar and a couple of cheers.

"Chip off the old block? Oh no, dear, I won't have it said!" Mrs. Thwaite put large red hands on her bony hips and gave another guffaw. "We've certainly got the cream of society staying with us this time—the corridor-creeping society, that is. And without mentioning any names, which I never do no matter how you twist me arm, I think there have been a few changes since they were last all here." More merriment among the kitchen maids, and Iris shook her head. "Yes, Iris, just you try helping out with the early-morning tea trays and see if I'm not mistaken. Why her ladyship doesn't arrange for a six o'clock bell so they can all get back to their rooms in time for tea, I can't imagine. Save the blushes of some of our nicer girls, it would." There was another gale of laughter from the kitchen element. They were getting loud, and this brought Mrs. Jackson fully in at the double to restore order, thinking as she did so that Mable Thwaite obviously believed she was back in some pub off the Mile End Road, where everyone threw back their heads and brayed with mindless laughter the cruder the evening became. Well, not in her servants' hall.

"What on earth is going on here? John, up those stairs and back to your work. Obviously, we need to have a little talk at the end of this evening. Now do I have to count to three?"

Order was immediately restored, but the image of John twirling his tray had a ring of truth, which was what had made his playacting so very unacceptable to her. Yes, of course

Mr. Barclay probably was . . . well, she couldn't bring herself even to think the word, respectability wouldn't allow it. But it was no reason for half the female servants to erupt in strident laughter. She stalked out of the servants' hall feeling doubly burdened by what was happening in their belowstairs world.

She had been aware that from the moment Sergeant Hawkins had walked downstairs to begin his investigation into the murder of Teddy Mallory, their lives would undergo a change that would bring no benefit. There would be questions asked and answers given that would chip away at the clear line that separated upstairs from downstairs. Loyalties would be tested and attitudes reversed, resulting in a shift in perspective and understanding. Once this line was crossed there would be no turning back, inevitably altering the long-instituted patterns of behavior between servant and master. She sadly came to the realization that John would never have behaved so disrespectfully a week ago. It was understood that footmen liked to play the fool, especially for the maids, but what had happened this evening was different. John had lost respect both for himself and for those he worked for. More troubling was that Mable Thwaite had had no problem in outwardly encouraging him.

Mrs. Jackson stopped and listened. She could hear the cook explaining exactly what *cinq à sept* meant—she pronounced it "sink or set"—for the edification of her kitchen maids. She was just about to turn around and go back into the servants' hall to reprimand her when she caught sight of someone moving at the bottom of the long corridor that ended at the scullery door. She leaned forward, peering into the gloom, and then walked down the corridor. It was Elsie in the shadows by the door, with a shawl up over her head.

"Elsie!" Mrs. Jackson's voice was sharp. "Where on earth do you think you're going at this time of night? Servants' curfew is at nine." She walked the length of the corridor rapidly. "Where were you off to, my girl?" Her voice was low so that no one would hear, but her tone was severe.

Elsie's face, insolent for only a second, became conciliatory. She caught her lip between her teeth; it didn't do to cross Mrs. Jackson.

"Just out to get some air, Mrs. Jackson." Elsie's tone was mollifying and she spread her hands, palms up, in a gesture of innocence.

"No, you were outside a moment ago, young lady, I saw you. I hope you are not off to meet someone." Violet's disappearance had made Mrs. Jackson more suspicious of all the younger maids. "I've got my eye on you, my girl." Her voice was low and cold. "You'd better be off to bed now and I'll talk to you again in the morning."

Mrs. Jackson was surprised to find herself so angry. She was quite sure that Elsie had been on her way to a meeting with someone by the guilty way the girl had responded. It suddenly struck her that Elsie often volunteered to run to the kitchen garden if something had been forgotten. Mrs. Jackson had assumed it was because she needed a break from the claustrophobic atmosphere of the servants' hall. Whom could she possibly be meeting at this time of night? Then she believed she knew who, and she felt the pain of jealousy so acutely that her stomach actually ached.

Chapter Twenty-two

The following morning Mrs. Jackson brought up Clementine's breakfast tray and with it a copy of *The Times*. As she struggled to wakefulness, Clementine was surprised to see that her housekeeper was still in the room.

"Good morning, Jackson. What sort of day is it?" she asked as Mrs. Jackson opened the curtains.

"A nice one, m'lady. I brought you *The Times* newspaper."

"Oh really?" Clementine caught Mrs. Jackson's encouraging tone and picked up the paper. "Oh . . . I see. Oh good gracious me, it's Lucinda!"

"Yes, m'lady, it most certainly is."

Lucinda Lambert-Lambert's whereabouts were proclaimed in heavy bold print on the front page, accompanied by a blurry photograph of her being manhandled out of, or into, a Black Mariah by three solidly built members of London's constabulary. Clementine read out loud:

PEER'S GRAND-DAUGHTER CHAINS HERSELF
TO THE RAILINGS OF 10 DOWNING STREET.
Miss Lucinda Lambert-Lambert, grand-daughter of Eamon
Geoffrey Parceval Squareforth, 5th Earl of Lanarkshire and

daughter of Northampton millionaire boot and shoe industrialist, Mr. Gilbert Lambert-Lambert of Clevellan Square, W1, was arrested yesterday afternoon at five o'clock, after chaining herself to the railings of 10 Downing Street. Miss Lambert-Lambert was wrapped from hat to toe in the suffragette flag and wearing a banner demanding "Votes for Women."

The Prime Minister, Lord Herbert Asquith, 1st Earl of Oxford and Asquith, is presently staying at Checkers, and was not inconvenienced by the young lady's attempts to draw attention to herself as a member of Mrs. Pankhurst's suffragette movement.

Miss Lambert-Lambert had manacled herself to the railings in front of the Prime Minister's official residence, where she remained until police cut through the iron links of her chains and placed her under arrest. She resisted all attempts to go quietly to the police vehicle and had to be dragged by three policemen into the carriage. A constable, assisting in her arrest, sustained a serious contusion to the side of his face and a broken nose from the chains that were still attached to Miss Lambert-Lambert's right wrist. During this time Miss Lambert-Lambert was loud in her exhortations for equality for women, and their right to vote.

While London constabulary worked to cut Miss Lambert-Lambert free, she called out to members of the public who had gathered to watch. "Our fight has been going on far too long. Women will not be trampled . . . we are prepared to die for our cause." It was thought Miss Lambert-Lambert was referring to the death of Miss Emily Wilding Davison yesterday afternoon as a result of injuries sustained when she threw herself in front of the King's horse at the Epsom Derby. Miss Lambert-Lambert shouted, "Rebellion against tyrants is obedience to God," as she was forcibly put into the police van.

Miss Lambert-Lambert will be held in Holloway Prison, and will be arraigned to answer charges of Disrupting the Peace, Causing a Public Disturbance, Obstructing the Police in the course of their duty, and the most serious of all, Assault on a Police Constable.

The Home Secretary, Mr. Reginald McKenna, was quoted earlier this week as calling for "greater measures to be taken against these lawless young women, who invade the privacy of senior government officials in their houses, and on our streets, causing danger to the public with their outrageous antics."

"Well, that's quite dreadful. What a terrible shock." Clementine finished the account of Lucinda Lambert-Lambert's debut into the attention-ridden world of the WSPU and read on. "It says here that everyone is sick to death of the suffragettes and the damage they do. Oh, and it says that poor Wilding Davison woman died of her injuries and her funeral is tomorrow.

"A good deal has happened in a very short time, Jackson. I simply can't believe that Lucinda has turned out so very badly. Her parents must be devastated."

"Lady Harriet and Mr. Lambert-Lambert are downstairs with Chief Inspector Ewan, m'lady. He has given them permission to go to London," said Mrs. Jackson as she rang for Pettigrew.

"What am I thinking?" Clementine started to scramble out of bed. "I have to get up, get dressed, and go down to Lady

Harriet. I expect they want to get up to London as fast as they can so they can set about helping Lucinda out of this scrape."

As Mrs. Jackson left, Lord Montfort arrived and heard her last remark.

"This is hardly a scrape, Clemmy, for heaven's sake!" he said. "I hope they don't make an example of Lucinda. The government is absolutely sick to death of these women causing trouble and destroying property. It is against the law to chain oneself to the railings of the prime minister's residence, and to thump a policeman on the nose." Clementine sensed that her husband had firmly allied himself with the ranks of outraged fathers and husbands, and sighed.

"Then Lord Squareforth will have to step in and intervene," she said. "It's the least he can do for Harriet."

"Well, let's hope he sees it that way too," her husband replied as Pettigrew bustled into the room, carrying Clementine's frock over her arm. "I'll leave you to get dressed and look for you downstairs. Harriet and Gilbert are leaving soon. They are just waiting to say goodbye to you."

Clementine arrived in time to find Lady Harriet Lambert-Lambert and her husband standing together in the hall as their motorcar pulled up into the drive. Gilbert looked quite ill and Clementine's first reaction was that he should not travel. Then she recognized the futility of this thought; when one's child was in trouble there was no staying away. Harriet looked drawn but determined nonetheless, and was clearly in full charge of herself, in an iron-woman kind of way that made Clementine feel nothing but concern for her friends. She took Harriet's arm and turned her gently toward her.

"Harriet, tell me what can I do to help?" she asked.

Harriet replied immediately, "Think who you know who can

influence them to drop the charges against Lucinda. Otherwise she will serve a prison sentence." It was evident that Harriet had no qualms about calling in all favors.

"Of course, I'll talk to Ralph. What about your father?" Clementine wondered if Lord Squareforth knew that his granddaughter was ruining the family's reputation.

"He is our only hope at the moment and he is quite beside himself." Harriet looked even more determined, and Clementine thought she had certainly inherited her father's powerful will. "I am hoping he will come round . . ."

"Harriet, what do you know about this terrible business?"

"I know that Lucinda chained herself to those damned railings. When she left on Sunday morning she probably drove to the Pankhursts' house straightaway and joined those bloody women. They must have been over the moon to see her. Can you imagine what a coup it was for them, a girl of her background joining their blasted cause? She must have been with them all this time . . . and then she did this terrible thing. We simply must get her out of there as soon as we can before the wretched girl decides to hunger strike.

"They usually throw the book at suffragettes who make a public disturbance these days. I am not sure at all what sort of sentence she could serve. Oh damn and blast, where is that motorcar?" Lady Harriet turned to her husband and Clementine felt alarm for Gilbert. He was looking old and vulnerable. Clementine was saddened by the overnight change in Gilbert; gone was the powerful captain of industry who had laughingly turned down Lloyd George's offer of a peerage for a mere fifty thousand pounds as being the last gambit of the desperate to belong to a class he had already married into.

"Ralph said something about Henry Fowler, he's a close friend of the prime minister, and he was in the same house at Eton as Ralph's father; he could talk to him, or perhaps the home secretary, Mr. McKenna?" Clementine said.

"McKenna hates the Pankhursts and the WSPU. I am hoping my father will persuade him on our behalf. Now I must go, Clementine. Pray for us. If Lucinda is to remain in prison I am not sure that Gilbert will be able to live with that."

Clementine and Lord Montfort stood side by side in the drive to watch their friends leave. As the motor disappeared around the corner they turned and walked into the house.

"It's the end of an age, the end of civilization as we know it." Clementine felt immeasurably depressed at the ugliness of it all. "It is simply not possible that a young girl of Lucinda's background could be put in prison for something as ridiculous as chaining herself to the railings of Number Ten."

"And I wonder if it is simply not possible for a young girl of Lucinda's background to have behaved with such impropriety as to chain herself to the railings of Number Ten," said her husband as he walked her toward the small dining room so that she could join him for his breakfast.

Hollyoak opened the door for them, but said just before they walked in, "Chief Inspector Ewan would like a word with you after you have breakfasted, my lord."

"Oh good God, what does *he* want?"

"I understood it concerns Haversham Hall. I think the chief inspector's intention is to drive over there to talk to the dowager countess and—"

"Mrs. Mallory? Well good luck to him." Lord Montfort laughed. "He must be either very brave or a complete nincompoop."

"I would say the latter, your lordship." Hollyoak bowed and left them to their breakfast.

As Clementine went upstairs to change for a stroll in the park with Gertrude and Constance, Mrs. Jackson arrived with more news for her. Oscar Barclay was having a wretched morning, so Agnes had reported when she had gone up to see to his room during breakfast and found him still in bed, looking rather ill.

"I was wondering if you had the time to see Mr. Oscar, m'lady," Mrs. Jackson asked with a look that said it would be worth a visit.

"Most certainly, Jackson, he's in the bachelors' quarters, right? Good. I'm on my way. Would you join me up there? And bring reinforcements in the shape of comforting food and sustenance."

As Clementine tapped on and opened the door to Oscar's bedroom, she could barely see him across the darkened room, where he lay in his bed.

"Oscar dear, how are you? Mrs. Jackson says you are not feeling well." Clementine stood at the foot of his bed, peering at him through the gloom.

"So terribly sorry you have troubled yourself, Lady Montfort. I just have this horrid headache, and I am so very cold, I can't seem to get warm." There was no fire in his room, which faced north, and she saw that Oscar had wrapped himself up in what looked like a flannel dressing gown over his pajamas and had wound a scarf around his neck. He lay there shivering, his face pale.

Clementine crossed the room and opened one of the chintz curtains that were drawn across the windows. Oscar turned his head on the pillow and she saw such misery.

"Oh my dear boy, you do look all in!"

"I don't feel too good actually." He tried to laugh it off but failed. "I had rather a desperate interview with Chief Inspector Ewan, it went on for nearly an hour. I decided to come back to bed."

Clementine laid her hand on his forehead. It felt incredibly hot, and she tried to decide whether he was really ill or had just come to the end of the line. Well, it amounted to the same thing, she thought. An hour with Ewan would have been grueling to a sensitive boy like Oscar, she had no doubt.

"Have you eaten breakfast at all, Oscar?" She kept her voice low.

"I have no appetite."

"Mrs. Jackson is on her way with something that should do the trick. I will look in on you again, but for now just rest and let nature take its course."

Oscar nodded his thanks and his eyes swam.

Clementine stroked his hair out of his eyes and off his forehead, smoothed the sheets and blankets comfortably across him, and eased a softer pillow under his head. Then she went to the wardrobe at the far end of the room, pulled out an eiderdown, and tucked it around him.

There was a tap on the door and Mrs. Jackson came in. With the calm efficiency Clementine so appreciated, Mrs. Jackson helped Oscar to sit up and gave him a glass of water with Beechams Powders. As he was shuddering the powders down, she slipped a hot-water bottle under his feet, the most comforting feeling in the world when one is clenched up with cold. Mrs.

Jackson took away the empty Beechams glass and gave him a two-handled cup from which small puffs of steam carried the deliciously rich aroma of hot, beef tea.

"Well, Mr. Barclay, it's been an upset for us all, no wonder you feel out of sorts," Mrs. Jackson said as she watched Oscar cautiously sip his beef tea.

"We'll leave you to rest, Oscar. Just give Mrs. Jackson a ring if you need anything and I'll look in on you again later." Mrs. Jackson opened the door for her and they left Oscar to sleep.

Clementine felt decidedly triumphant as she turned to her housekeeper.

"I will pop along and see how the poor boy is doing after luncheon. Please be sure that a tray of something delicious and heartening is taken up to him at one o'clock. Something comforting, tell Mrs. Thwaite. What did the boys love when they were home from Eton, apart from treacle tart?"

"They liked sausages and mashed potatoes with pickled onions, m'lady," was Mrs. Jackson's unhesitating reply.

Clementine shuddered. "Well, I am sure Oscar wouldn't. Ask Mrs. Thwaite to come up with something tempting. I always like a little roast chicken when I'm feeling off. You set him back to rights again; afterward I can have a nice little talk with him and find out what he's all about."

Chapter Twenty-three

Before she changed to go down to the dining room for luncheon, Clementine paid a visit to Oscar, who had just finished a tender *blanquette de veau* and had obviously rallied considerably under their kind attentions. Always appreciated for his beautiful manners and fastidious appearance, Clementine was pleased to see that Oscar had bathed and was sitting by the fire, dressed in a velvet-and-silk padded robe over his pajamas; he had even had the energy to shave.

"My dear boy—how are you feeling now?" she asked, taking a seat in the chair next to him and looking appreciatively at his made bed and the overall tidiness of the room.

"I feel so much better, thank you for your kindness, Lady Montfort. Your housekeeper has taken such good care of me." Clementine noticed that although he had lost the reduced look of bone-tired weariness, there was a resolute grimness about him now.

"Maybe you should continue to rest until tomorrow. But in the meantime is there anything I can bring you? Books, newspapers? Please ring for anything you need. I am sure your friends will want to look in on you later!"

"Thank you—you are too kind to me, as you always have been." He was genuine in his appreciation, she thought. Oscar had always been such an effortlessly nice boy.

"Goodness, Oscar—don't mention it, my dear. You must have had a pretty rough time of it with that ghastly policeman. What a nasty bully . . . worse than being back in school I should imagine," and she laughed so that the bogeyman didn't creep into the room and their conversation.

"Quite," agreed Oscar, though rather weakly.

"Just doing his job, Oscar, after which he will up and leave us alone. You see, they have to carry on as if we are all suspects—that is the purpose of an investigation." She laughed again, inviting him to join in. "Did he grill you so very horribly?"

"Yes, he did rather. Made me feel I hadn't a leg to stand on." Oscar believed quite evidently that he didn't, Clementine thought.

"Oldest trick in the book," she said, as if she were interrogated every day of the week for all sorts of crimes. "Wants to throw you off guard, make you feel panicky, trick you into all sorts of indiscretions. He was awful to poor Ralph."

Always confide in the person you want information from, she said to herself. She instinctively knew that if you wanted to invoke other people's trust, you extended trust to them. Another wily trick absorbed by osmosis from her father, the adroit governor general; she mentally sent her thanks.

"Really?" cried Oscar. "Good to hear I'm not alone."

"Oh yes, practically accused him outright, said he had all the motive in the world."

"No! What a nerve."

"Yes, all nerve but no brain. What about you, did he nail you up as his favorite suspect?"

"Well, I think I am a suspect, by my situation alone, you see." She watched him jump nervously to his feet and straighten his brushes on the dressing table; then he turned to her. "I have no alibi for the time of Teddy's death. I was not with Harry and Ellis, who were playing billiards until breakfast, or with anyone . . . really. I left the ball towards the end and went for a stroll to clear my head. Walked through the gardens, it was a beautiful night before the storm came. I ended up in the orchid house just before dawn. We used to play there when we were young."

"Anyone see you? The gardeners as you were leaving, perhaps?" Clementine was on alert, hoping that Oscar would confide.

"No," Oscar said. "It was all quiet, I didn't see a soul. It was warm and the tropical plants made me feel as if I were somewhere else entirely other than England. When we were boys, Harry, Ellis, and I played Rafting the Amazon, in the orchid house. We used to catch hell from the gardener in case we damaged something . . . All that seems so long ago now."

Clementine caught the longing in his voice for a time when he had been sure of his friends, and comprehended that all Oscar needed was to talk to someone—someone who was not going to judge or criticize him. Hard though it was not to ask questions, she took a leaf out of Mrs. Jackson's book, contained herself and waited.

"One summer, when we were about eight or nine, we made an enormous anaconda from bird netting, which we stuffed with newspaper and painted a lurid yellow with black bands. It had a great floppy head, and must have been about fifteen feet long. We went up to the orchid house with Lord Montfort's old canoe: Teddy, Harry, Ellis, and I. Teddy liked to be the snake. The game was to get us out of the canoe and then he would try to sneak up behind us, wrap the anaconda around us, pulling tight. If we couldn't fight free by the count of twenty we were crushed to death and eaten. It was great fun."

Clementine reached out and patted him on the shoulder.

"Those days will return, Oscar, the pleasant and simple ones. Not the way they were when you were boys, but the straightforward days of living everyday life. Studying at Oxford, being with your friends. You will earn your degree and find your place in the world, meet a lovely young woman to share your life with."

"No," said Oscar, "not for me."

"No return to Oxford?" Clementine wondered if Oxford held many bad memories.

"I don't see the point really, now it's all gone so wrong."

"Maybe not immediately, but perhaps you need to finish it off, just for the sake of it. To help put you back in the swim of things."

"Yes I suppose . . ."

"What are you reading, law?"

"Greats . . ."

"Ah, the classics. Perfect for a career in the diplomatic. That would be such a wonderful life, full of travel. You could revisit your Amazon adventures." She was being as careful as she could be.

Oscar smiled. "I don't want to be defeatist, Lady Montfort, but I am not sure the diplomatic would take someone like me."

"Oh, because of the gambling thing you mean? You know Ralph is pretty close with the chancellor; he could have a word on your behalf, and maybe square things there for you, when most of this fuss and bother has died down. All undergraduates get up to silly nonsense. People do understand, you know."

She was not sure they did. More than likely, Oscar would end up somewhere like Kenya, along with all the other untouchables whose families didn't want them around.

"Oh, the gambling is one thing, but I basically don't think I fit very well, and the diplomatic is all about that . . . y'know . . . fitting in."

"Why do you say you don't fit in, Oscar?" She thought she knew. She thought she had it buttoned down the other evening, but she wasn't too sure.

"Because I don't. I fit in to half a life but not a whole one. I am at ease in a certain type of world, but not one that everyone accepts. I am not bad at games and sport, but I don't make friends easily . . . I . . . Oh, God, listen to me, I sound so self-pitying. That's what Teddy used to say: 'Don't be such a bloody girl, Oscar,' and stuff like that."

"Well, Teddy was a frightful bully sometimes," said Clementine, grateful that Oscar had brought up Teddy, "and probably not your kindest friend."

"No, he wasn't always kind, but I certainly knew where I was with him. Teddy didn't care about a thing. I care too much about far too many things. I was useful to Teddy, but I don't think he cared for me really, not the way I did for him."

A warning bell was clanging away in Clementine's head, so she said nothing but nodded.

"Teddy included me in all of his life, whether I wanted to be included or not. I went along with it because I didn't want him to exclude me. I had no choice: it was accept the bad with the good. He made me unhappy and he often scared me, but his friendship counted more than anything else. Now he is gone I feel rather lost."

Clementine decided that now was the time to push him.

"Is it friendship when someone makes you feel scared and unhappy, I wonder?"

"What? No . . . well, no . . . probably not. He could be so very cruel, but so much fun."

"And you loved him very much, Oscar, in your good, loyal way." She said this with such genuine understanding that Oscar could only nod. She leaned forward and put her hand on his arm and gave it a firm and sympathetic squeeze.

"I cared for our friendship more than anything else in the world, and look what he did to me. He betrayed me. He knew I cared about him and he betrayed me. I wish I could find some way to forget that part, but I can't seem to."

She was appalled. Like most women of her background and upbringing, it was hard for Clementine to cope with the sight of a man falling apart in front of her. It made her feel panic-stricken. But she had learned a thing or two about getting a grip in the last two days: "And," she said quietly, "he blackmailed you."

Oscar's head came up—and he looked at her in horror.

"Oh my god, how did you know? Who told you?"

"You did just now, my dear. You see, Teddy was a blackmailer by nature: he was ruthless, opportunistic, and unprincipled, all perfect attributes for a successful blackmailer. You were not his only victim, you know. I am so sorry you have been through such a terrible time of it." She looked away, giving him time to compose himself.

"Yes. I am heartbroken he is gone, and quite devastated he died in such an awful way, but there is such incredible relief that he has no power over me anymore. Do you understand what I'm saying?" He got up from his chair to find a cigarette, but did not light it, even though Clementine indicated that he might smoke.

"Yes, I think I do understand. You gave this young man your friendship and trust and he treated you shamefully. Very charismatic young men like Teddy can be lethal unless they have honor and compassion to balance out all that easy charm— qualities which you have, Oscar, but Teddy lacked. Young men who are narcissistic and selfish usually create absolute havoc in other people's lives, especially those who are unfortunate enough to love them. You know all of this, Oscar. Allow yourself to see Teddy for what he was, and accept it, so you will be free to go on with your life. There is no blame." But she added to herself, *Unless you killed him.*

It was almost as if she'd spoken her last thought. Oscar's face sharpened and he straightened up.

"But go on as what . . . Teddy's murderer? Because that is what that policeman is trying to prove."

"But how can he? Just because you don't have an alibi for the time of Teddy's death."

"Because I have a perfect motive. You said it yourself, blackmail."

"Not all victims kill their blackmailers, Oscar. If this were the case, perhaps there are half-a-dozen people in the house who could have killed Teddy. And anyway, Ewan doesn't know about *your* blackmail, does he? No, I didn't think he did. Well, my dear, you must simply keep your head and remain calm. It is a pity you were alone in the orchid house."

"Well, I was until about half past four."

She saw him wince; he had given himself away.

"Oh really?" She resolved to tread carefully.

"I may not say who, because I would get someone else into terrific trouble if I said anything."

"Would that person be able to give you an alibi?"

"Yes, they would. But at the moment, my opinion of myself stands pretty low and I don't want to sink lower by splitting on someone who has every reason to trust me." She saw an obstinate expression set in and worried that he was shutting down.

Clementine felt almost agitated at this point. She yearned for five minutes with Jackson, she would know how to winkle this out of him. Clementine knew she had to go carefully and not panic him.

"Well, think about it, Oscar. Rest now, eat a good dinner, and get a good night's sleep. Think about what we can do next to clear your name." Clementine got up from her chair and walked to the door, where she turned.

"Whoever it is you are protecting, Oscar, might need you as an alibi too. After all, wandering around the grounds between four and six o'clock would put anyone on the top of that policeman's list, unless you were with someone who can vouch for you. Now I must run."

As soon as Clementine got back to her sitting room she rang for Mrs. Jackson and waited for her impatiently. When Mrs. Jackson came, she related her conversation with Oscar. She was not going to let Ewan arrest a young man she had known since he was a child, just because there was no one else. The man must accept that Teddy's unsavory life had been the ultimate cause of his death and leave her friends and her servants alone. Oscar had a perfectly sound explanation for where he had been at the time of Teddy's death, silly boy, but he was determined to be a martyr. She was amazed at how men behaved quite stupidly and then called it being honorable.

She became aware that Mrs. Jackson was only half listening to her.

"I'm sorry, m'lady. Yes, I was listening to you, but I was also following my own train of thought. What time would that have been do you think, m'lady, when Mr. Oscar was in the orchid house?"

"He got there at just after four and was there until just after a quarter to six. I think it was perhaps Violet he might have been with. Do you think it could have been Violet?"

"No, m'lady, I somehow don't think it could have been Violet. Before I say anything, I would just like to pop downstairs and follow up on a few things."

"Yes, well, Jackson, go ahead, but try and get this thing sorted out before tea. Chief Inspector Ewan is probably about to make an arrest, so we must hurry. The very last thing we need is for Oscar to be taken out of the house in a Black Mariah. It would be quite awful."

Mrs. Jackson practically ran to her parlor. Her mind was flitting about in an irritating way, so she sat down to order her thoughts. And when she was quite sure what she was to do, she rang for Elsie, who arrived looking both worried and defensive. Mrs. Jackson didn't waste a moment.

"Elsie," she said, "I think it would be better for everyone if you told me the truth about where you were on the night of the ball when you finished work in the anteroom, and," here Mrs. Jackson took an enormous risk, hoping not to scare Elsie into shutting down, "who you were with in the orchid house."

Mrs. Jackson knew the lower servants joked that she could see through brick walls, and now Elsie would no doubt believe it to be fact. She saw Elsie's surprise and panic and knew the girl was not a natural liar. *This is too easy,* she thought as she watched Elsie's pretty face crumple.

"Please, Mrs. Jackson, don't dismiss me. I can't lose my place here."

"Well, my girl, you should have thought of that before. Now I think you had better tell me what you were up to." Mrs. Jackson hardened herself; most of her really didn't want to hear what Elsie had to say next.

"Nothing. I was up to nothing, Mrs. Jackson. I was just spending a few minutes alone in the orchid house to take a breather. I know it's against the rules. But please don't tell on me. I can't lose my place here, please, Mrs. Jackson."

Elsie looked so desperate that Mrs. Jackson felt disgusted with herself. Why did it matter after all? It wasn't as if she cared for Ernie Stafford; his manner could be intrusive and she didn't ever feel at ease around him. But now she had to know, if not for herself then for poor Mr. Oscar, sitting upstairs in his room, willing to be arrested so he could feel he'd done the right thing.

"Come on now, Elsie. Just tell me the truth. What were you doing in the orchid house at half past four, and who did you meet there?" Mrs. Jackson kept her tone cool and her face expressionless.

Elsie snuffled and wept into her handkerchief but Mrs. Jackson sat in impassive silence and waited her out.

"It was Horace, Horace Wobbley, first footman at the hall. Henry, his working name is. We're stepping out together . . . sort of. We want to be married . . . one day."

"Horace Wobbley? You were seeing Horace Wobbley?" Mrs. Jackson was so taken aback that she almost got to her feet.

"Yes, in the orchid house. That's who. Oh, I am so sorry . . ." Elsie burst into tears.

"Elsie, stop crying and don't make such a fuss." Mrs. Jackson was so surprised and relieved to hear the name Horace that she forgot for a moment what the real purpose of this exchange was. "Who else was there, who else came into the orchid house?"

It was as if Elsie had given up, it hadn't taken much. She knew she was for the high jump. It was forbidden for the lower staff to have followers. It was even worse that she was seeing a male servant from the dower house.

"It was Mr. Barclay, he was already there. We got into chatting with him, told him all about our plans for our shop. He said we should stick at it, that it was a good idea." This was said with some spirit. "Such a nice gentleman, I thought he was. He said he would never tell on us, and I trusted him." Mrs. Jackson noticed that Elsie didn't think much of Oscar's promise.

Mrs. Jackson laughed. She laughed with genuine pleasure, a full-throated, delighted laugh.

"Mr. Barclay didn't say a word, Elsie, you silly girl. Not a peep. He kept your promise. The reason I know what you were up to is because I can see through brick walls. Now here is what we are going to do."

She sent Dick off on his bicycle with a note for Mr. Stevens, the butler, at the dower house, asking if Horace would come over to Iyntwood to help Dick load up the red couches that had been on loan from the hall for the ballroom for those who could not or would not dance.

There was a tap on her door and Horace put his head in. He was looking particularly red-faced and anxious, having ridden over on Dick's bicycle as fast as he could. His face dropped when he saw Elsie, who was still sniveling into her hankie. Mrs.

Jackson quickly filled him in and watched him relax. He was onboard, as long as his Elsie didn't get the chop, thought Mrs. Jackson.

"No one in the house or at the dower house will know about your meeting with Elsie, and anyway you have no choice in the matter. You have to be accurate and truthful with Chief Inspector Ewan, otherwise Mr. Barclay will be compromised. Come on, Horace, pull yourself together. Just tell him the truth. Then you can have a nice cup of tea with Elsie in the servants' hall. If you are stepping out together then stop skulking around. It makes you look untrustworthy. Just be straightforward and stick to the facts when you talk to the chief inspector. Oh, and by the way, you need to help Dick with the couches in the ballroom before you go."

Half an hour later, Mrs. Jackson, Horace, and Elsie came out of the morning room after a brief talk with Chief Inspector Ewan. Mrs. Jackson did not like the man; he had behaved quite unpleasantly when Elsie had told him that she and Horace had been with Mr. Oscar in the orchid house.

"That won't do at all, Mrs. Jackson," he had said. "I know the family has a feudal hold over all their servants, but this is too much. I have had to put up with this sort of collusion from the moment I stepped through the front door. Why didn't you come forward earlier?" He shot Horace an ugly look. "Looks to me like you have been properly squared away. Who put you up to it?"

She was impressed with Horace's dignity. "I had no idea that we were withholding important evidence from you, sir," he said. "I have not been interviewed by any policeman since Mr. Mallory's death and Elsie here was just scared stiff of speaking to you alone." Mrs. Jackson smiled at his implication of police bullying. She noticed that Ewan's sergeant was already thumbing through his copy of Bradshaw.

"There is the half-past-four express leaving from Market Wingley station, sir, which will get you into Marylebone at just after five o'clock," she said to the sergeant. "If you wish to catch that one, his lordship's chauffeur will drive you to the station."

As the two men left the house in Lord Montfort's chauffeur-driven Daimler, Mrs. Jackson stood in the drive. She saw Ewan's face looking suspiciously at her from under the brim of his hat as the motorcar drove slowly up the drive. She was quite enjoying herself and turned back to the house with a light step, to find Oscar Barclay and let him know that he was in the clear and could expect to hear nothing more from the chief inspector.

Chapter Twenty-four

"Lord Squareforth has done his bit for the Lambert-Lamberts," Lord Montfort announced to his wife as she awoke from a deep sleep, to find him perched on the edge of her bed, sipping a cup of tea and eating toast and marmalade from her breakfast tray. She moved a crystal vase of sweet peas to one side and took her teacup from his hand.

"Where is she now?" she asked, trying to clear her head and deal with her husband's teeming energy as a result of an early-morning ride and interesting news to impart.

"Lucinda spent all yesterday and last night in Holloway Prison." Lord Montfort's eyebrows went up and the corners of his mouth came down, an expression she recognized that meant he wished to express regretful behavior. "She is now recovering at Clevellan Square, all charges dropped."

"All charges?"

"Well, the worst ones. She's been bound over to keep the peace, so she had better be a good little girl from now on."

Clementine pushed the tea tray away. This all sounded very unsatisfactory somehow. She did not approve of Lucinda's behavior; it was unutterably selfish. But she didn't approve of women being brutalized in prison because the government was still too stupid to give women the vote. She felt tetchy and irritable.

"Poor Harriet and Gilbert, what a mess," she said in what she hoped was a neutral tone of voice, because she didn't want to start an argument with her husband about women's suffrage this early in the morning.

"Yes, it is. Harriet is coping admirably of course, but Gilbert is devastated." Lord Montfort got up and walked over to the window, his face disapproving. "Christina wants Teddy's funeral for the day after tomorrow, early in the morning at about eleven."

There were more things to organize before this terrible week was over, thought Clementine, and she swung her legs out from under the covers and got out of bed. "I'd better have a word with Jackson about our helping out with the funeral arrangements at the church. The least we can do is organize the flowers." She rang for Pettigrew.

Mrs. Jackson had already heard about the funeral plans from Mable Thwaite and had walked over to the kitchen garden to look over flowers with Mr. Thrower. She had hoped that Stafford would be around, but he was nowhere in sight, and Mrs. Jackson decided to loop around the back of the orchard and return to the house by way of the new sunken garden. It had been a while since she had visited the now transformed old chalk- and flint-excavation and the morning air was sweet and warm, perfect for a walk.

When she arrived at the lip of the old quarry she found herself gazing down into a lush new world. Tips of young trees planted last autumn in the garden's terraces, to disguise the sloping sides of the pit, were doing their best to soften the edges of the quarry's scarred edges. Its rim was planted with gold, orange, and white azaleas now at the peak of their bloom, which scented the air and provided a softened edge to what had been a craggy crater two years ago. Within this ruffle of bright green growth, steps led down to planted, tiered terraces and pathways, through shrubs and small herbaceous garden plantings, gradually descending to the floor of the original excavation, nearly forty feet below.

Mrs. Jackson, standing at the top of the steps, felt as if she were looking down into a mountain valley in miniature, and she found the prospect entrancing. She walked down the first flight of steps to the path and paused to look around. At each terraced level the path took her around the interior wall of the old pit before it dropped down again and took her back the way she had come on a level below. Each turn was concealed by an outcrop of large boulders, a grove of trees, or the flinty wall of the pit itself. From northeast to southwest, a small stream traversed the garden, guided so that its course ran at a slower, more meandering pace; it dropped in a fall of water to form a pool, overwhelming it and continuing on until it reached the floor of the garden. Because the plantings were still immature, she could easily see there were two other flights of steps descending to other paths from the rim. As the plants grew, the pathways would become concealed and secret. All she heard in the quiet of the morning was the call of birds, the drowsy hum of bees, and the breeze ruffling the leaves of the treetops near the rim.

When she arrived at the bottom, she experienced a brief moment of disappointment. Stafford didn't appear to be here, and there was no sound of work being done in the garden. In fact it appeared to be quite empty. She came down the last few steps, followed the path around, and found him under the shade of a stand of newly planted birch saplings. He looked up at her approach and tipped his hat in greeting.

"It looks wonderful, Mr. Stafford, the early spring really helped it along." She stood beside him under the trees, feeling a little awkward. Stafford gestured for her to take a seat on an old bench in the sun. As she sat down she noticed that his lunch basket and a jug of cider were parked underneath it. This was probably where he sat for his noonday meal, she thought.

"Now then, Mrs. Jackson, just look up from that spot," Stafford said, gesturing upward, and Mrs. Jackson lifted her eyes.

The whole garden looked like an irregular oval bowl with cliffs on three sides. She allowed her gaze to travel the lush walls of the garden and then she pivoted on the bench to take in the view from its base as level ground flowed out to meet an undulating sweep of parkland down to the river's edge several hundred feet distant. Mrs. Jackson raised her face to the sun and inhaled the scent of new green leaves, pollen, flowers, and the rich earth, which smelled like plum cake. She heard the stream as it chattered along its stony bed. No wonder Stafford was so at ease when he was at work—he had created this extraordinary world. She turned to look at him. He was following her gaze with his arms folded, trying to look critical of his creation; he succeeded only in coming off as rather smug. She laughed.

"It is quite beautiful, Mr. Stafford, quite, quite wonderful."

"Just give it three years and it will begin to look like something." His self-satisfaction was evident and Mrs. Jackson was struck again with how straightforward Stafford was. She had never heard him be insincere for the sake of convention, and he had a disarming way of speaking his mind.

But he was never unkind, she thought, because he was a thoughtful man, aware of what others might feel. It was a nice change after the servants' hall.

"I would like to ask you something, Mr. Stafford," she said, taking his example and coming straight at it. "This last week has been . . ." She paused and he finished for her.

". . . A real strain, I can tell just by looking at you. I'm so sorry, it was a terrible thing to have happened."

"Yes, it really was a terrible thing," she said, and found herself telling him about Lucinda, about Violet's running off, about Oscar's tangle with the police, all of which he knew of course, gossip being what it was. But he heard her out without interruption or impatience. Most of all, she told him how troubled she was about Violet.

"I think I knew there was something upsetting her, but I was so busy, I put off dealing with her homesickness. If I'd taken the time perhaps I could have done something to help." She shrugged her shoulders and shook her head, uncustomary gestures from one who was usually so still. "Now it's too late."

"What did you want to ask me?" he said, but in such a kindly way that Mrs. Jackson knew his question was from real concern and that he would do his best to help her. He picked up his rake and began to lightly work the surface of the earth under the trees.

"What makes a young village girl of fifteen leave her home and run off from the only place she has known all her life?" she asked. "I can't fathom it."

"Iyntwood is her home?" he asked, putting aside his garden rake and walking out from the shade of the grove of young trees.

"No, of course not, but the village is, her father lives here."

"But Iyntwood is not the village. How long had she been up

at the house? Two months is it? The only newcomer to the staff in how many years?"

Mrs. Jackson felt herself stiffen a little. He made it sound as though coming to work at the house had been a hardship to overcome, not the great opportunity it was for a village girl. Stafford smiled as if he knew what she was thinking. "Must have been a tough go," he went on, "adapting to the strange ways and rules of the great house, and learning new skills at the same time. Perhaps you forget how it is, because it's been *your* home for quite a few years, and you are the housekeeper. How did your life in service begin?"

Mrs. Jackson flushed and looked away from his direct gaze. Her beginnings in service had been unhappy ones. She had come from a parish orphanage, left there when she was seven, when times were a lot tougher than they were now. She would never be able to forget the five years she had spent living on the charity of the parish. It had been cruel and calculatedly demeaning, but she had learned to endure it. Then she had gone into domestic service when she was twelve. She was certainly not going to discuss her lowly beginnings with Stafford.

He came over and sat next to her on the bench and took off his hat; she could see his face from the corner of her eye. It was a nice face with strong, even features and a firm mouth, and his eyes were clear and bright as they regarded her with intelligent humor. She relaxed as he continued.

"We often think others have it easier than we did, but it's rarely true. Instead of asking yourself the questions everyone else is asking: Did she run off with someone? Had she stolen something? Was she in the usual trouble? All the questions asked when young girls go missing. Oh aye, I have a good idea what they might be, Mrs. Jackson." Stafford ran his hand through his dark hair and thought for a moment. "Ask yourself, what did you know about that young girl that would help you understand the *reason* for her going?"

Mrs. Jackson thought that Violet had been rather a shy girl, a little timid when she had first come to work in the house, but she had adapted well, and the other servants liked her. She learned quickly, worked deftly and quietly, and even as Mrs. Thwaite reluctantly admitted there was no side to her, no impudence or pertness. She had done her best to fit in. Mrs. Jackson told Stafford all this, and he listened staring down between his knees and twirling his hat slowly between his hands. He got up and walked over to several shallow rectangular baskets, stacked like trays on the ground. He bent down and lifted off the top one.

"Sounds to me like she really did her best to do a good job for the family, so what changed? Something must have happened to make her throw over everything and run off. Running away would be a scary business for a young village girl. What would she know of the world and where could she have possibly gone? Must have been something really bad, something that made her risk leaving the known for the unknown and a world where she knew no one at all. Life in Haversham village does not prepare anyone for life outside it. So think about the worst things that can happen to a young helpless girl in service that would make her take such a risk. I wonder what that could have been."

Mrs. Jackson felt he was putting her on the spot and she was uncomfortable. "I can't, really I can't. She was not a reckless girl." Her thoughts went back to her own first years in service. Sometimes it had been unendurably hard: years of endless toil as a scullery maid working for a critical kitchen maid. But there had been good parts. The cook had been kind, had helped her learn her letters and encouraged her to read and write. She had worked hard, though, harder than any of the girls at the house did. The family she worked for had not been as well-to-do as the Talbots, so the few servants they had worked excruciating hours. She had dreamed of a better place, but there was nowhere for her to go until she had the skills to offer. It was this that had pushed her on. Remembering her youth made her feel acutely miserable. It had not been youth in the way the young lived now, even those in service.

"Ah, well, I see you probably have to do some more thinking on it. You've a smart head on your shoulders, I've noticed. Remember yourself at fifteen, and don't let duty to the family and your job take away your compassion for what it was like to be scared, out of your depth, and vulnerable." Stafford stood aside from his collection of mosses and looked across at her, sitting on the bench in the sun, confounded and uncertain, and he said, "Violet was a good girl. So why did the poor little thing run off, leaving her sick dad all alone? I heard at the Goat last night the poor man's taken another turn for the worse. It always happens with these lungers—worry and distress can break them down faster than anything." He returned to the bench and sat down next to her. She felt his nearness and liked the scent of his freshly laundered linen shirt, which was open at the neck, where she saw three gray hairs. She looked away, rigid with embarrassment and shame. She wished he would go back to his mosses; his nearness was disconcerting and her heart was beating rapidly. She stood up and smoothed her hands down the front of her dress.

"Thank you, Mr. Stafford, you are most kind, really. Yes, you are right, I must think about this from another angle." She glanced at her watch. It was half past nine. "Oh, I must be getting on."

"I know you'll come to it, Mrs. Jackson. It might take a bit of work, but I'm sure you can do it." He turned back to planting his moss garden.

An hour later, she was standing in front of Lady Montfort with the most surprising request. "I would like the day off, m'lady. It will not inconvenience Mr. Hollyoak." Mrs. Jackson then briefly explained her reasons.

"Well of course, Jackson, I am surprised we didn't think of this before. Of course you must go. We'd better get Simpson to drive you to the station if you want to catch the next one up to town. Take all the time you need," Lady Montfort replied as she rang for the chauffeur.

Chapter Twenty-five

Sitting alone in her second-class compartment, Mrs. Jackson looked out of the window as the train, sending out a plume of thick, oily black smoke and cinders into the pure air, trundled heavily through a shallow valley of fields and copses.

Over the hill to the north lay Haversham Hall and Iyntwood, and to the south, over the brow of another hill, lay Cryer's Breech. Market Wingley was already several miles distant and she had been on the train only five minutes. It had taken just five minutes to cross the only world she had known for nearly twenty years. It had been nearly two years since Mrs. Jackson had traveled alone by train up to London, so her sense of adventure was almost overpowering. The train rocked in a comfortable rhythm as it picked up speed and Mrs. Jackson gazed unseeing out of the windows. In her mind she saw Haversham village: the church on the edge of the green; village women as they gathered at the pump; the men grouped at the forge as Bernard Oldshaw shod the great, round feet of shire horses while the plowman leaned against the door of the Goat and Fiddle with half a tankard of cider, enjoying a moment of respite from his labors. It was an idyllic image and Mrs. Jackson knew it was one much prized in the hearts of the English, especially when they were abroad. She was also aware, however, that behind it lay narrowness and an insularity that prevented any comprehension of life in a wider world.

Her thoughts of the village led her back to Violet. Since her conversation with Stafford, she reflected that she was perhaps rather intransigent when it came to stepping outside her own experience and what she considered the proper way of doing things. She had acquired status in the house of an important family by often having to squash down her personal needs and sensitivities, to accomplish her lofty status. She had perhaps sacrificed almost too much to attain her position, and now she found it hard to step away from the rigid conventions she clung to and find compassion for the likes of Violet. She had forgotten how hard it was to fit in to a strange new culture with its own language and government.

She had initially believed that Violet had chosen to run off, but around the edges of this belief now crept the beginning of doubt. Wouldn't it be too daunting for a village girl to leave this known rural backwater and venture out with no idea of what was waiting for her in the great wide world? What if Violet had been forced to run away by something she had witnessed on the night of the ball, perhaps the murder of Teddy Mallory? Mrs. Jackson was a practical woman. She was on the whole well meaning and kind, but she was not blessed with a rich imagination. She left all that sort of stuff to Lady Montfort.

Her train pulled into Marylebone station on time at seven minutes past one. As she got down onto the platform it took her a moment to adjust to the noise and throng of passengers alighting from the train. It was hard to get her bearings with carriage doors slamming like volleys of gunfire. The harsh hiss and clash of steam engines pulling out from other platforms was disorienting. She startled at the train conductor's shrill whistle and the whir of a flock of pigeons as they flew up to roost in the vaulted glass roof. She joined the orderly crowd walking toward the ticket collector and stopped to look for the Bakerloo Underground sign, causing people to step around her. Her tuppenny tube ticket was tucked into the inside of her glove so that she didn't drop it as she clutched the handrail of the escalator, steeply descending deep into the underworld.

She hadn't ridden on an underground train in well over five years. The Bakerloo line was new, she now remembered. At the bottom of the escalator she turned left and walked along the brightly lit, white-tiled tunnel to the station. On the platform, she had to hold on to her hat as a gust of warm, stale air preceded the hum of the train in the tunnel before it clattered into the station, shining with lights, glossy painted maroon coachwork, and gleaming glass. Twenty minutes later she rose to the street and a mass of traffic. The noise was deafening: horse-drawn cabs, motorcars and omnibuses, errand boys on bicycles, and pedestrians—all competed for right-of-way as they swept past her, dexterously weaving in and out among one another, and another horde of the same spun by in the opposite direction. A tall police constable blew his whistle and threw up his right arm to stop traffic, and she joined a group of people crossing to the other side of the street, where she asked directions to Clevellan Square.

When at last she arrived at the house and walked down the area steps below street level to the servants' entrance, she felt she had come a thousand miles from another country and had made every step of the way as a pioneer in some foreign land.

It was a scullery maid who answered the door and indicated

with a wrinkled, soap-stained hand that Mrs. Jackson should walk through into the butler's pantry. Mr. Evesham greeted her with great civility, unusual in butlers to domestic staff from other houses; Lady Montfort must have called ahead. She followed the butler down the dimly lit central corridor to the far side of the house. He opened the garden door and out she went and up steps to arrive at last in the house's large walled garden, which took up the entire center of the square. There among the trees, sitting in a lawn chair, as pretty as a watercolor and as if Holloway Prison existed only on the front page of *The Times,* sat Lucinda Lambert-Lambert.

"Good afternoon, Mrs. Jackson," she said politely, sitting up a little straighter and indicating a chair next to her. "I hope you had a pleasant journey." She sounded like a little girl playing at tea parties; her words came out self-consciously, almost haltingly, as if Lucinda was listening to them carefully and checking herself for adult inflection and manner.

Mrs. Jackson sat down but did not presume on the invitation; she sat on the very edge of the chair, her hands in her lap. She returned Lucinda's greeting just as carefully.

"I am very relieved to see you looking well, Miss Lucinda, after that awful experience. It must have been quite dreadful in . . ." Mrs. Jackson was careful to keep any judgment about Lucinda's recent doings out of her expression and voice.

". . . Prison," Lucinda firmly finished for her. "Actually, that was the point of it all, to go to prison. Yes, it was an awful experience. I believe it is supposed to be." This condescending statement was in such contrast to Lucinda's pretty-picture-book appearance that Mrs. Jackson was jolted out of her tactful consideration toward the girl. *Goodness me,* she thought, *what a self-righteous little prig.*

She remembered the Lambert-Lamberts patiently standing in the hall at Iyntwood, waiting for the telephone to ring. Feelings of annoyance and impatience began to gather and then evaporated when she noticed that Lucinda looked very pale, and there were dark smudges under her eyes and her lips were dry and cracked. Lucinda must have felt her sympathy rather than her irritation, as she continued with little less bravado.

"The whole thing was frightful, but I had to do it, had to do my bit," the girl muttered and folded her thumbs into her fists. Mrs. Jackson had already noticed how bitten-down the nails were. She understood that Lucinda had naïvely taken on what she believed to be a just and deserving cause out of a passionate need to be useful. The poor girl was probably under the impression that she had joined a noble crusade and that right would prevail over might. Mrs. Jackson's understanding of the political machinations of their modern world was limited, but she understood human nature. She knew enough to recognize the pitfalls of the hidden ambitions involved where the suffragette cause was concerned—the Pankhurst women on one side and the home secretary, Mr. McKenna, and the government on the other. Nothing was as it seemed; there were always hidden agendas.

"Holloway was hellish, but they'd told me it would be," Lucinda went on. "The noise was the worst because you can't see what's going on. They keep WSPU prisoners in the horridest part of the building, poor, brave things. Most of them were striking."

No doubt she was referring to the hunger strikes, thought Mrs. Jackson. Accounts of them in the newspapers had been hair-raising. Now there was this Cat and Mouse Act, which meant that they released starving women from prison before they died, to allow them to recover, and then put them back in prison. It was a form of suicide or murder in itself, depending on how one looked at it. It got the government off the hook if their prison inmates starved themselves to the point of death in prison but died conveniently at home.

She listened as Lucinda spoke of her forty-nine hours in Holloway. Female wardens built like men, who smelled of sweat and greasy unwashed hair, and their refusal to let her be with other political prisoners; the oppressive silence that fell between the sound of heavy footsteps on hard stone and the ceaseless slamming and locking of heavy doors; and, worst of all, the voices of women calling out in entreaty, pain, or outrage. It would have been an appalling experience for gently reared Lucinda, Mrs. Jackson thought, alone in her cell, left to imagine the worst . . . The girl was evidently still suffering the effects of her ordeal.

Mrs. Jackson was not unsympathetic but she was in London for another reason, and it was one that mattered far more than the self-induced fears of an indulged girl who had spent a couple of nights in prison before her father rescued her. She leaned forward with her eyebrows raised in polite inquiry; it was an expression that worked well on housemaids, and she found it had its effect on Lucinda.

"You didn't come to hear about all of that, Mrs. Jackson." She watched Lucinda push back a long lock of hair that had fallen out from under her hat. It refused to stay put and slid down again, and she spun the end of it around her forefinger.

"I am very sorry for everything that happened to you, Miss Lucinda, but I am sure you have heard what happened at Iyntwood." She sat in her chair, back straight, signaling that she had heard enough about Holloway.

"Yes, I have, Mrs. Jackson. Terrible news about Teddy, I had no idea. Mother says there was a gang of people who had followed him down from London. It was an awful, terrible thing to have happened." Lucinda's voice was flat and expressionless.

"Yes, quite dreadful." Mrs. Jackson kept her voice neutral, as if she were talking about missing a bus, or dropping sixpence down the drain. It sounded too dismissive, so she added truthfully at the last moment, "Poor young man, he certainly didn't deserve that end."

"Poor young man my foot! He was a thug and a dreadful bully. Do you know what he did to Violet?"

Mrs. Jackson did not know, but in the last few hours she had groped toward the possibility of what might have happened to Violet, and then shied away from the thought. But this was why she was here, to find out, so she nodded, encouraging Lucinda to continue.

"If you knew, why didn't you stop it?" Mistaking Mrs. Jackson's nod of encouragement as one of knowledge, Lucinda's tired, blank face became animated and more hair slid down from under her hat.

In a reasonable and quiet tone Mrs. Jackson assured her that no one had had an inkling of what had happened to Violet, not even now.

"I can't imagine how they didn't— When I saw her on the night of the ball, she was terrified, incapable of speech. How could you have not known? It was a continual thing, you know . . . his . . . his, well . . . what he did to her. She was desperate, with no one to go to in that blasted house."

Mrs. Jackson tried to slow things down. She said quietly, "Of course something would have been done to protect Violet, had we known. But she . . ."

"Somehow," Lucinda shot her a reproachful look, "the poor girl had got it into her head that Teddy's wicked treatment of her was her fault, that she had behaved improperly." Lucinda's voice was low and she almost spat the words. There were two bright spots of pink on her cheeks and, to Mrs. Jackson's wary eye, something almost deranged in her fervent expression.

"He was at it almost as soon as Violet started work at the house." If she had wanted to see Mrs. Jackson flinch, she was rewarded. "You had no idea, did you?" Mrs. Jackson shook her head. "Apparently you told her not to catch anyone's eye when she was working upstairs, and to avoid conversation altogether with the family. She hoped that if she steered clear of Teddy, he would leave her alone. But of course he didn't. He stalked her through the house in the early morning when she was working, when she was cleaning the fireplaces, when he was sure she was alone, the little weasel. He always waited for her in the dark. It makes me ill to think of the terror she endured and the pain she suffered. She told no one at all. She was ashamed, you see, petrified every time she heard that Teddy was coming down to Iyntwood. Can you imagine living like that? I can't." Lucinda was completely out of breath. She licked her dry lips and frowned off into the shrubbery.

It dawned on Mrs. Jackson that having just spent a couple of the most frightening days of her young life, Lucinda had given herself Violet as a cause to strive for and perhaps as a justification for the crushing embarrassment she had caused her kindly and well-meaning parents. Evidently Lucinda was not done.

"There are so many of them: young girls, working long hours in factories, sweatshops, on farms, and in houses; alone, afraid, and abused by little scugs like Teddy." Lucinda's voice sounded too shrill, her sharp face looked angular and mean, her eyebrows were down, and she glared at Mrs. Jackson from under them.

Lucinda's escalating wrath caused Mrs. Jackson to become very still. Her heart beat at an alarming rate and her blouse collar cut into her neck. *Oh dear God,* she thought, *here it is. Now she's going to tell me.* She fought down a rush of panic. *How stupidly I have blundered in here. She's going to tell me how she manhandled Mr. Mallory's tied and gagged body up onto that dray and hid it in the storage box. She's tall enough, she's strong enough, and she's angry enough. She could have done it given the time, and Mr. Mallory was such a slightly built young man. She walked over to the stable block to meet him, knocked him on the head, and then tied him up. Then she drove the dray up to Crow Wood, and hanged him from the gibbet. All she had to do was drive forward.* She jumped as Lucinda laughed.

"If you could just see the expression on your face, Mrs. Jackson, it's almost laughable. What do you think I did?"

"I can't imagine, Miss Lucinda." She heard the whisper of her voice and tried to pull herself together. She squared her shoulders and waited.

"Oh yes you can imagine, Mrs. Jackson. You can imagine very well what I did, and that is why you are here, isn't it?" Lucinda had regained some control of herself. Her face was still white but her eyes were not as fierce as they had been. She was fully in control now.

"You don't want to say?" She laughed cheerily, just like she had when she was a naughty little girl. "All right then, I'll be a good sport and tell you what happened.

"As long as Violet worked in the house, Teddy would hurt her and bully her, until he got bored and moved on to some other poor girl. No one could stop him but me."

Mrs. Jackson exhaled slowly, a long, shaky breath.

Lucinda laughed. "Oh no, Mrs. Jackson, you are quite wrong. I didn't need to kill Teddy. There were plenty of other people who wanted to do that. They were practically lining up."

"Well, I didn't think you had . . ." She was gratified to hear that her voice was as smooth as glass, despite the pounding in her ears of her fast-beating heart.

"Oh yes you did!" Lucinda laughed again. "On the night of the ball I was outside alone at the front of the house wondering when I could decently leave, and Violet came running along in the dark. Teddy had got his hands on her again, and all she could think of was getting as far away from the house as she could. Luckily I was there to stop her. I knew she hadn't a hope of finding a decent place to go to, that she would be in as much danger out there as she was in the house. But I knew I could help her. I told her I'd take care of her. I told her to go and change out of her uniform and then I took her up to my room and we waited there for the ball to be over and when it was quiet and the storm was over, I took her with me up to London."

Mrs. Jackson felt relief wash through her like a drink of cold water, and she heard herself ask, with understandable trepidation, where Violet was now. She imagined Violet chained to railings outside the Houses of Parliament or filling bottles with petrol in the basement of some suffragette stronghold; even worse, languishing in Holloway with other women encouraging her to go on a hunger strike.

"She's quite safe, you know, she's with friends of mine."

Here was Lucinda's triumphant moment, and privately Mrs. Jackson would have liked to give her a good slap. Neither did Lucinda's news reassure her. *Which friends?* she thought. *Where?* She swallowed and tried to keep her voice even.

"I hope you'll trust me with Violet's address. I'll understand if she doesn't want to come back to Iyntwood, but I would like to talk to her and tell her how sorry I am we let her down. All of us."

"Yes," said Lucinda, "all of you—all of us in fact. All women, all let down. Women like you, Mrs. Jackson, and young women like me." Mrs. Jackson could tell that Lucinda was about to embark on the suffragette cause and the plight of the working-class woman again. She didn't think she could bear another political harangue. If Lucinda wanted to spend her life fighting for women's suffrage and the rights of the working poor, that was her choice to make. All Mrs. Jackson wanted to know now was where Violet was. She said quickly before Lucinda could get going, "Her father is desperately worried too . . ."

"No, he's not, Mrs. Jackson. Jim Simkins knows exactly where Violet is. You didn't really expect me to spirit her away and leave her father to wonder for the rest of his life where she could be?"

Lucinda was quite calm now; no doubt she saw her motives as beyond reproach, thought Mrs. Jackson. Rescuing Violet was Lucinda's redemption for her outrageous behavior and in her mind she had done a very good job of it.

"Violet wrote him a letter while we were waiting up in my room to leave the house. She reassured him that she was being taken care of, and had been given a splendid new start in her life, far better than being a working skivvy for indifferent employers, at any rate."

Oh Lord, back on the soap box again, thought Mrs. Jackson as Lucinda continued. "Employers who take advantage of women with overwork, poor pay, terrible working conditions, and abuse. With the right government, voted in by women themselves, we can begin to make . . ."

Mrs. Jackson closed her eyes momentarily as she sat in the sun-filtered shade. The garden's high walls shut out most of the noise and hubbub of London traffic, but it was a dull, irritating hum in the background. She had worked long hours and days all her life, days of monotonous drudgery when she was younger. There was no trade union for domestic service and she wasn't sure that if there were, it would make a huge difference in the long run. She allowed Lucinda's voice to join the background drone of London traffic.

The garden door from the kitchen swung shut and she opened a wary eye. A white cap and a lacy apron fluttered crisply against a smart, violet gingham dress, as a young maid walked across the lawn carrying a large silver tray. She was very young, about fifteen years old, a pretty girl with dark brown hair and large deep blue eyes that flitted from Lucinda to Mrs. Jackson to the garden table laden with newspapers, pens, pencils, and books. She stood for a moment, apprehensive and unsure. Mrs. Jackson rose from her chair and cleared the clutter off the table so that she could put the tray down. The maid did so without speaking or lifting her eyes. She stepped backward, hands behind her back, eyes down, as she had been trained to, then turned and walked briskly back to the house, hands by her sides. On the table were a jug of lemonade, two glasses, and some little things to eat.

Lucinda's voice became less animated and Mrs. Jackson sat back down.

"I would tell you where she is, but I think it would be wrong to burst in on her and frighten her with apologies. She doesn't want to return to the village, or the house. She has a much better job near Cambridge, working in a bookshop, and she's very happy there; she's made friends . . ."

"So quickly, in the space of less than a week?" was all Mrs. Jackson could think of to say.

"Yes, Mrs. Jackson, in less than a week. Now that you know how Violet got away from the house, and why she had to leave, I suppose you'll have to tell Lady Montfort . . ." There was not an ounce of self-blame about her, thought Mrs. Jackson as she prudently maintained a respectful silence.

"I expect you could do with a glass of lemonade after that." Lucinda leaned forward in her chair. "Now tell me I did the right thing."

Chapter Twenty-six

Mrs. Jackson left Clevellan Square in a sort of trance and walked back along the Bayswater Road. Before she got to Lancaster Gate she crossed the street and turned into the Marlborough entrance to Hyde Park. Almost immediately the stink of petrol fumes and the racket of engines and horns receded. She was feeling light-headed and hungry; the glass of lemonade she had had with Lucinda had been too tart, and it was sloshing around in her empty stomach, making her feel queasy. Now that her initial alarm about Violet was allayed, she was not pleased that Lucinda had spirited Violet away from the house, leaving everyone to believe that anything could have happened to her; in fact, she was furious with her. Lucinda's rescue had denied them all the right to have helped Violet in their own way; she felt it was a vengeful act, an act of spite on the Lucinda's part.

She stopped for a while and stood under a large plane tree, engrossed in her thoughts. Perhaps Lucinda had taken Violet to provide a distraction. Perhaps she had taken Violet to conceal her as a witness to Teddy's murder. It was quite possible; there had been almost a spark of madness about Lucinda when she had talked about Teddy, and her hatred of him had been palpable. If Lucinda had murdered Teddy, she had to have had help and taking Violet away had been part of her overall plan. Mrs. Jackson wondered about Lord Haversham. She didn't want to think of him in connection with Teddy's death, but he could have been involved. Since childhood he had always been under Lucinda's sway and they were still the greatest of friends. Lady Montfort would have been perfectly happy for her son to marry her, until Lucinda started demanding independence and said she wanted to study medicine and be an independent working woman.

If Lord Haversham had known about Mr. Mallory's treatment of Violet, that would have been enough to stir him to action. She remembered Lady Montfort's account of Lord Haversham's rage toward Mr. Mallory at the boathouse. Yes, of course it made sense to his mother that he was angry about his dog. But she remembered quite clearly the young Lord Haversham whacking the living daylights out of the Boswell boy when he pushed Lady Althea out of the tree house. He was so incensed by the boy's bullying that Mr. Thrower had had to pull him away.

Her stomach lurched and Mrs. Jackson looked at her wristwatch. *What was she thinking? She was so tired that she had lost her sense of proportion.* Lord Haversham was incapable of murder. She needed food and she needed the quiet of her train ride home for reflection. She had plenty of time to eat a late meal and then catch the half past four from Marylebone. She quickened her pace and turned right down the West Carriage Drive and alongside the Serpentine.

When Mrs. Jackson had been in service as a very young housemaid she had spent her one afternoon off a month in Hyde Park if the weather was fine. Now, she stopped at a drinking fountain to dilute the acidic taste of lemonade, and then walked on up the Broad Walk. There were the usual crowds at Speakers' Corner. Without stopping, she brushed through several groups; someone was shouting that the end of the world was nigh, as usual. The Salvation Army was packing up their trumpets, trombones, and drums, having spent a profitable morning saving sinners from the evils of drink. The crowd around them dispersed and re-formed around another soapbox evangelizer. This time it was a woman. Actually there were three of them, and they wore the purple, white, and green sashes of the WSPU. The older woman started to speak, and two police constables who had been hanging around, enjoying the Sally Army band and their hymn singing, now stood to attention. The woman was a good speaker. She had a strong voice and spoke with conviction, but Mrs. Jackson had heard it all before, just twenty minutes ago from Lucinda. The crowd at first glance appeared unsympathetic and there was jeering from the lower element, but Mrs. Jackson noticed that a great many quite respectable men and women listened attentively and were annoyed at the continued interruptions from the louts and layabouts in the crowd. She shouldered her way around the outside of the crowd, her stomach growling, and made her way out of the park to the Lyons' Corner House at Marble Arch. She would treat herself to a jolly good mixed grill before she caught the train, and with a full stomach and hopefully a quiet compartment she would be able to think through what she had learned from Lucinda and her new fears at the possible involvement of the Talbots' son and heir.

She caught her train with minutes to spare. A little breathlessly she took out her Bradshaw to check at which time she would arrive at Cryer's Breech. To her horror, she found that she was on the Manchester express train, which was now clattering through the dreary outskirts of London and gathering speed. She would be in Market Wingley in twenty minutes and then there would be . . . she thumbed desperately to the next page . . . there would be a connection from Market Wingley to Cryer's Breech an hour and twenty minutes later via Little Buffenden. Her journey home had just stretched into nearly two hours. Now she would be hanging around in Market Wingley for an hour, what a waste of time. But being the resilient soul she that was, she thought perhaps it could be turned into a useful hour. She could walk to Harper's drapery, just ten minutes from the station, and spend some time looking at the new things they had for summer and pick up the black crepe for the servants' armbands for the funeral tomorrow. She relaxed and enjoyed the reckless sensation of traveling at high speed; someone had told her that the express could run nearly sixty miles in one hour.

She turned her mind to considering the business of Lucinda and her determination to rescue Violet in such a strangely unpredictable way. Try as she might she couldn't understand how Violet had been accosted by Teddy on the night of the ball in the garden. She had accepted that Violet had been out and about, because she now knew that it had been Violet on the backstairs. But what was the girl doing outside at that time? Of course she had been rather dense about Elsie's involvement with Horace Wobbley so perhaps she needed to address this issue a little more thoroughly. Had Violet had an assignation with someone? Remembering Stafford's advice to her, she instructed herself to think about the situation from a different angle entirely, and she was still deep in thought when the train pulled into Market Wingley.

* * *

Mrs. Jackson liked Market Wingley. It was a quiet, prosperous country town with a large open market square, empty today, and a hotel and ostlery on the south side. From the cobbled square pleasant streets radiated out into the town, with plenty of shops selling useful items. She never went to town on Wednesdays, when the streets were packed with farmers and their families up to town for market day. All the taverns and pubs were full of red-faced farmers drinking beer, and the teashops were crowded with their wives and daughters. But today the streets were quiet and it took Mrs. Jackson just a few minutes to walk to Harper's, which was in a narrow street that backed the market square.

The bell tinkled as Mrs. Jackson walked into the shop's deep and narrow interior. She looked down the tall mahogany and glass counter that ran down the right-hand-side of the shop, with display cases underneath presenting a fascinating array of numerous sundries: crochet hooks, darning needles, buttons, clasps, hooks and eyes, embroidery silks, and skeins of wool. Mrs. Jackson particularly liked the wall behind the counter with its rolled bolts of fabric on shelves. A captivating array of colored materials carefully graded in color and fabric from serviceable drab wool to crisp white linen, brightly printed cotton, and vibrant glossy silks, all exuding the particularly pleasant, stringent, sharp smell of formaldehyde used in the fabrics' dressings: the smell of newness. Pausing to admire a bolt of shot blue silk on display in the center of the room, Mrs. Jackson looked around for an assistant to help her with her simple purchase. She knew most of the people who worked in the shop, but they were busy measuring, cutting, and parceling materials for their customers. She was turning back to a display case of machine-made lace that was almost as good as the real thing, if you hadn't seen the real thing, which Mrs. Jackson had, when she noticed Mr. Wallace at the end of the shop. He had just finished serving a customer and was sliding a tray of black shoe buttons under the display top of the counter.

"Mr. Wallace, good afternoon." Mrs. Jackson approached the counter.

"Good afternoon, madam. It's Mrs. Jackson from Iyntwood, isn't it? You must have come in about the crepe. It's all ready for you, if you will excuse me a moment."

He returned with a neat stack of black crepe strips. "Not particularly heavy, Mrs. Jackson, but it's funny how parcels seem to get heavier the further you carry them. Far to go? Oh I see, to the station. Well, David will accompany you."

Mrs. Jackson thanked him.

"There is no need to tell you how very sad we were to hear the news of Mr. Mallory's . . . terrible accident," said in a low voice, his eyes downcast. "Everyone here offers the family our sincerest condolences."

"Thank you, Mr. Wallace, and how . . ." She looked down at his nimble hands as they made a tidy portable package of brown paper tied with string, and a loop for carrying. There was no sign of a bandage on his injured wrist. "I heard about your unfortunate accident and I'm pleased to see that your wrist is on the mend." He looked up at her, a little surprised perhaps that she had noticed.

"Doing very nicely, thank you, Mrs. Jackson. It was nothing at all, really, just a silly rick. Hurt like the dickens at the time, of course. Thank you for asking. I was so disappointed not to be able to play at the ball. I heard it all went off very well." He finished with his parcel and called to the errand boy to accompany her back to the station.

It was a mystifying little moment, but one that didn't cause Mrs. Jackson a second thought. She was far more preoccupied with how she would find the words to explain to Lady Montfort the reason why Violet had had to run away from the house.

Chapter Twenty-seven

Clementine was up very early the morning after Teddy Mallory's funeral. Careful not to appear too eagerly enthusiastic, the Talbots and their house guests all assembled after breakfast in groups in the hall and on the drive, the women exchanging last cries of regret at having ever to leave at all. Gertrude, particularly, wanted to reassure Clementine that indeed she was grateful for their friendship and for Clementine's loyalty and kindness. She drew her friend away from the throng of departure.

"Going to the Desboroughs' ball next Friday in town?" Gertrude asked her friend as they said goodbye.

"Oh no, Gertrude, I don't think we will; so much to take care of here. But please say hello to Evelyn for me."

"I will, if we go. Hugo is in bate, and I am playing it by ear right now. I feel so drained, I just want to sleep for a week."

"Rest and take some time."

"Yes, all very well for you to say, but I end up being so terribly bored. Well, my dear Clemmy, kindest of friends, thank you—it was undoubtedly memorable." They laughed self-consciously and Clementine knew she would not see Gertrude for a few weeks. There was a lot they both had to erase from the memories of the last week.

"Gertrude, please take care," she said as her friend turned and walked toward her waiting husband and the motorcar.

"Don't you ever worry about me . . . too much, Clemmy," said Gertrude.

Standing next to her husband by the front door, Clementine spent the next hour saying fond goodbyes to their guests as if nothing untoward had occurred during their stay.

"Goodbye, and thank you," she said to the Ambroses. "See you at the Waterfords'."

"Goodbye, it was delightful," the Ambroses called out, leaping happily into their motorcar; with so much luggage, they had brought the Lanchester just for that.

"Goodbye, Sir Wilfred and dear Olive, goodbye. Yes of course, if you have left anything at all we will send it on . . . no problem at all."

Downstairs, Mrs. Jackson watched Mable Thwaite, who was leaning up against the scullery door, shouting instructions to Mary and alternatively calling out to Iris in the pantry. Strategically placed as she was, there was no need for her to move an inch, so as she issued her commands she barely turned her head in either direction. Mrs. Jackson gritted her teeth. Mrs. Thwaite would be needed in the kitchen to supervise luncheon in a moment, she thought, as she tried to give instructions to Agnes, Dick, Elsie, and two women from the village who had come up to help put the house back to order for the next few days. She turned in irritation to ask Mrs. Thwaite to lower her voice, then decided not to. Mrs. Thwaite had news and it was important that she was the first to relay it. As Mrs. Jackson had learned the hard way, it was important to keep abreast of belowstairs gossip.

"Did you hear about Northcombe House? Didn't think you had. They had a burglary there on the night of our ball. Yes, thought that would catch your interest. Saw Mrs. Cumberbunch at the church for the funeral and she told me everything; all the Staunton family jewels, which were worth a packet—gone just like that. They weren't even aware they had been burgled until the maid went to put the jewels Lady Staunton had worn to our ball back in the silver safe the next day, and it was wiped clean. Not one of the servants saw or heard a thing. Their butler is practically a geriatric so that would explain it. Course, they are covered by Lloyd's of London, but you can't replace tradition and history, can you?"

Mrs. Jackson listened to exclamations and a babble of excited chatter from maids and footmen alike; it was a joy to hear bad news that didn't feature Iyntwood. The strain of the last week was beginning to lift, she thought. There were no more policemen asking nosy questions and insinuating violent and improbable behavior. Visiting servants had mercifully gone, and one could actually move around the servants' hall without having to say "pardon" all the time. There was an atmosphere of holiday in the air.

As Mrs. Jackson started once again on her instructions to her group, Mr. Hollyoak came into the servants' dining room. He was drawn up to his full height and was patently upset and offended.

"Well, Mrs. Jackson," he said, his face quite red with annoyance. "Horrid, nasty little animal! If you could see the state of Lady Booth's room, dog hair everywhere. Behind the sofa . . .

yes, Mrs. Jackson, behind the sofa, are dog droppings; must have gone there this morning. It's like having a pig in the house."

Did Hollyoak mean the pug or Lady Booth? Agnes obviously thought so, because she bent over in a fit of giggles.

"Agnes, stop it at once." Mr. Hollyoak had had enough. His voice, sharp with irritation, cut across the servants' hall, and Mrs. Jackson hastily went over to the maid as Agnes gulped down tearful laughter. "The events of the last week have had a disgraceful impact on the discipline in this house."

"Yes, indeed they have Mr. Hollyoak." Mrs. Jackson took Agnes by the shoulder and steered her away. "Pull yourself together, Agnes. Now go up to the room and clean behind the sofa; open the windows and spread baking soda on the carpet. Later this evening, dust it up and wash the area with a *very* dilute solution of vinegar and warm water. Agnes? Agnes? Are you listening to me?"

"Yes, Mrs. Jackson, I am on my way now . . . baking soda and later diluted vinegar water . . ." Agnes stuffed her apron in her mouth to stop herself from another bout of hilarity.

Mrs. Jackson turned back to Mr. Hollyoak. He was still fuming.

"What is it about some guests, Mrs. Jackson? I mean, letting a dog go in the house!"

Mrs. Jackson listened with sympathy; she could tell Mr. Hollyoak was exhausted. How old was he now, fifty-eight or fifty-nine? This week had been hard on all of them, but it had taken its toll on her old comrade. She closed her ledger, tucked it under her arm, and walked behind the butler toward his pantry.

"Time for a sit-down and a nice cup of tea, Mr. Hollyoak. Everyone is working to your directions, perhaps you can take a little time? I'll get Elsie to bring in a tray to you. Been a long week, and considering everything that's been thrown at us, I think everyone has stood up very well. Training will out, as you so often have said."

Hollyoak turned at his pantry door as he said, "Yes indeed, Mrs. Jackson, they have done a sterling job, every one of them. I am especially pleased with young Dick. You know something? He was completely in step with me on the night of the ball, I didn't have to ask twice, he pulled out all the stops . . . anticipating every single thing." Remembering Dick's sterling performance helped him return to his stately manner. He nodded to her, knowing she would understand the importance of proper training. A disciplined and trained army was how Baden-Powell had triumphed at Mafeking; it was why the empire continued to prosper. Training, discipline, and pride in the work one did. Mrs. Jackson had heard it a hundred times. But Hollyoak was proudly remembering Dick's victory on the night of the ball, which in some way reflected his own dedicated service in the Boer War.

"Yes, he's a bright lad, Mr. Hollyoak, and shows promise. Worth the extra effort to bring him on, don't you think?" she said, hoping to circumvent Mafeking.

"Oh yes, I think so. Of course he needs to learn the importance of punctuality. Almost perfect performance throughout that night, but went missing towards the end. Couldn't find him anywhere, but I kept *that* to myself, what with all this nosiness going on in the house."

"Oh really, Mr. Hollyoak, went missing when?"

"Must have been right at the end, just before four o'clock. One moment he was in waiting on the terrace, the next moment he had vanished, reappeared about twenty minutes later of course. Have to have a little word with him about that . . ." He sat down at his desk and closed his eyes for a moment.

"Well, he'd been at it for eighteen hours at that time; perhaps he needed a little break," she said, knowing that he would understand the need to get off your feet at the end of a long day. But no, she had miscalculated Hollyoak's belief in discipline, order, and obedience—they were precepts to die by.

"I give the little breaks in this house, Mrs. Jackson," he reminded her.

"Yes, of course you do, Mr. Hollyoak. I'll go and get you a nice cup of tea."

Having spent the greater part of her day confronting the stark truths that had emerged as a result of her visit to Lucinda, Mrs. Jackson felt drained by the enormity of this new intelligence, but her day in London had at least given her the opportunity to leave the stifling atmosphere of the servants' hall for a while. Now on her return she found it almost impossible to order her thoughts, and even with the departure of the visiting horde of servants, belowstairs still felt crowded and claustrophobic. She knew that at any moment Lady Montfort would ring for her and want to hear the outcome of her visit to London, and she dreaded this moment.

She realized that for the first time in over a week she had not had a moment to enjoy her usual late-evening walk. A turn in the grounds would clear her head and give her a moment alone to decide on the proper approach to take over the subject of Violet, she decided, as she wrapped a shawl around her shoulders and stepped out into the cool night air of the kitchen courtyard.

James and John were standing in the dairy-room door, smoking and laughing at the sort of joke that footmen particularly enjoy. Dick was sitting on the top step of the scullery door, cleaning his boots, his face turned expectantly toward them; one day Dick would wear house livery, smoke his cigarette cupped protectively in his hand, and laugh at some shared observation that only footmen are privy to—the footman's world of upstairs gossip and intrigue.

But Mrs. Jackson had had enough of servants'-hall gossip. She walked out of the courtyard in the direction of the lake. It was a beautiful night, with enough of a moon to light the way.

She paced along the path, immersed in thought. At the edge of the shrubbery she stopped and gazed out onto the dark surface of the lake. A cool breeze ruffled the surface, causing the reflection of the moon to shiver and jump. She unclenched her jaw, took a deep breath, and rehearsed her opening words to Lady Montfort: *It would seem that Violet had every reason to run away . . .* and stopped. Perhaps it would be better if she let Lady Montfort begin; her ladyship was always brimming with questions. *Get a grip on yourself, Edith, for heaven's sake,* she told herself. *Just open up your mouth and get the words out. There's no right way to say them. And you do have to say them, so just get on with it.*

Far off in the woodland she heard the sharp, eerie territorial cry of a vixen hunting, and a nightjar churred in the park beyond the lake. Behind her she heard a slight rustle in the rhododendrons as field mice went about their business. She returned to her thoughts, immersed in an imaginary conversation with her ladyship. Again a movement behind her, and she almost wished she had brought one of the dogs.

She was about to turn when the rustles in the undergrowth

behind her coalesced into one definite and solid sound as something altogether heavier and larger than mice came up directly behind her. A cold, strong hand closed over her mouth and her head was jerked back to rest against the chest of a tall man, wearing what felt like a heavy tweed overcoat. She felt herself lifted easily by a powerful arm around her waist as she was pulled backward into the shrubbery, off the path.

Her neck was stretched so far back that she could barely swallow, and she felt her heart convulse in a bounding leap to fill her throat, where it seemed there was no space to contain it.

There was silence, except for his harsh breath in her ear and the sound of her own thudding pulse in her head. Mrs. Jackson tried not to give way to an overwhelming flood of fear. She could barely breathe as adrenaline coursed through her in painful, prickling waves.

Finally he spoke: "Keep quite still; one twist will have your neck." He tightened his hand on her mouth, and she felt stifled.

Keep still? She was too frightened to move. *Find calm,* she instructed herself, *be calm.*

He spoke again: "Now then, Mrs. Nosy Parker." The voice seemed familiar but his tone certainly wasn't. No one she knew ever spoke to her like that. She felt the beginning of indignation and it helped her push back against unreasoning fear.

"You be a good girl now. Keep quiet and listen hard." The hand on her mouth was clean; it smelled of soap, its skin smooth. The coat her head was pressed up against was of good quality. This wasn't the tramp, the London stranger. But it wasn't the voice of a gentleman, either.

"Been prying, haven't you, Edith?" *He knew her name, then.* "Been poking that long nose about and we don't like that."

Her mind struggled to remember the many men who had

been at the house in the past week: visiting servants, chauffeurs, and valets. She waited for him to speak again.

"Now, Edith, we know what you've been up to and we don't like it. No more of this taking an interest. No more running nosy errands for her ladyship sitting up there in her big house. Understand? Otherwise . . ." he stroked down the length of her taut throat, reached the hollow at its base, and tapped hard twice, "we don't know what we'll do.

"Now then, girlie, just stand there nice and quiet. Don't turn around until I've gone. Count to a hundred, then you can go back to the house and fold your napkins and arrange some flowers, and everything will be all right. The very last thing we want is for someone to get hurt. Just say 'yes' if I have made myself quite clear." He lifted his hand off her mouth.

She obediently said yes and was released. She gasped in cool air, her mind racing through possibilities.

Two hands descended on her shoulders and held her still for a moment, and then he was gone.

Now she felt fear, real fear. It swept through her in ice-cold waves. Her knees buckled and she fell to the ground. She remained there on all fours like a frightened hedgerow creature. She felt faint, giddy, and powerless. How long she crouched there she was not sure, but when she summoned up enough energy to move and got to her feet, she found to her relief that training will out after all. Her childhood had been a tough one: the workhouse and the orphanage had been full of bullies; she had long ago learned to keep all signs of fear in check, because to show it was fatal. To her complete surprise, she discovered that she was no longer frightened. Her mind was clear, and if she remained calm it would come to her whose voice she had heard. And if he was the murderer, had she just escaped becoming his second victim, or was that moment still to come? The thought was enough to send her gibbering at the run for the servants' hall, but she made herself stand still, forced herself to remain quiet.

She didn't have the answers right now, but given time something would help her to recognize that voice. Because, she realized, their investigation had stirred up enough mud at the bottom of the pond to alert the man they were trying to identify. But she had also been warned, and she must be very careful. There was terrible danger here and at the moment it was directed at her.

Years of dressing in the dark of early morning came to her aid; she automatically combed her hair with her fingers and found enough hairpins to make herself respectable. She took her handkerchief and dipped it into the cold water of the lake and washed her face, scrubbing her mouth where she could still feel his hand, and she shuddered. Then, squaring her shoulders and taking a steadying breath, she straightened her clothing and brushed the dirt off her knees.

It was hard to walk back through the night alone. *You're not in danger,* she told herself. *He may be watching you but he has delivered his warning, you're safe for the time being.*

No one felt as reassured and welcomed by the lights of the great house spilling out across the lawn as Mrs. Jackson did that night. As she walked toward the back stairs, acknowledging Dick's call that Lady Montfort would like to see her as soon as possible, she told herself that one thing was certain: telling Lady Montfort about Violet would be a piece of cake in comparison with her other news.

Chapter Twenty-eight

Clementine's sleuthing hour with her housekeeper last night had so thrown her off-balance that she had been unable to sleep. Conflicting emotions of fear and remorse were all that remained to torment her throughout the night after Mrs. Jackson returned to the servants' hall.

Teddy's vicious treatment of Violet had been devastation enough and had left her senses reeling, but the news that her housekeeper had been accosted so aggressively on the grounds of her house was such a shock to her already stunned sensibilities that her self-recriminations knew no bounds. How could she have put her loyal and trusted servant at risk? How could she have been so utterly naïve as to suppose their questions would not arouse the interest and intervention of violent men? She replayed the last of her conversation with Mrs. Jackson over and over in her mind.

"We should stop all this, Jackson, right now. I can't run the risk of your being hurt. What was I thinking?" she had said to her housekeeper, who stood before her, frighteningly composed and seemingly detached from everything she had told her.

"Ordinarily I would agree with you, m'lady. But I believe it was a threat and nothing more than that. How could I possibly be in danger in this house? If you are in agreement, I think we should continue, that is, if we can. Deep down I have a feeling that this is all linked. We are closer than we think. We are missing one small piece."

How could she have allowed her housekeeper to talk her into continuing? It was sheer madness. Ralph would be furious if he found out what had happened. She felt her confidence ebbing away the darker the night became. She turned restlessly in her bed as the hours slowly crept by, her head hot, her feet cold. By dawn she had arrived at no intelligent conclusions and was even more distraught than she had been on retiring. By eight o'clock she was up and dressed, after a fashion, and decided she would go down to breakfast in the dining room. She needed the reassuring presence of her family around her.

As soon as she entered the small dining room she knew she had made a mistake. Her family, together with Ellis and Oscar, were gathered together, happily eating great platefuls of food and going over their plans for the coming day. She felt immediately awkward and alien among them, with her ugly secrets.

"What are your plans for the day, Mother?" Verity asked.

"I think I'll drop in on Stafford," she answered automatically, relying on her usual summer pursuits when she had time for recreation during the day. Yes, she thought, it would do her good to get out of the house; a day spent in the garden would order her thoughts.

Daylight and a good breakfast helped to strengthen her resolve and dilute some of her dark nighttime fears. She tuned in to the lighthearted chatter around her, looking for a momentary distraction from the leaden sadness and anxiety that she felt within.

Harry, Oscar, and Ellis were off to play cricket at Northcombe House. The Iyntwood Cricket XI had played Northcombe for sixteen straight summers and was made up of all the cricketers that Haversham village and the Iyntwood estate had to offer, including Fred Golightly from the Goat and Fiddle; the first footman James, second footman John, and young Dick Wilson; Mr. Hollyoak, Horace Wobbley from Haversham Hall, Ernest Stafford, and Tom Makepeace; and Dr. Carter and the Reverend Bottomley-Jones.

"I'm surprised Staunton is still going ahead with his cricket match after this wretched business." Lord Montfort was not a cricketer; her husband didn't enjoy games that involved a ball. They were an important part of boyhood and school, they taught teamwork and strategy, but he found them tedious to watch. He considered polo a terrible sport, hard on the horses' legs and backs, and refused all invitations to Hurlingham.

"I'm a bit surprised Valentine never let on our neighbors had been so thoroughly burgled while they unsuspectingly danced the night away at our ball," said Harry. "It wasn't very sporting of him to be so secretive. He must have known about it when he came back from London. They lost all the good stuff apparently, the Staunton emeralds and the diamonds, some rare pieces of very old silver. I hope they were backed by Lloyd's." He returned to his smoked kipper.

"How far are we from Northcombe? Five, six miles? Do you wonder about the stranger the locals all saw hanging about? I bet you anything he was part of the . . ." Ellis looked up and caught Clementine's frozen stare across the table. Evidently embarrassed at having brought up an unsavory topic at breakfast, he got up to help himself to more bacon and sausage and another heap of mushrooms.

"You're going to be pretty low in the batting order if you eat all that," said Oscar as he crunched his toast and scrambled egg and gazed critically at Ellis's rather solid middle. Everyone laughed.

"Yes, but he's a crack bowler and he's going to be spinning bosies at you all morning, so perhaps you'd better have a bit more than toast," Harry replied. Oscar had drawn the short straw and was to bat for Northcombe as they were one man down on their side.

Lord Montfort was paying attention only to part of the conversation; he was reading *The Times* and shook it every so often when the noise at the table became too loud. Clementine hoped her husband would take himself off to the stud farm after breakfast. She remembered that Mr. Broomstock was coming over to take a look at his favorite mare, Flossie, whom her husband intended to breed to Bruno. She needed an empty morning with no interruptions.

She heard an exclamation from behind the newspaper. "No wonder Shackleton looked tense all week, did you read about the White Star Line? Not doing too well and it looks like Cunard is waiting in the wings to scoop them up if things get any worse." He half lowered his newspaper and looked at her over the top.

"That'll make Emerald Cunard even more detestable than she is now." Verity looked across at her mother for agreement as she ate her scrambled eggs.

"And that would explain Wilfred's preoccupation all week, poor man. Is it bad, darling?" Clementine asked her husband.

"Probably a hiccup; I'm just a farmer, you know I don't understand these things. White Star had a lot of problems with the *Olympic*'s collision with the *Hawke*, it says here. I don't remember that, do you? Oh yes, and then there was that strike over lifeboats, that was nasty. The *Olympic* was steaming out of port, and the crew turned the ship round—they said none of the lifeboats were seaworthy, so the ship has been out of commission for a refit, taken months apparently. The legacy of the *Titanic* still haunts White Star, I'm afraid. Too bad all this publicity . . . Still, Wilfred's up in town now taking care of things, I expect." Her husband, financially secure, with his eighty thousand fecund acres, could afford to be offhand about Sir Wilfred's financial responsibilities in the City.

So this was why Sir Wilfred had been so preoccupied and anxious, she thought, and she wearily crossed another minor suspect off their list. More bad news to share with Mrs. Jackson.

All their suspects for Teddy's murder had dissolved, with questions left unanswered and only the sordid facts of Teddy's mistreatment of Violet laid bare. And now this most disconcerting new element, this man in the shrubbery who came out of God knows where. Their investigation was foundering.

"When we go to war with Germany, won't that put a stop to passenger ships to America?" asked Ellis, and she could have screamed. *Not war talk at breakfast surely; this was why women had breakfast in their rooms.* She harrumphed to herself.

"*If* we go to war . . . you've been listening to Winston again, Ellis. I can't believe how much money we are spending on building dreadnoughts. Pray we do not go to war with Germany. It is not the answer, my boy. But yes, if we do, then all our ships will join the navy, passenger liners included. Our best defense has always been our huge navy." Lord Montfort hated the thought of war.

She was turning to her daughter when she heard Harry and Ellis enthusing about the merits of aeroplanes and their possible usefulness in wartime, and her irritation knew no bounds. She made a point of catching Harry's eye, frowned at him in a most repressive way, and, ignoring his hurt look of entreaty, changed the topic of conversation to something a little less controversial.

"Well, as the morning appears to be my own, I think I will pop down to the quarry garden. Mr. Thrower will be there, and we can enjoy a nice ramble among the new plantings. If this lovely weather holds, I think we should have a picnic there for luncheon tomorrow. Verity, what about you, dear, would you like to come with me?" She had made a supreme effort to conceal her irritability and succeeded.

To her relief, her daughter, who was not as much interested in gardens as she was in the displaying of beautiful things in houses, said she thought she might rearrange the furniture in the tapestry room and rang for Mrs. Jackson to ask for help from Agnes, Elsie, and Mary, as the menservants were off to Northcombe.

Twenty minutes later, Mrs. Jackson and the maids arrived in the tapestry room to find that Lady Verity de Lamballe had collected up all the pretty things she could manage alone and now stood contemplating chairs and other small pieces of furniture. Mrs. Jackson was used to Lady Verity's passion for rearranging the rooms in the house. She had developed a wonderful eye for beautiful things and had made great improvements on her visits to Iyntwood. According to Lady Montfort, she had transformed her house in Paris, bringing in exquisite pieces from dusty old forgotten rooms and arranging them simply and with great balance to bring out the best of the lovely rooms and the de Lamballe family's superb collections of porcelain and Gobelins tapestries.

"We have to get rid of this heavy furniture it makes the room feel stuffy and overcrowded. But we can keep this." Lady Verity tapped her fingertips on the surface of a delicate pier table. "It's beautiful when you get it away from that monstrous chair. So we'll move this baroque sofa to right here under the window, and then balance it by getting rid of both those hideous wing chairs and moving the Hepplewhite pier table to here."

Mrs. Jackson was slender, but she was strong, and she smiled at the red-faced silence, except for grunts and muttered instructions as they heaved the furniture around. The sofa was long and heavy and it took a lot of effort to move it across the room. Finally they had it in place and were able to straighten up, breathless and giggling at a little squeal from Mary, who had barely escaped getting her foot mashed.

"Ah yes, now that's much better. But it needs . . . I know—I thought of this last night. Agnes, pop along to the library and bring the lapis-covered vase with gilt handles for this table and the Sevres porcelain figure. They are far too elaborate for the library and will look perfect on the gilt wood console against this gray wall. I don't know why Mama says the console is Louis the Fifteenth; it looks very Fourteenth to me."

Mrs. Jackson hurriedly said she would go to the library, as the thought of Agnes bumbling alone with 150-year-old porcelain was too much to bear.

An hour later Mrs. Jackson and her crowd of helpers stood in the doorway to take the room by surprise. Lady Verity reminded her of Lady Montfort at this moment, all enthusiasm and determined that everyone enjoy the fruits of their labors as much as she did.

"Oh yes, so much better. Don't you think, everyone? Agnes, would you move that a little to the left, thank you . . . yes, perfect. Well done, all of you. Mrs. Jackson, please don't let Mama move it all back again. Don't you think it better this way?"

Mrs. Jackson thought it was, and she said so. She didn't ask what they should do with the two heavy Victorian chairs parked outside the door or with the little *bibliothèque* and four petit-point footstools, proudly stitched by the dowager. They crossed the room to the windows and Mrs. Jackson opened them to let in the soft summer air to cool down their hot faces as the housemaids trooped back downstairs.

"The ball is such a huge amount of work for you all," said Lady Verity, evidently feeling bad after she had made them all puff up and down the room. "What a tragic end to it all. I felt so miserable I couldn't come this year, but now I'm glad I wasn't here. When we were children the ball was the biggest event of our summer, you know."

"I remember you gave Nanny a good run-around," Mrs. Jackson replied, laughing at the memory of Nanny's ample form trying to round up her charges before bedtime.

"Poor Nanny, she was never very quick on her feet. Harry was the worst, he would pretend to play along, and then we would double round the east portico and creep through the gardens to the rose garden and hide in the north pavilion. No one ever looked for us there."

Mrs. Jackson was happy to join in her laughter. She had known Lady Verity since she was a little girl and was particularly fond of the eldest Talbot daughter, who was pure sweetness and light. Lady Althea was younger by two years, and because she was such a tomboy she had often sided with Lord Haversham against their elder sister, making Lady Verity appear to be as good as gold, when in fact she had always been the ringleader. Lady Verity continued recounting the escapades of her childhood.

"If Mr. Ellis was staying here, he would join us. We would hide out in the north pavilion because we could easily see into the ballroom across the terrace—and all the misbehaving that went on in the rose garden." Lady Verity smiled at her recognition of social naughtiness and Mrs. Jackson quickly looked away as memories of Lady Waterford loomed. "Lord Haversham and Mr. Ellis would creep through the gap in the yew hedge and bring us back pasties and ale from the dray. One year Lord Haversham drank so much rough cider that he was sick all over the pavilion floor!"

"How old were you then, Lady Verity?" Mrs. Jackson asked.

"Oh, I was about twelve, the boys would have been nine. If we thought Nanny was coming or Hollyoak, we would jump over the side and hide at the back of the pavilion. We could make our getaway through the yew hedge into the woods if it looked like someone was onto us, but we were never caught."

"The secret lives of children." Mrs. Jackson laughed. "You were all such a handful, I don't know how poor old Nanny coped."

"She didn't really, but she did give the boys a good walloping with her slipper when she caught them smoking Father's cigars. I think Mr. Oscar was with them that time, or perhaps it was Mr. Mallory, I don't remember now."

"I had no idea you could get through the yew hedge behind the north pavilion. That hedge has to be at least four feet thick," Mrs. Jackson said, making Lady Verity backtrack.

"Oh yes, it's cut that way, straight in almost to the middle, a sharp left turn and a right turn to come out the other side. Unless you are looking for it you can't see it. You have to squeeze anyway. It was made so anyone working in the rose garden could leave without crossing the garden or the terrace."

Mrs. Jackson understood what she meant. Outside staff worked in the early hours of the morning, before the family was up and about, so they were not seen or heard. If a gardener was raking leaves and someone in the family came that way, he retreated into the nearest hedge. Most of these concealed places in the gardens had long ago grown over. Lady Montfort liked to talk to her gardeners, and she was more likely to put on her gloves and prune alongside them than to expect them to disappear when she was outside. But when the house and some of the gardens had been built, more than two hundred years ago, all servants were expected to work behind the scenes.

Mrs. Jackson experienced a little flash of excitement. In one moment she saw how everything had happened on the night of the ball and with that understanding came the identity of Teddy's murderer. It was at once a truly frightening and exhilarating moment.

She heard Lady Verity say, "I had better go and change for luncheon, and then I can surprise Mama with the improvements to the room. Thanks for your help, Mrs. Jackson; you have such a good eye for balance." She turned and surveyed the effect of her work with satisfaction.

Walking back through the hall of the house, Mrs. Jackson heard the telephone ringing and changed direction to answer it. It was Mr. Hollyoak's job to answer the telephone from his pantry, but he had already left for Northcombe, so she went into the house telephone room. She picked up the listening piece and the operator announced a call from Colonel Valentine. Mrs. Jackson's heart sank. He asked to speak to Lord Haversham.

"This is Mrs. Jackson, sir, the housekeeper. Lord Haversham is over at Northcombe today, playing cricket."

"I have been asked to bring Lord Haversham with to me up Scotland Yard, Mrs. Jackson; nothing terribly serious, nothing to worry about. Chief Inspector Ewan spoke with Miss Lucinda and some of her testimony is confusing. It doesn't quite fit with Lord Haversham's for the night of the ball and Ewan needs some clarification before he moves on. If Lord Haversham would telephone me at my house this evening when he returns, we can decide which would be the best train to catch tomorrow, unless he would prefer to drive."

"Yes, sir, I will give him the message. They are expected back from Northcombe at about six o'clock."

"Please do so, Mrs. Jackson. Goodbye." She heard a click on the line and replaced the earpiece.

Oh yes it is terribly serious and something to worry about, Mrs. Jackson thought as she walked quickly across the hall to the terrace door. Serious if Lucinda got carried away with her own sense of self-importance and said something stupid; dangerous because the eagerly listening Ewan would jump all over an opportunity to rope in Lord Haversham.

The sun was hot on the flagstones of the terrace, and she walked as fast as she dared, breaking into a little run when she knew she could not be observed. She went along the south terrace and turned right to the west portico of the house. The gardeners had finished working in the rose garden long before breakfast, and the rest of the servants were focused on preparations for luncheon. This side of the house and gardens were completely empty.

The rose garden lay before her, with its rich tapestry of golds, buffs, creams, and soft pinks, blending into deeper carmine pinks, reds, and burgundies in an intricate parterre of beds and a careful palette of color. Grass pathways divided the beds and at their intersections were stone terraces with wooden benches. At each end of the garden there were small marble temples: the north and south pavilions.

Mrs. Jackson walked along grass avenues, banked on either side by roses, their heads heavy with bloom and their fragrance soft and creamy. By the time she reached the north pavilion she felt almost giddy from their heady scent. The north pavilion, like its counterpart, was circular with open columns on one side of the sphere that looked out into the garden, and a closed column wall at the rear. An ornate stone bench stood in the center. Mrs. Jackson noticed that it was very clean; the marble had been thoroughly scrubbed quite recently. There was not a trace of garden vegetation anywhere on the pavilion floor, not a leaf, not a twig. Mrs. Jackson mounted the shallow steps and stood in the middle of the open room. Yes, Lady Verity had been right: you could sit on the balustrade and look across the rose garden and the terrace straight into the great windows of the ballroom. She wrapped her long skirt tightly around her legs, swung them over the side of the balustrade, and dropped down into the garden. She walked directly around to the back of the pavilion, where the yew hedge towered ten feet overhead. Very little daylight penetrated here and it was damp. The earth was still squashy from the rain. She trod carefully at the edge of the path, her right hand brushing the wall of the hedge.

Her hand disappeared into the gap; it was only eighteen inches wide. She pushed herself into the hedge and found that the gap suddenly widened considerably. She reached out her right arm; the opening into the hedge turned to the left and then almost immediately again to the right. She pushed on and found herself on the other side of the hedge, in the small service area for the ballroom. She looked around the area. Here on the ground, in the sunlight, she saw the tire marks of the dray: here was where it had been parked, here was where it had been driven from the drive, and here was where it had been driven back onto the drive at the end of the ball. There was a confusion of footprints in the trampled grass where people had gathered around the dray to eat their pasties and drink ale.

Mrs. Jackson turned back and inspected the ground at the concealed entrance to the hedge. She saw two deep grooves in the soft earth; the hedge had protected them from being washed away by the rain. She felt a thrill of terrific excitement. What had she found? She walked back through the gap in the hedge to the other side and got down on all fours behind the pavilion, carefully lifting her skirt up so that her stockinged knees pressed into the cool, moist earth. Yes, she could see two long grooves here, and here again there were some broken boughs at the base of the hedge. She peered under the hedge to her left and right. Her eye caught something bright in the gloom underneath, where the lowest yew branches of the hedge were thinnest. She reached out and, with her cheek pressed into the earth of the path, groped back under the hedge, trying not to scrape her arm on the rough lower branches. Her hand closed over something smooth, hard, and cold. Something metal. She drew out her hand. It appeared to be a silver cigarette case. *Careful now,* she thought, *keep calm.* She rose swiftly to her feet, tugged her skirt down. and walked back to the pavilion. In the strong afternoon light she looked at what she had found. Indeed it was a cigarette case, beautifully engraved with a central monogram.

"T.E.D.M.," she read aloud. "Theodore Edward David Mallory." She sat down on the bench and looked at her watch. Nearly one o'clock; the maids would be serving luncheon in the dining room.

She opened the case. Inside were three oval Turkish cigarettes, still quite fresh. She sniffed the tobacco, which smelled rich and sweet. On the other side of the case was a square of folded ivory bond paper. She carefully drew it out from behind the silver latch that held the cigarettes in place. It was a letter. Mrs. Jackson hesitated. As an upper servant she lived within a strict code of honesty and discretion, especially where the family was concerned. Loyal to the Talbots, her job was to ensure their comfort, to serve their needs, and protect their privacy. Reading private letters was something for the servants of lesser mortals, loyal only to their weekly wages. After a struggle, Mrs. Jackson unfolded the letter. It was written in black ink, the writing forward-slanting and bold. There was no crest or designation at the top of the page; there didn't need to be. She saw what was written and blushed. She made herself read to the end. It was Lord Booth's letter to Lady Waterford and in it he told her how much he enjoyed her company, and in detail how much he would enjoy seeing her again at Iyntwood. This was the letter Teddy had used to blackmail them. Embarrassed and feeling rather disgusted with herself, and with Lord Booth, Mrs. Jackson carefully folded the paper and put it back in the cigarette case. She snapped it shut and slid it into her pocket.

Mrs. Jackson returned to her parlor, drank a cup of tea, and organized her thoughts as she waited for the Iyntwood cricket team to come back from Northcombe. When she was quite sure they had returned, she rang for Elsie.

"Ask Dick to come up to my parlor for a moment, would you? He can bring up my supper before he has his."

Dick was prompt. He arrived with her tray and was his usual pleasant and attentive self.

"I want to talk to you for a moment, Dick," Mrs. Jackson said in her crisp, matter-of-fact manner when he came into the room. "Just put that tray down. My goodness, your knuckles are still bruised, must have fetched them quite a wallop . . . how did you hurt your hand again?"

"Ice cream churn, Mrs. Jackson." He didn't like reference to his knuckles, she noticed, as he slid his hand behind his back.

"Ah yes, the ice cream churn, how on earth did it get into the north pavilion do you think?" Dick, completely caught off-guard, looked stunned for a moment, and Mrs. Jackson felt mean; it wasn't fair to be flippant.

"Dick, I know what happened. I know what Mr. Teddy did to Violet. I know where Violet is. You see, I talked to Miss Lucinda."

Dick was silent, and his face was very pale. The look he gave her was not just guarded. There was something else, a wistful glance, almost apologetic. It was not lost on Mrs. Jackson. *I'm with you, boy,* she thought. *Just tell me the truth.* And then she said, "What I couldn't work out was who was in the north pavilion when Mr. Teddy walked up the steps and into it, just before four o'clock. After that no one saw him again." She didn't add "alive" because she already had the surprise of a frontal attack; she saw it in Dick's frozen stillness and his anxious eyes as he waited for what was to come. He reminded Mrs. Jackson of a hunted animal that bursts out of its hiding place too soon, then realizes its error and stands in vulnerable, paralyzed horror out in the open.

"I guessed you took Violet to the north pavilion so she could watch the ball. You wanted to give the girl a treat and you knew you were safe because no one ever goes to the north pavilion. Violet sat there with a glass of lemonade to watch the dancing, as you worked on the terrace. Then the worst thing imaginable happened—you saw Mr. Teddy walking across the rose garden to the north pavilion. You knew you had to get Violet away before he found her there. You went through the house, out of the front door, and along the north of the house to the service area where the dray was parked and squeezed through the gap in the yew hedge. You must have run like mad, Dick. But you weren't quite quick enough, were you?" She waited. Dick said nothing at all. He was such a nice boy, she thought, such a straightforward lad. She repeated herself in a stern voice: "Were you?"

"No, Mrs. Jackson."

Mrs. Jackson almost let her shoulders relax.

"So you hit Mr. Teddy."

"No! I had to get him off her. He was . . . he was . . ." Dick looked away. "He had his hand across her mouth. He . . . I pulled him off her. He took a swing at me and then I . . . well, then I hit him and he went down. He hit his head and didn't move. I knew I was in for it." She noticed that his country accent was stronger. His careful enunciation was gone and he looked like a scared village boy.

"I didn't know what to do. We both thought he might be dead. I told Violet to get out of it. Run, I told her, and whatever you do, don't come back."

"So what happened next?" Somewhere in Mrs. Jackson's mind

she was reminded of unraveling an old sweater to reuse the wool for another purpose. You teased out a loop of wool from the hole in the edge of the cuff and then very carefully pulled, and before you knew it you were winding up the yarn into a nice tidy ball.

"I needed to get help." He looked away from her, off into the corner of the room.

Ah, she thought, *now he's going to lie.* She waited until he had lost his evasive and persecuted look.

"Dick, sit down." She pointed to a nearby chair. He sat on it and stared down between his hands. After a while he looked up at her and continued.

"I knew after Vi had gone that he wasn't dead, but he was knocked out cold. I didn't kill Mr. Teddy, though I know you won't believe it." His voice was low and she saw a look of defeat beginning to take hold on his frightened face.

"I believe you, Dick. You were only missing for twenty minutes—the time it took to get Violet out of the north pavilion and give Mr. Teddy a good punch on the nose. But you have to tell me what happened next so I can help you." And then she simply sat there, her hands still on her lap, and waited.

"You see, we had to get him out of there. I had to tie him up and gag him, in case he came to. I took him over the pavilion wall, and dragged him round the back. I laid him down and checked the dray. No one was there." Dick paused and licked his lips. "I went back and picked him up again, and dragged him through the hedge. I got him up onto the dray and put him in the tool-storage box . . . because, he was going to have to be there awhile." He paused again and looked at Mrs. Jackson out of the corner of his eye. She nodded her head slowly in sympathetic agreement.

"I went back to work on the terrace. The rest I only know because I was told what was going to happen. At the end of the ball, when the orchestra went back to the stable block for the night in the dray, Mr. Teddy was handed over to the man who had been looking for him for the last two days. Mr. Draper I think his name was, you know, the strange man from London. I didn't know he was going to kill him!" Sweat had broken out on Dick's forehead and he looked white and shaken. "He was to take Mr. Teddy away, and we would never see him again. I believed it because that was what I was told!" He stopped and stared down at his hands, and eventually managed to meet Mrs. Jackson's gaze. She nodded again, encouraging him to go on.

"Next afternoon we heard that Mr. Teddy had been found dead. And I didn't know what to think. I knew it were the man from London who did it, because . . ."

"Because that was what you were told?"

"Yes! That's what I was told."

"And who told you that, Dick?"

Dick started to shake his head and his face became sullen. He was shutting down, Mrs. Jackson thought with desperation. She stopped herself from pushing him too hard.

"Does Violet know what happened after she left the pavilion?"

"No, she don't, nor did Miss Lucinda. That night she saw Violet running along the front of the house and went after her, and Vi told her what had just happened with Mr. Teddy. Miss Lucinda hid Violet in her room. They left early in the morning, before anyone was up." He paused and took another look at Mrs. Jackson, who kept her face neutral as she risked another question.

"Why do you call him Mr. Draper? How do you know his name?"

"I don't know who he really is. I never even saw him."

"So who was it who helped you? Who was it who handed Mr. Teddy over to Mr. Draper?"

"Who are you going to tell? Not Mr. Hollyoak?"

Mrs. Jackson appreciated just how innocent Dick really was. "No, Dick," she said patiently. "Not Mr. Hollyoak."

Chapter Twenty-nine

Lord Montfort went for a walk when the late afternoon faded into early evening. The light turned to golden-green as the sun slowly sank in the western sky; it was the time of day he loved best. His dogs were trotting beside him as he walked into the village and crossed the green, where the two younger dogs peeled off on their own paths, enticed by new scents and bored with obedience. He slowed his pace so that the oldest dog of the three could keep up with him. As he walked past the church, he called out a good evening to the verger who was locking up after evensong.

Twilight deepened to dusk and the lane softened to dull greens and purple shadows as Lord Montfort arrived at Jim's cottage. He told the dogs to stay and they sank into deep, damp grass, watching him through narrowed eyes, mouths opened wide to pant, as he turned to knock on the closed door.

"Good evening, your lordship." Jim opened the door, and his hand automatically lifted in salute as he recognized his visitor.

"Good evening, Jim. I've come to tell you we've found Violet." It was hard to see Jim's face in the half-light. Inside the cottage, lamps had been lit for the coming night. Jim opened the door wider and stepped to one side.

If Lord Montfort had expected tears and cries of relief when he told Jim Simkins that his daughter had been found, he was disappointed.

"How long have you known where she was?" he asked Jim as they walked farther into the cottage's main room.

"Since she first went to Cambridge, the morning after she was taken there by Miss Lucinda." Jim was standing in shadow and was quite motionless. "She had written me a letter that night, and they posted it on their way."

"Yes, they left before Teddy was found. Of course, Miss Lucinda thought she was doing the right thing, since we had been so lax in our responsibility to Violet. A sort of punishment, I think. There you have it, Jim, the arrogance of the young. How much better it would have been if Lucinda had come to me. How much trouble, heartache, and worry it would have saved." He noticed that Jim did not react to his frustration, but was watching him, his face composed, disinterested almost.

"No one could have saved Mr. Teddy, your lordship. He was already on his path. The boy had caused nothing but misery and hurt his entire life. It was his time to go." Jim's voice sounded remote. It was not shaded with blame, anger, or concern.

Lord Montfort was not prepared to hear the beginning of a confession so easily and his response was far brusquer than he intended. "It was not your decision to make," he said.

"He was a parasite: corrupting, weak. Men like him eventually destroy everything; they destroy hope and the future. It was a natural end. " Again Jim sounded distant, removed from the moment.

He accepts his fate, thought Lord Montfort. *He has been waiting for this time.*

"Not for revenge, not by murder." Lord Montfort kept his voice even.

"Not murder . . . justice . . ." Jim started to reply. But got no further. Lord Montfort saw his face gleam with a sudden slick of sweat as he reached into his pocket and pulled out a strip of cloth. He buried his face and started to cough deeply, hacking for a long time. Lord Montfort watched Jim make his way to the high-backed chair by the fireplace. He walked to the sink and poured water from a pitcher into a cup, then took it over to Jim and waited until the old man's chest heaved less and he regained his breath. Jim laid his head back against the chair and looked up at him. When he was sure that Jim had caught his breath, he handed him the mug and took the only other chair in the room; turning it to face Jim, he sat down and waited.

"Everything seemed to start well enough for Violet up at the house. She was adapting well and was learning fast; I think she was almost enjoying it in her own way. On her day off she would come home for tea and tell me about her new life. Then she started to miss a visit or two, and after a while I knew things weren't going too well, because she stopped her visits altogether. I never guessed how badly things were going for her, though.

"By chance Mr. Wallace, from the drapery, asked me to take his place in the orchestra for the ball, because he'd hurt his wrist. It was an opportunity to see Violet and reassure myself she was all right."

In the brief pause as Jim caught his breath, Lord Montfort heard one of the dogs scratching at the cottage door. It whined, but he did not move. He waited for Jim to continue.

"Well, it was worrying to see how she'd changed. She looked thin and I knew something was wrong, but she didn't tell me what." Jim paused and Lord Montfort made himself meet his gaze. Jim's face was pallid and there was an expression of deep pain that was not from his illness.

"I decided that after the ball I would tackle Mrs. Jackson about her. I had almost decided that I would take her away, something was not right." He paused, and Lord Montfort watched him hack into his handkerchief, his shoulders heaving. He forced himself to sit quite still without saying anything as he waited for Jim to continue.

"Well, later that night, things got more complicated. Violet was watching the ball from the little temple in the garden and Mr. Teddy came along and found her there." Lord Montfort nodded as Jim repeated almost word for word what he had been told earlier that evening by his wife.

"Well, as you no doubt already know, Dick knocked Mr. Teddy down and thought he'd killed him. Dick didn't know what to do. He lost his nerve and came to me for help. He told me what he had seen in the pavilion, what Teddy had been trying to do to Violet. He told me she had confessed Mr. Teddy had raped her. Raped her repeatedly after she had come to the house. And there it was, the opportunity to clean up this nasty mess completely." Jim bent forward and again pulled the cloth from his pocket. Lord Montfort looked away to avoid seeing the bright stain glistening on Jim's handkerchief and waited until the man had recovered himself enough to continue.

"I did what I had to do: Dick wouldn't get sent to jail for assault, Violet would be free to start her life over, and Mr. Teddy would not be able to damage any more young lives."

"How did you do it?" Lord Montfort had a pretty clear idea

from his wife's account, but he needed to hear Jim's side of the story.

"I had to get Dick to put Mr. Teddy onto the dray. The boy was in a panic. If he knew what I had in mind he would have caved in. And so I told him I'd hand Mr. Teddy over to the man who'd been looking for him—the 'stranger' that had been hanging at the back of the pub that afternoon. I'd seen the man myself walking from the station to the village and I saw him later that afternoon getting into Mr. Teddy's motorcar in the lane behind my cottage. I told Dick no one in Haversham would see him again and he believed me. So he hauled Mr. Teddy through the hedge and stowed him in the toolbox of the dray. I went back to play violin for the last dance of the night."

Short of breath, Jim stopped. Lord Montfort got up and poured him more water, and he noticed the that Jim's eyes were sunken deep in their shadowed sockets, as he took a cautious sip, and then another, before he could carry on.

"At the end of the ball we were driven over to the stables in the dray. When the rest of the musicians had gone to sleep, I went back outside and drove the dray up to Crow Wood. When I got to the wood the rain was heavy, the storm was coming in fast. I managed to tie off a length of rope to the gibbet. I made a noose, put it around his neck, and drove the dray forward."

Jim's face was the color of wet putty. Lord Montfort got up from his chair and laid his hand on Jim's shoulder. More than anything he understood why Jim had killed the man who had so harmed his daughter. It was understandable but not forgivable. What kept England's "green and pleasant land" the most civilized country in the world were its laws. The first Baron of Mountsford had been present at the signing of Magna Carta, which had led to the rule of constitutional law in England. Laws had been written and refined over the centuries, laws that people of Lord Montfort's education and background had worked hard to instill and maintain. Without law, without order, England would just be France.

Clementine stood by the open window of the music room and looked down on the drive. It was late and she had just left her husband and Colonel Valentine, who were tying up the details of Jim Simkins's arrest. Watching from the window, she saw the two men walk out of the front door. As they moved away from the lights of the house they disappeared into the shadow of Valentine's motorcar. She heard the car door slam shut and her husband's voice as he called out a last good-night. She watched the lights of Colonel Valentine's motorcar disappear around the last bend and with a tremendous sigh of relief she closed the window.

The day had been enormously long and she was still trying to come to terms with the fact that one of the gentlest men she knew had committed murder. Because she was blessed, or cursed, with an abundant imagination, images of the frightened, vulnerable Violet had crept into her conscious thoughts wherever she went in the house. They had been quite vividly with her earlier that day, when she had laid the facts of her investigation with Mrs. Jackson before her husband.

Clementine had not expected congratulations and relief that she had saved the Talbot name from disrepute when she told her husband that she knew who had murdered Teddy Mallory. She had carefully rehearsed beforehand what she was to say, touching minutely on the process and prudently skirting around Mrs. Jackson's actual contributions. But Lord Montfort had asked questions and had kept asking them until Clementine had described every step along the way of their quest. It had been a relentless interview. As her story unfolded, his look of puzzled concern had given way to one of incredulity and then to shocked embarrassment. She had known all along that colluding with a servant to discover information about their friends and servants was in poor taste. But to have shared the secrets of their friends' intimate lives with Mrs. Jackson was a definite no-no. Her husband had made his disapproval quite clear, leaving Clementine feeling a bit grubby. In his opinion, she had forgotten her position and by doing so she had rather let the side down.

He ended by saying, "I'm rather surprised that you involved Mrs. Jackson." His face and manner were chilly. He was covering annoyance and confusion by being distant.

"I could not have done it without her." Clementine would not justify colluding with her housekeeper out of loyalty to Mrs. Jackson. She had made her apologies for her unconventional behavior earlier, and had no intention of repeating them. To grovel at this point would mean losing all self-respect.

"Then perhaps you shouldn't have done it at all." This was his first direct criticism and it had hurt.

"I'm sad you see it that way, darling. I believed it was the right thing to do. As for Mrs. Jackson, the more I worked with her, the more I found I could trust her. She is a woman of remarkable integrity and loyalty, and awfully clever in her practical way. I think I trust her more than I would one of our friends." This had been a startling concept for him no doubt. The loyalty of servants and friends was clearly divided in his mind.

"That all remains to be seen. I will have to square Valentine. I trust he will keep your name out of things, he is a gentleman after all." He was coming around, but still a bit stiff and sniffish.

She did not say that Teddy, a gentleman only because of his position in society, had completely broken the code most gentlemen live by. She also understood that although her husband enjoyed and respected her natural intelligence, he was probably wistfully wishing for the days when she had used it only for planning gardens, organizing balls, and smoothing over spats on the boards of the charitable organizations she belonged to. They had parted politely, if not amiably, and Lord Montfort had trudged off to the village for his talk with Jim Simkins.

Now that Colonel Valentine had gone, Clementine would go downstairs and join her husband so that they might begin the business of being friends again. But before she did that she had one more thing she wanted to take care of.

The door opened behind her and Mrs. Jackson came into the room.

"Ah, here you are, Jackson. Yes, please shut the door. My goodness, you have had a long wait; Colonel Valentine had to have his say, of course." Clementine settled herself in a chair and looked up at her housekeeper. "Jim Simkins confessed to the murder, it was just as you said."

To her credit, Mrs. Jackson received this news quietly, with not a flutter of self-congratulatory pride, no display of vulgar excitement. She nodded, and Clementine heard the faintest sigh. "What a terrible business, m'lady, so very sad," Mrs. Jackson said, and Clementine knew she was not referring to the death of Teddy Mallory.

"Yes, indeed it is. It's late, Jackson, and you have had a long day." Clementine indicated the chair to her right. "Please take a seat, Jackson. Now, I should fill you in on the missing bits. Where should I start?"

"If you would be so kind, m'lady, was it perhaps Mr. Wallace in the shrubbery that night?" An inquiry, rather than a direct question.

"Yes, Colonel Valentine is sure it must have been. As we suspected from the drawings Oscar described to me and gave to the colonel, Mr. Wallace was a sort of go-between for a gang of thieves in London, run by a man called Baker. They specialized in country-house break-ins: good jewelry, old silver, and valuable paintings. Mr. Teddy provided information on the houses, the staff, how to get in and out, and what was worth taking. Mr. Wallace set up the burglaries. The police investigation must have prompted Baker to contact Wallace, and so when you came into the shop and noticed that his sprained wrist was miraculously healed, he worried that you had made the connection. It's quite amazing really. I still can't take it in. Mr. Teddy was up to all sorts of tricks it would seem."

The distress Clementine felt at her husband's annoyance with her was beginning to fade and she warmed to her story.

"Colonel Valentine thinks that Teddy had planned to double-cross Baker and do a burglary on his own at Northcombe. The money to be had from the Staunton diamonds alone was stupendous. He'd found a man in London who would do the actual burglary, the man seen walking towards Haversham by both Stafford and Theo Cartwright. Mr. Teddy met him in the village and drove him over to the Northcombe estate on Saturday evening. The colonel thinks that Mr. Teddy planned to meet up with his burglar after the ball to pay him off and collect his haul.

"But Mr. Teddy underestimated Wallace and this Baker fellow. He didn't make it to the rendezvous at Northcombe at the end of the ball, of course, but Wallace did. Most likely Wallace took the loot from Teddy's burglar and went up to town to hand it over to Baker. By the way, Colonel Valentine will arrange for Mr. Wallace's arrest tonight, so we have no need to worry about him skulking around here anymore. That was a horrible moment, Jackson, I am so sorry."

For the first time since she had come into the room, Mrs. Jackson's face showed something other than mere polite inquiry. She sat back in her chair and look of supreme self-satisfaction crossed her face. Clementine suspected that everything she had told her about Teddy's involvement with the Northcombe burglary was confirmation of what Mrs. Jackson had pieced together this evening. *What a brain,* she thought with admiration.

"I don't know how you worked it all out, Jackson. I mean, how did you get there?" Clementine leaned forward as if waiting for a word from God.

"I knew Violet had been out in the garden during the ball, m'lady, and Dick had bruised knuckles, afterwards. After my talk with Miss Lucinda I understood something of what had happened that night. But the timing was all off. I couldn't work out how Mr. Teddy was bound and put into the dray when he was last seen in the rose garden. It was Lady Verity reminiscing about watching the ball from the north pavilion when they were children. The minute she said they could come and go from the rose garden to the service area through a gap in the hedge, everything was quite clear. For the first time I knew how someone could have got Mr. Teddy to the dray without being seen from the terrace. I knew Dick was involved but he had to have had help. Whoever had helped him had killed Mr. Teddy."

Clementine couldn't help herself: "Yes, it took two of them, didn't it? Dick could not have done it alone. He was in a scrape and he went to someone he trusted for help, giving Jim Simkins his opportunity. Poor Jim was desperate, his time was running out, and there would be nobody to look after . . ." Clementine couldn't bring herself to finish.

"What will happen to Dick, m'lady?" Clementine was grateful for Mrs. Jackson's tactful interruption.

"Not much, at the most he'll be bound over to keep the peace. After all, Jim made a full confession to Colonel Valentine that he hoodwinked Dick."

"And Mr. Simkins?"

"Jim is terribly ill, so ill we doubt he will live to come to trial. He will stay in his cottage until then and not go to prison in Market Wingley. Lord Montfort will see to that." Lady Montfort stopped for a moment and Mrs. Jackson saw her look down and away.

"Dr. Carter is arranging for Violet to come to be with her father. He doesn't have long to live, Jackson. It all ends here."

They sat silently together for a few minutes. *Yes, it all ends here,* Mrs. Jackson thought as she saw Lady Montfort's distress and unhappiness at the unspoken failure of the Talbots to protect a young girl who had worked for them.

"So Lord Haversham didn't know anything about this at all, m'lady," Mrs. Jackson said, so that they did not have to linger over the Violet business.

"Nothing! Lord Haversham's head is always firmly in the clouds." Lady Montfort laughed and Mrs. Jackson watched her turn and fill two glasses from the decanter on the table next to her. "I know you have a soft spot for amontillado." Lady Montfort offered her a glass of sherry. "Here is to your very good health, Jackson, and my heartfelt thanks for everything you have so cleverly achieved. Well done!" She raised her glass to her housekeeper.

"Thank you, m'lady. It was nothing at all." Mrs. Jackson took a small sip of sherry; it warmed her throat as it slid down, such delicious stuff, amontillado. She was barely listening as her ladyship continued.

"Yes, Lord Haversham is in the clear all right; except of course he is in hot water with his father. Silly boy has gone and got himself a job, as he calls it, flying for a friend who makes . . ."

Mrs. Jackson nodded her head obediently as she acknowledged Lord Haversham's little ways. She thought perhaps she might pop down to the sunken garden and find Mr. Stafford tomorrow morning. She had a lot to thank him for. Without his prompting she would never have made that trip to London. For the first time, she didn't feel hesitant about him.

". . . Lord Haversham will just have to write and put him off." Lady Montfort's voice brought her back to the present. *Good Lord,* Mrs. Jackson thought as she put down her glass on the side table next to her chair, *how on earth could I have forgotten?*

"There is just one more thing . . ." Mrs. Jackson rose to her feet.

"Surely there can't be!" Lady Montfort exclaimed. "Haven't we got it all tied up?"

From her pocket Mrs. Jackson took out Mr. Teddy's silver cigarette case. She opened it and offered it to Lady Montfort. "I'm not quite sure what do with this."

A perplexed Lady Montfort stared at the cigarette case until she saw what was neatly folded within it. "Oh, really no, it can't be!" She looked at Mrs. Jackson, who said nothing at all. Lady Montfort burst out laughing. "Ah, I see it is. Well, I know what to do with it. Just take that awful thing downstairs to the furnace and sling it in."